The Blood Oranges

Also by John Hawkes

Is there then any terrestrial paradise where,
amidst the whispering of the olive-leaves, people can be with
whom they like and have what they like and take their ease
in shadows and in coolness?

—Ford Madox Ford: THE GOOD SOLDIER

John Hawkes

The Blood Oranges

New Directions

LIBRARY OF CONGRESS CATALOG CARD NUMBER: 74-152516
(ISBN: 0-8112-0061-2)

Portions of this book first appeared in *The Dutton Review,
The Harvard Advocate, Tri-Quarterly* and *Works in Progress,*
to whose editors grateful acknowledgment is made.
The author is grateful for generous help given him by
The Rockefeller Foundation.

Manufactured in the United States of America.

First published clothbound in 1971.
First published as New Directions Paperbook 338 in 1972.

Published simultaneously in Canada by Penguin Books Canada Limited

Designed by Gertrude Huston.

New Directions Books are published for James Laughlin,
by New Directions Publishing Corporation,
80 Eighth Avenue, New York 10011

ELEVENTH PRINTING

For James Laughlin

The Blood Oranges

LOVE WEAVES ITS OWN TAPESTRY, SPINS ITS OWN GOLDEN thread, with its own sweet breath breathes into being its mysteries—bucolic, lusty, gentle as the eyes of daisies or thick with pain. And out of its own music creates the flesh of our lives. If the birds sing, the nudes are not far off. Even the dialogue of the frogs is rapturous.

As for me, since late boyhood and early manhood, and throughout the more than eighteen years of my nearly perfect marriage, I always allowed myself to assume whatever shape was destined to be my own in the silken weave of Love's pink panorama. I always went where the thread wound. No awkward hesitation, no prideful ravaging. At an early age I came to know that the gods fashion us to

1

ıd the legs of woman, or throw us together for no
ɔn except that we complete the picture, so to speak,
and join loin to loin often and easily, humbly, deliberately.
Throughout my life I have never denied a woman young
or old. Throughout my life I have simply appeared at
Love's will. See me as small white porcelain bull lost in the
lower left-hand corner of that vast tapestry, see me as
great white creature horned and mounted on a trim little
golden sheep in the very center of Love's most explosive
field. See me as bull, or ram, as man, husband, lover, a tall
and heavy stranger in white shorts on a violet tennis court.
I was there always. I completed the picture. I took my
wife, took her friends, took the wives of my friends and a
fair roster of other girls and women, from young to old
and old to young, whenever the light was right or the
music sounded.

Now there is only my little South European maid. She
speaks an ugly language that will never be mine, she cannot understand a word of my lengthy erotic declarations.
She does not smile, she has never known my sexual embrace, may never have known the sexual embrace of any
man, this small solemn girl who appears to have been
created only to draw water and build fires. But together
we live in our otherwise abandoned villa which is one of
a pair, long and single-storied, with broken red tiles and
fireplaces like abandoned urinals, live together in our
drafty and sometimes muddy villa where I knew my last
mistress, sang my last song, last spread the legs of my
wife. I have named my maid Rosella because the calves
of her legs are raw, unshaven, and because she wears thick
gray woolen socks. She cooks, she draws water, I spend my

time attempting to inflame Rosella with words she does not understand, attempting to surround the ignorant virginity of Rosella's spirit with at least the spoken tones of joy and desire. I have made myself rules: no touching, nothing overt. Only the spoken tones of joy and desire.

Why, after more than eighteen years, does the soft medieval fabric of my tapestry now hang in shreds—here the head of a rose, there the amputated hoof of some infant goat? Is it possible that in purging her field of Hugh's sick innocence Love (impatient Love) purged me as well? Eliminated even her own faithful sex-singer from the joyous field? It is possible. The villa that is twin to mine and that lies just on the other side of the funeral cypresses is empty.

But I am patient, I am faithful, perhaps one day I will reach out and close my fingers on Rosella's thigh, perhaps my last mistress may again become my mistress. It is possible. We shall wait and see.

Y ESTERDAY I PAID MY WEEKLY VISIT TO MY LAST MISTRESS. She has been given refuge in the sanctuary, that small white cluster of Moorish-looking buildings above the town. Each week I visit her. My ritual, my weekly ritual of hope and fidelity, and in the process I suppose I reveal vestiges of the former lover, the former man of good taste.

Yes, in these visits and in my personal habits which involve crude but elaborate baths, the selection of a shirt and

3

faded tie for the day, the trimming of thick waves of hair around the ears, the care of fingernails as well as exercises for the body, and even an effort to pay some attention to shoes (to brush or knock the dried mud from them if not to polish them), yes, in visits and habits I tell myself and my indifferent and backward world that this abandoned man survives the period of his uselessness, that no catastrophe can destroy true elegance. Each night I wear my nearly ruined black dinner clothes, Even though I expect never again to travel, still I keep in the stone loft above my bed those old cowhide suitcases now covered with mold. Weekly visits, personal habits, a very nearly aesthetic memory—to me it is worth something to know that if circumstances ever gave me back my last mistress or my wife Fiona, I would be as attractive to both these women as I was in the days when, to both of them, I was the white bull brightly fired in Love's kiln. To me fidelity is the most masculine trait of all.

Yesterday the small white cluster of Moorish-looking buildings above the town looked exactly as it had the week before, and as usual the little fat women in their white dresses, blue aprons and worn-down sandals were expecting me. Even while I was chaining the bicycle to the stunted tree (the bicycle is old, rusted, with large wheels and rotted tires and a pair of narrow handlebars without grips, a pathetic machine yet still functioning, so that if left unchained it would be stolen by the first man, woman or child who happened to see it leaning unguarded against the tree) and even while I was reaching for the thong that hangs from the clapper in the bell that is like a baby's head cast in iron, even in the midst of these preliminaries, one of the little fat women was already staring at me over the low wall.

I smiled, nodded, threw away the small wet butt of my precious cigarette, and through a series of gestures (lifting of eyebrows, baring of teeth, a rolling motion of the hand) tried both to ask if I was to be admitted safely this morning and to make it clear that I knew perfectly well that I was.

Each week it is the same. My slow bike ride takes me from the villa where I live by choice with Rosella, through the poor coastal village with its ruined aqueduct and small houses of charred bone (that wet dark place always fetid with the faint bulbous aroma of sewer gas still rising from the deep pits dug by ancient barbarians), then out of the darkness and up the crusted slope of the hill and on to these white Moorish buildings and clean fat women and stubby men lolling in their constricting uniforms. The same each week, from dead snails and sediment and the stately gloom of the funeral cypresses to the sudden light, peace, charm of this walled sanctuary. The yellow fountain, the orange sand of the courtyard, the white walls and deep-set windows, the tobacco-colored trees with their enormous leaves in the shape of fat supplicating hands, the low balconies, and above everything the pale blue tile roofs that suggest a bright powdery fusion of sky, sea, child's eye, a soft lively blue unlike any other blue I have ever seen. Each week I find all this waiting at the end of the bike ride, and enjoy it, delight in it, my sophistication only enriching if anything the aching candor of the blue tiles. The sanctuary is simple and mysterious too, is antithetical to the brambles and broken tiles of the primitive landscape above which it is set. Surely the sanctuary was conceived and built by

5

someone who could never vocalize the harsh unimaginative language of this terrain.

Aching candor. Though I am a dispassionate man, the phrase is equally appropriate to me and to the blue tiles roofing the sanctuary. Aching candor describes exactly what I felt yesterday, and feel each week, when we crossed the remaining portion of the orange courtyard, passed into the shade of the trees, at last turned to the right and approached the nearest balcony where my last mistress sat wrapped in a large thick woolen blanket. I smiled, stood close beside her low balcony wall, stared at her apparently sleeping face until my own head, eyes, mouth, chest, felt saturated with aching candor. Once my mistress, now Hugh's widow, perhaps some kind of essential invalid, though I think not, there sat Catherine merely feigning sleep, I knew, and in her silence still basking, blazing, bristling, collapsing in the invisible aftermath of our long adventure.

I spoke to her softly, as I do once each week: "Come on, Catherine, you know you still want me to woo you." And then my voice filled with the honeyed sweetness of the golden lion or white porcelain bull: "Stop being a child, Catherine. Take the flowers."

To her, I knew, my admonitions were like chocolate stars, chocolate half-moons, dark balls of honey. I knew she was listening, waiting, watching me behind those closed eyelids, in her mind was clutching at the gentle sounds of my voice and once again was slipping, rolling over the edge and falling among the shadows of her past life and mine.

The matrons were gone, my usual half-hour of peace with

Catherine was mine once more, though nearby one of the small swarthy men in uniform was sitting on a low urn containing the ashes of a Roman lover. On the air I smelled a mixture of citrus leaves and the transparent secretions of pale and disintegrating roses. I had only to begin swinging my leg over the balcony wall to arouse the sentry to angry shouts of *croak peonie.* But I had discovered on previous visits that I could talk to Catherine, smoke, laugh, even sit on the wall, as long as I, the godlike foreigner suspected of being connected with her trouble and who in small dark smoldering eyes was too tall, too strong, too blond, too handsome, much too elegant and good natured, made no effort to cross the wall perhaps to do the large sick woman some further harm. But I could sit on the wall and did so, lit one of my precious puffy cigarettes that smelled of nitrates, burning paper, animal stains, sex. In my mouth and nose I bottled up that smoke, that tumultuous pungent smoke of the cigarette of my tragedy and good humor. And thanks to burning lips, burning eyes, thick golden cough, yesterday I was best able to study Catherine feigning sleep in the same hot woolly blanket that Fiona used to spread across our bed on cold nights in the villa.

I started to blow smoke rings. Tiny and egg-shaped, large and ragged, out they came from the casual oval of my pursed lips and then smashing one into the other, piling rapidly one on top of the next, soon they turned into silver cornucopias, silver wreaths, large ghostly horns of invisible rams. For I was an artist at blowing smoke rings, from an early age had delighted the little girls I knew with my swans, my elephants, my beach balls all blown in smoke.

And between puffs: "Why don't you open your eyes, Catherine? I know you want to watch your old smoke ring artist hard at work."

But of course she was already watching me, I knew, behind those closed eyelids of hers, was watching every move I made and every thick gray acrid creation that sprang or floated from my large and sympathetic lips. And all this time, as I drew one foot up and rested it on the wall and crooked my right arm around the upraised knee on top of that low wall in the warm sun, all this while I was studying Catherine as she feigned sleep, through the luxury of my loosely packed and hotly burning cigarette was nodding and squinting attractively, scrutinizing each feature for the mere pleasure of the sight, but also hoping with my eyes alone to appeal to her as I had once appealed to her with all my unlimited gentleness, on those dark licorice-smelling nights in their villa or ours.

Sinuous smoke, sun on the back of my hand, smile reaching out for the pain that lay behind the skin of her face, the sound of my voice already gone, frames of golden eyeglasses warm on the bridge of my nose and behind the ears, and smiling in silence, leaning forward, waiting, receiving no answer. Then my shoe scraped, my eyes became heavier and larger with concentration and good humor, became even darker brown in color: "Listen, Catherine. There's comforting silence, there's childish silence. Yours is childish. I don't even need to say it, do I?"

I saw what I had seen for weeks, the shape and substance of the woman both familiar and unfamiliar, both young and old, and I kept staring at her with admiration, remoteness, aching candor. Only her head was visible, the large head always seen in comparison with the head remembered on the pillow, gripped between my hands, rippling in Fiona's little mirror, clouding over suddenly with her uncertain laugh. The body itself was hidden. Yet no blanket was thick enough, rough enough, dense enough, or so wildly colored or so grotesquely patterned or so filled with other associations (the sensations of Fiona, say, on a cold night) as to prevent that large female torso and the arms, legs, hips from taking solid and in a way maximum shape under my first glance.

I knew what lay beneath the blanket. I knew quite perfectly the hips and calves and thighs somewhat fallen and still minutely falling, spreading from classical lines, knew well indeed the navel oddly sculpted, as if her belly had been sealed with a final flare of some hot iron. I had seen and always would see beneath old blankets or behind black funeral cypresses the heavy knees and feet and hands, the placid buttocks, all the immensity of the plain flesh that still suggested classical lines. The large but ordinary body, then, of someone who had borne children and overcome self-consciousness, body of someone who had never been aware of the statuesque design the ancient artist had in mind for it, a body so plain and big, so close and yet so far from the target of beauty that to me it was the richest beauty of all. I knew Catherine's body, saw it, loved it for its totally unconscious grandeur.

She moved, something trembled (or so I thought) beneath the ugly folds of Fiona's blanket. And once again, smiling, reaching out to her with silent smoke, all this awareness came back to me as it does each week. My finger tips were burning but my mind was filled only with this vision of the body of my Catherine lying before me in pretended sleep.

It was a knee that moved. And had it not been for the squat man seated upright on the urn, I would have thrust out my hand, placed it firmly on the sloping forehead of Catherine's knee and given her great uplifted knee a tender shake. It would have pleased me to touch the blanket just as it had pleased me when, in the stillness of absolute sexual purpose, I first swung her big plain body into the arc of my life.

Another amusing creation out of poisonous smoke, another silent sequence of meditation, and then I lifted my chin, stretched heavily, and nipped the undulating smoke ring with the very lips that had blown it. And softly laughing, in my own ears hearing the appealing sounds I knew she wanted to hear from deep in my diaphragm, hearing my own sympathetic laughter even while it was yet riding the tide of smoke in the dark resonant hollows of my nose and throat: "You can't forget me, Catherine. Why try?"

All this awareness, all this richness of feeling came back to me. As it does each week. And now the emotion that was clouding Catherine's face was pain (I could see it like schools of microscopic black fish drifting just beneath the skin), and now my precious cigarette was nothing more than the taste of black ashes and a small livid blister on my lower lip, while the last of the smoke was already dissolving in the sunlit peppery-looking leaves of the nearest tree. The blue tiles appeared to be white with frost.

And smiling, touching my burned lip with my tongue, slowing still further the cadences of my rich appeal: "I might have prevented our—what shall I call it? Idyl? Yes,

I might have prevented our idyl. Maybe I could have stuck my hands in my pockets instead of using them to remove my golden eyeglasses. I didn't have to climb into my dressing gown and silk pajamas and cross from our villa to yours and turn down the pink percale sheets on your bed. After all, I could have walked down to our pebbly beach and thrown pebbles into the phosphorous wash for a couple of hours. But a steady, methodical, undesigning lover like me really has no choice, Catherine. The eyeglasses come off in my hands, the skirts of the dressing gown fall open, I fold the wings of the glasses. No choice. And don't forget you were waiting for me. You wanted my slow walk, my strong dark shadow, my full pack of cigarettes, the sound of my soft humming as I approached your villa. We both knew you were waiting, Catherine. Neither one of us had any choice that first night. It was inevitable."

I shifted my position so that I was sitting sidesaddle, so to speak, on the low wall. I licked the small painful spot on my burned lip. And now a different bell was ringing. I listened to it, recognizing it, between its strokes I heard the silence that fell between Catherine and me like a festering marsh whenever I stopped talking.

Pain is saddest, I thought, on plain features. The dark swiftly floating schools of grief and bitterness were far more visible on Catherine's round face, for instance, than they would have been on the proud and youthful face of my Fiona. Fiona had the face of a faun, an experienced faun, and its elegance would have obscured or leavened or enriched her pain. Catherine's broad cheeks and heavy lids merely gave pain room to play—alone, unadorned. Pain, beneath Fiona's eyes or in the corners of her mouth, would simply have become a kind of spice to her beauty. But when the shades of pain were drifting across Catherine's face, as they were drifting now, there was nothing else to see, to marvel at, to desire. Catherine's pain was her beauty.

The bell I listened for each week was ringing. From far below the sanctuary, from the top of the squat and crumbling tower in the center of the smashed shards of the little coastal town, it called to us faintly, tonelessly, not in firm even strokes as if the ringer meant to announce the hour or send forth a summons, but with an irregularity that to me sounded like the soft dispirited voices of all those who were dead. I listened and heard the ringing of Catherine's soul, the toneless calling of Hugh's voice. It continued to ring, to vibrate down there through empty windows and black olive branches, the faintly metallic sound so distant and pointless in this bright sun that it made me smile deeply, seriously, in the midst of these meditations with my big-limbed and heavy-hearted Catherine. Then softly: "Remember how Hugh's coffin made that poor wreck of a hearse sag in the rear? I guess I like endings. I like flat bells, don't you?"

And at that moment I stood up, as I do each week, and stretched, glanced away from Catherine where she lay at my feet, glanced swiftly at the blue tiles, the dark clumps of peppery leaves, the blue of the sky, and then breathed in an enormous amount of that sweet air and abruptly leaned down with my two hands spread on the wall and my two eyes once again cradling Catherine in their brown benevolence. The vest was tight around my heavy ribs, the black jacket was hot and heavy on my shoulders. Would she ever open her eyes and look at me, say my name, ever again hang around my neck in graceless confusion?

"Arise, arise, Catherine," I whispered then, leaning on the wall and staring at her through golden eyeglasses, "climb to your feet, and let's comfort each other."

But she could not arise, or look at me, or say my name. It was in her power to help me speak for the past, to help me see the future. Her voice might have reinforced my voice, her eyes might have met mine. And yet I knew it was not to be. She still preferred to remain only the inert supine center of my life, the sun that neither sets nor rises. The bell had stopped ringing. I sighed, again I pushed off from the wall and smiled down at her in a way that said I had endless strength and patience to give her in small doses once each week. She could not have mistaken the sound of my breath or the meaning of that distant smile. I dug the toe of my left shoe into the orange sand, shoved both hands into my torn pockets. Nearby a finch was covering itself with pale dust.

No doubt she heard my breathing long after my heavy footsteps had died away. Perhaps she expected to see me or at least hoped to see me standing there when the little fat women approached her wearing their blue aprons and carrying their terra-cotta bowls and stiff brushes. Perhaps for a moment she did in fact see me, though I was already gone. Perhaps after today she would think more about me and less about Hugh, perhaps now would begin to prepare herself more agreeably for my next appearance. When next I saw her, wouldn't she be digging happily among the flowers that grew in the little stone pots along the front of her balcony, or standing with her eyes open and her hands clasped together and a vague hopeful smile drawing the top lip from the bottom? I thought so. Soon I would move her back to the villa, soon she would be able to join me arm in arm beside Hugh's grave.

And slowly riding back down the narrow path from Catherine's sanctuary to the broken stones of the empty town, beyond which waited my silent villa and Rosella, squeezing the rusty hand brakes with my aching hands to keep the bike from tearing loose on the hill and pitching over the nearest shaggy precipice, squeezing the brakes and hearing the rusted spokes going around and the soft tires humming like inflated snakes, amused at the thought of the perfect beauty of my large formally attired self mounted on the rust-colored bike, and then thinking of Catherine, already planning my next visit to her balcony while my lip burned and while a mildly rancid breeze played about my face—suddenly in the midst of all this I went around a turn in the path and bumped through a cleft in the mossy rock and applied the brakes, put down both feet, held my breath, forgot all about Catherine and myself.

There on a low wall of small black stones that resembled the dark fossilized hearts of long-dead bulls with white hides and golden horns, there on the wall and silhouetted against the blue sky and black sea were two enormous game birds locked in love. They were a mass of dark blue feathers and silver claws, in the breeze they swayed together like some flying shield worthy of inclusion in the erotic dreams of the most discriminating of all sex-aestheticians. Together we were two incongruous pairs frozen in one feeling, I astride the old bike and hardly breathing, the larger bird

14

atop the smaller bird and already beginning to grow regal, and all the details of that perfect frieze came home to me. Exposed on the bare rock, lightly blown by the breeze, the smaller bird lay with her head to one side and eyes turning white, as if nesting, while above her the big bird clung with gently pillowed claws to the slight shoulders and kept himself aloft, in motion, kept himself from becoming a dead weight on the smooth back of the smaller bird by flying, by spreading his wings and beating them slowly and turning his entire shape into a great slowly hovering blue shield beneath which his sudden act of love was undeniable. Grace and chaos, control and helplessness, mastery and collapse —it was all there, as if the wind was having its way with the rocks. There before my eyes was the infusion itself, and the birds remained true to nature and undisturbed by the infinite rusty sounds of my old bike until it was all done and the larger bird loosed his claws, made a bell-like sound, then rose slowly and vertically on the hot breeze. Some time later his small partner toppled off the wall and half fell, half flew down toward the burnt clay roofs of the village, while I rode off slowly on my now humbled bike.

Obviously the two birds mating on the horizon were for me a sign, an emblem, a mysterious medallion, a good omen. They augured well for the time I had spent with Catherine and for my own future in the electrified field of Love's art. But as I pedaled once more between the funeral cypresses and approached the villa, I found myself wondering if in the brief twining of that dark blue feathery pair I had actually witnessed Catherine's dead husband and my own wife clasping each to each the sweet mutual dream which only months before had been denied them by the brief gust of catastrophe that had swept among us. Yes, Hugh and Fiona in the shape of birds and finding each other, so to speak, in final stationary flight. Could it have been? I smiled to realize that the pleasure and truth of the vision were worth pondering.

Youth has no monopoly on love. the sap does not flow solely in the young. In all my adventures and in all my diligent but unemotional study of sex literature I found nothing to justify the happy expressions of total self-confidence we generally read in the superficially attractive faces of so many younger men and still younger girls. Jaunty, spritely people with trim bodies and unclouded eyes are not necessarily the most capable of those thrust into the center of the pink tapestry. After all, at the height of our season Fiona and Hugh were almost forty, Catherine had passed that mark by several years, while I was already two or three long leaps beyond middle age. Furthermore, we were a quartet of tall and large-boned lovers aged in the wood. Too big for mere caprice, too old to waste time and yet old enough to appreciate immodesty, we were all four of us imposing in height, in weight, in blood pressure, in chest expansion. All except Hugh perhaps, who always said that his long thin legs were the legs of the Christ and whose spare fishy chest was actually day by day collapsing, though like me Hugh was nonetheless capable of carrying either Fiona or Catherine across one naked shoulder without stumbling or shortness of breath. Body to body, arms about each other's waists, our undergarments and bathing apparel dangling together on a line strung hastily between the two villas, or each standing separately and exhibiting his characteristic gesture—Catherine with her hands at her sides, Hugh clutching his impertinent camera, Fiona unconsciously holding her breasts in hands as bold and sensitive as Leonardo's, I bare-chested and cigarette in mouth and staring with bland eyes at a full wineglass lifted high in my weathered fingers—at the height of our brief season and in the four fully matured figures of our quartet, anyone with an eye for sex would have recognized an experience, purpose and continuity only hinted at in the poignant stances of young girls with thumbs hooked in bikinis and brown legs stiffly apart. There were four of us then, not merely two, and in our quaternion the vintage sap flowed freely, flowed and bled and boiled as it may never again.

Can youth make such claims?

ONCE AGAIN WE SEPARATED IN THE DARK EMPTY NAVE OF the squat church, Fiona and I, once again went our separate ways, each to the altar of his choice. The windows were cut through those deep walls as if for the arrows, lances, pikes and small cannon of sturdy peasants who might still attempt to defend this church from the barbarians, and without glass, never intended for glass, exposed us, hidden though we were, to the smells and harsh light of the rocky village around us. The windows, mere rude rectangular holes left high in the moist walls, were themselves barbaric, and made me smile. Yet I smiled not only because the windows were unsymmetrical and gave a feeling of ancient violence to altars, cross, shaky wooden seats for solemn populace, as if the dungeonlike church had been abandoned before they had even morticed the last volcanic stone in place, but smiled also at the symmetry of taste and feeling that pulled Fiona and me apart and drew us to altars so nearly opposite in color, mood, design. Hands in pockets, I could hear Fiona breathing quietly and could hear the sharp sounds of her footsteps as she bent all the energy of her tall and beautiful and impatient self toward finding still better angles from which to view the altar.

"Cyril, baby, why don't you put out the cigarette? For God's sake."

And I smiled to hear Fiona's voice clipped and imploring, harsh and sweet, a mere whisper filled with the richest possible sounds of assurance in the ear-ringing silence of the stone vault. It was like Fiona to talk without turning her head, to respect the sanctity of old stones in a whisper that ruffled the little moth-eaten dress of the infant in Mary's arms, to comment on my cigarette in her distracted way while squatting all at once to examine a pair of short yellow bones crossed at the base of her favorite altar. Everywhere Fiona was in lovely character, yet nowhere was she more herself than here in the stone crypt where we joked about some day being buried together alive. Her graceful agitation, her girlish fixation on the altar of the dead, the absolute self-possession of a woman so large and yet so faunlike and hard—I could only smile to hear the soft silver of her

18

voice and to see my athletic angel merging her fluted flesh with those cold shadows.

"What's the matter with my cigarette?" I whispered across the nave in a deep and gentle echo as rich in reverence as Fiona's. "The little boys have been relieving themselves back there in the darkness. Smell it?"

"Cyril, you're making me nervous. OK?"

Then my own slow, bemused, vigorous whisper: "If the little boys can make water, I can smoke."

How like the two of us to spend each day these long minutes together and yet apart in this little medieval church of cold passion, how like us to choose these different altars. Hands in pockets, brief cigarette still in my mouth, I lounged against my own small altar which was of white marble and was devoted to gold, to fresh flowers, to the wooden Virgin recently lacquered in bright blue paint and stiffly cradling the crude doll dressed in his rotting gown of real lace. The two crowns, the sightless eyes, the feeling of water sprinkled over the whole thing and the sunlight that warmed altar and shoulders alike—here I could lounge suspended in a childish array of cheerful artifacts quite appropriate to my luminous good nature, here laugh aloud and take my time watching Fiona trying to penetrate the secrets of that other altar so absurdly opposite from mine.

"My God, I've found the skeleton of a child. Head, ribs, hands, feet—the whole works. How could they do it?"

A moment before she had been sitting on her heels, with the open coat of yellow suede drawn tight across her widened buttocks, but now, never at rest, she was standing on tiptoe directly in front of that black and white altar, while with my usual pleasure I noted her straight legs, her narrow calves stretching with a kind of girlish muscular determination, her hands spread wide and resting firmly on the black marble. Even stock still she was trembling, I thought, even motionless appeared already to be wheeling and running on naked white feet toward her next confrontation with bright light, old stones, new lovers.

"He's beautiful, poor thing. I'm going to kiss him, Cyril. Shall I?"

Yellow was Fiona's color, as in the case of the almost tissue-thin suede coat which, in her stretching efforts to reach the skull of the child, was now lifted high above the tight skin behind her knees. And for more than eighteen years she had been most obviously true to character and to her color yellow in the act of kissing, and had spent those years kissing each letter she wrote, each book she enjoyed, kissing flowers, shadows, dead birds, dogs, old ladies, attractive men, as if only by touching the world with her open lips could she make it real and bring herself to life. So even while I was grunting my approval and pleasure, which was the only way to reply to any of Fiona's questions about kissing, she had already found the small white skull with her eager mouth, and I could only smile still more broadly at the sight of Fiona lavishing one of her brief floods of compassion on the tiny cold features of a grinning relic. It was like Fiona to leave her jasmine scent perfuming the mere skeleton of some unknown infant embedded along with thick-lettered unreadable injunctions against frivolity and sex in their unfrequented altar. To her, no expenditure of her own affection was ever wasted.

But I smelled wax, dust, flaking wood, rusting iron, all the effluvium of devotion and religious craftsmanship. Taking my left hand from my pocket and between thumb and first finger rubbing half-consciously the hem of the tattered dress on the Virgin's doll, at that moment I found myself looking not at Fiona, who had forgotten me in her brief moment of frenzy in front of the dark altar, but up at a small pulpit lacquered with circus colors of blue and gold and somehow fastened high on the stone wall opposite me. The sun, as on my altar, warmed the pulpit and struck with fire a life-sized wooden arm that protruded over the edge of the pulpit and was extended, as in some kind of benediction, in the wet air. Except for the arm, with its crack near the elbow and its flowing wooden sleeve and pasty yellow hand, and except for the two altars and little peculiar pulpit, I might have been standing in some gutted cellar of the ancient world, some pit giving onto secret viaducts packed with the old world's excrement.

"Look, Fiona, a wooden arm!"

Barefooted, wearing only her bra and brief for the beach, as well as the yellow coat, of course, which was her concession to the disapproving village and intended to spare us both from muttered threats of *croak peonie*, and alert, unappeasable, quick-breathing, austere and supple, the only woman I have ever known who, as sex-aesthetician, was nearly my equivalent, woman whose aging body was nonetheless a young green tree—how like my wife, Fiona, to thrust her proud chin and hungry mouth into the crumpled face of the sightless dead and then to fly on, magnificent and quite oblivious to my own discoveries, my own passing sensual interest in a wooden arm. Perhaps the aesthetic pleasures of the wooden arm were subtle, even for Fiona. Because now she spoke again in her whisper that was firm and clear, submissive and peremptory, and already her mind and eyes were elsewhere, had not comprehended the comic miracle of the arm in space, the wooden hand that no one would ever hold.

"Cyril, I want to light a candle. OK?"

She had turned, was facing me, the coat hung open, her stomach appeared to be unusually small and round above the wide hips and wonderfully frank pelvic area bound up in the tight spongy whiteness of her brief for the beach. So I drew the smoke back in through my heavy nose and took my time, once again admired myself for thinking to bring this woman into the humorless solemnity of empty nave and squat buttressed church, once again tried to follow the new course of her flight.

"Sure. But who on earth would we light it for?"

"Oh, Cyril, does it matter? I just want to light a candle, baby."

And Fiona would have had her way, would have sailed in long quick strides to the other end of the nave, would have selected the perfect thin white candle and kissed it, impetuously kissed it, and then would have watched while I slowly took the candle from her firm hand and impaled this, Fiona's candle, on one of the little upright spikes set in rows for that purpose, would have had me strike the match and light the wick for the benefit, perhaps, of the infant whose ancient and miniature skeleton she had already made her own—would have caused all this to happen, would have had us standing side by side and inhaling the long black strings of smoke and appreciating together the honeyed scent of the wax, had not the candle-lighting idea been destroyed the very instant Fiona was beginning to move by a sudden ominous clamor in the cobbled alley just outside the church. We heard men running and grunting, heard the sound of boots on the stones. Simultaneously the nave was filled with the sharp clanging of the bell in the squat tower above our heads, and with the ugly blasts of the obsolete mechanical horn always blown by some village official in times of crisis.

"Is it a fire, Cyril?"

"Button your coat and we'll find out," I said, smiling at the disappearance of the flame that was never lit.

In the next instant we fled fragile bones and rotting lace and wooden arm, fled the rows of little upright spikes that were spattered with dusty clots of melted wax and on one of which a single crooked candle was, as a matter of fact, already burning, hand in hand ran from the cold nave, appeared together briefly against the sagging and worm-eaten wooden church door that we pushed shut behind us, and then took up the chase after two squat men in rubber boots and crude black leather helmets. Fiona's coat was closed, the black horn was blowing. From a short distance ahead came gruff intermittent shouts, commands of *croak peonie* and, oddly enough, the sound of laughter.

"What the hell," I said, pacing my breath, holding Fiona's hand and restraining somewhat her flight, "they're laughing."

"Come on, baby. Please. I want to see."

One more booted and helmeted figure, short and fat and carrying some kind of boat hook, thundered up from behind and passed us, despite his clumsiness, and sped on after the other two and disappeared. Broken tiles, the familiar stone cups filled with poison and set out on empty window ledges and in empty doorways, the closeness of the narrow walls that magnified every sound so that we could hear distinctly the choppy breathing of the three stunted men who were, I knew, members of the much-feared and openly hostile fire brigade—through this brief stretch of dismal labyrinth we ran, the elegant woman who dared show to all the village her hard naked feet and the spectacular man who, in actual sight of the church, had been seen to blow from his mouth disrespectful shapes in blue smoke.

But then we emerged from the hollow darkness of a low arch into full view of the black canal whose simple low cobbled embankment was wide enough to accommodate roving dogs, sullen families on foot and, one at a time, those rare engine-powered vehicles that appeared, now and again, from beyond the mountains. Here the crowd was gathered, we saw, not for fire or bicycle accident or fist fight between children with slack jaws and bloodshot eyes, but instead was pressing toward the edge of the canal in anger or with laughter because a large khaki-colored motorbus had somehow found its way off the sloping embankment and now sat, floated, right side up on the still water black with pollution.

"My God, Cyril, they're going to drown!"

Her hand was long and white and cold in mine, gently I maneuvered myself so that Fiona could see—it was always essential that Fiona see the cruelest accident, the smallest catastrophe, the gravest incident—but would not be able to pitch us without warning into the midst of the little factioned crowd or into the way of the rescuers. She pulled, I held her firmly, she leaned as far as she could toward the bus that was imperceptibly rocking now about ten feet from the embankment where the nearest brute-shaped member of the fire brigade stood shouting out his furious commands.

"It's going to sink, Cyril. Isn't it?"

I frowned, waited, and with pressure on her hand and a movement of my shoulders and a soft thoughtful sound in my nose and throat tried to convey that it was a question no one could answer.

"But people commit suicide that way, baby. It has to sink."

In the air a handful of slim white pigeons circled the scene, on the embankment half the crowd bent themselves into lewd positions and laughed at the occupants in the bus and at the bus itself, while the other half scowled darkly and pointed to ropes and boat hooks and flimsy ladders. Across the canal a woman in a shuttered window was calling for someone to come and look. And there on the water before us the old high-bodied motorbus still floated. Derelict, obviously painted and repaired endlessly by lazy unskilled workers, khaki-colored and smeared here and there with swatches of lurid purple and smoky black, heavily dented from its long life of collisions (with stone fountains, cornices, rocks in the road, unlucky animals) still it floated in a kind of majestic dementia, though steam was hissing up from its hood and an oil stain was rising from all its submerged gearboxes, tanks, iron pockets packed with grease. I could see air bubbles where the tin body met the water, a drifting orange bobbed against the side of the still floating old machine.

Here, I thought, were several different modes of incongruity. In a matter of minutes we might be left staring at nothing more than the little orange drifting on the dark and apparently currentless flow of sewage. The pigeons, of course, were small and sweet and serene, while the helpless crowd and remnant of the fire brigade were clumsy, violent. But what of Fiona and me? In all their shock and fear, did those in the bus give a passing thought to Fiona and me? For one terrible instant did it occur to them, driver and passengers, that the tall man and woman on the edge of the crowd might be precisely strong enough and elegant enough to save them, since even the bulky members of the fire brigade were hopelessly entangled in the slick coils of their age-old brutal ignorance and despite all their activity could in fact do nothing? But what of the woman screaming behind the slatted shutter? And how did the motorbus arrive in its present state of danger and momentary suspension on waters more fetid than any waters I had ever smelled? A failure of brakes? Some physical or psychological failure in the stricken driver?

A single gasp went up then from the serious faction of the crowd, Fiona squeezed my hand and held her breath as if all her fear and courage and sweeping empathy were now mounted forever in still marble, across the canal the screaming woman burst open her shutter, glared out, and as quickly smashed it shut again, the brute-backed leader of the fire brigade fell to his knees, stuck out his arm, waited—because with a sucking sound the front of the old bus started down, dipped with sudden unalterable purpose toward the stinking depths of the timeless pestilential canal. Dipped, started down, but was then somehow relinquished by the deep intestinal tug of the canal and slowly, slowly, rose again to its original horizontal position with nothing to mark the near disappearance of motorbus and occupants except a thin ripple spreading out from the front bumper, some agitation in the orange, and a sigh from those of us who did not suffer from the abnormal attitudes born of the bad blood carried to this warm coast centuries before from central Europe.

"Do something, Cyril," she whispered then. "Please, baby."

All those on the embankment were quiet. Several of the leather-garbed stumping firemen began, like lunging turtles, to tie together two slender ladders with strips of wire. Fiona put her lips to my cheek.

The occupants of the bus were unaware of Fiona's efforts on their behalf, were apparently unaware of the will power she was now exerting. Yet might not the power of Fiona's psyche have been as much responsible as anything else for the continued presence of the motorbus on the viscous surface of the historically significant canal? And, as far as I could see, they were unaware of the disaster which, a moment before, had all but concluded. Pigeons, ladders, Fiona's white face and yellow coat, an old man with a stack of twigs on his back and determined to tell someone that they should tie a rope to the head of a pike—none of it meant anything to the pathetically small group of occupants inside the bus. The driver gripped his wheel, the man and woman were holding the edges of the seats in front of them, only the heads of the three female children and the black dog were visible. but those few faces were cold, expressionless, unusually small, and were, all seven of them, including the dog's, forced rigidly to the front. As I bent down to get a better look through the windows it occurred to me that driver and passengers did not in fact comprehend that they were afloat precariously in an ancient canal, but rather were expecting some more conventional catastrophe and were still looking ahead toward the as yet invisible landscape of the impending crash. It occurred to me also that beneath the water those six people and the small black animal would be lost, so to speak, in so large and so nearly empty a motorbus.

And then it sank. Again the crowd gasped, the old man threw down his twigs, Fiona with one round movement of her shoulders tore free of my hand. But of course I was familiar with all the bright severity and wildness of Fiona's spirit and now was ready for one of her stronger displays of grace and determination. So in my left arm I caught her slender waist exactly as the motorbus went down.

"Wait a minute," I whispered, feeling the fight going out of the stomach muscles against my arm, "just wait a minute, Fiona. It's all right."

Then once again the laughing faction of the crowd was laughing, and even while she felt my soothing voice in her ear and the comforting tension of my forearm drawn tight across the central portion of her body, still Fiona must have understood the laughter and forced herself to see what was actually happening to the old bus before our eyes. Because now it sat more firmly than it had ever rested on dirt road or cobbled street, sat immobile with all four wheels solidly positioned on the hard bed of excrement which, down through the centuries, had accumulated like lava in the bottom of the black canal. But windows, roof, luggage strapped to the roof, spare tire, hood—all the upper half of the old high-bodied machine rose above the water, would no doubt remain emerging from that motionless water as long as the canal walls stood and there were sudden figures to shout *croak peonie* and tip the contents of stinking buckets into the holes and stone gutters that fed the very smell of time. The waters were not deep (how like these villagers and members of the fire brigade and the old men not to know the depth of their own canal), not deep, yet deep enough to rise well above the wheels, to flood the interior of the bus at least as high as the knees of the still unmoving occupants, with its black weight to anchor the motorbus where it sat forever. In all the village there was no hoist to lift it, no barge to drag it down to the mouth of the canal. But even if they could, would red-eyed peasants ever take the trouble to remove the enormous old motorbus from a canal that had once been choked with the bodies of dead barbarians? I knew they would not.

"Baby, look! That little girl is waving at me!"

Then Fiona snatched my face into her two hands, kissed me, wheeled about and waved back at the child, while even above the shouts and clatter of the fire brigade we heard, suddenly, the muffled terror-stricken yelps of the black dog that was now jumping from seat to seat up and down the long water-filled interior of the half-sunken bus. Momentarily out of sight, it reappeared with wet shredded ears and tail, with wet fur slick on its belly and on its short black sturdy legs, had obviously fallen, had been swimming and barking in the fetid water between the seats. And now the woman was attempting to wade to the help of the smaller children who were kneeling, apparently, on the wooden seats, the oldest girl was waving timidly at Fiona, the tall black-haired man was stooping and holding to his chest an armful of photographic equipment and grinning.

"Oh, Cyril, he's handsome! And look at his wife!"

The sucking of the boots of the brute-backed leader of the fire brigade, the sound of shattering glass, the wheezing and laughter and shouts of the crowd, all of whom clearly suffered from some congenital rasping respiratory disease, the thin high cries of the sopping wet dog—suddenly through all this abrasive noise I heard, as if directly into my left ear, the strong but milky vocal qualities of Fiona's voice which told me, in sense and tone, that she was once more making one of her aesthetic evaluations.

"My God, he's handsome. Just look at him!"

She had twisted her head in one direction, her shoulders in another, at the same time twisted her hips in the same direction as her sharp-featured and happily agitated face, and out of all this sinuous exertion and equilibrium had come her voice, her judgment, another fresh gift of discovery which, as usual, she gave to me swiftly and without hesitation. So now I listened, lit one of my clumsy cigarettes, glanced around at all the illiterate faces and powerful but sagging shoulders, and then leaned down again for another and better look at the man in the half-sunken bus. Fiona was already waving again at the white-faced girl.

Stroked my chin, leaned down, frowned a little and got some intensity into my large brown eyes, until suddenly I caught him there knee-deep in the excremental waters, from all the chaos of dog and children and large unsmiling wife was able to isolate his grinning face and for a moment to hold him still, so to speak, for appraisal.

30

She was right. As usual Fiona had made another good aesthetic judgment. Because the tall black-haired man stooping in the bus window was dressed, I could see, in a powdery blue tweed jacket and black turtleneck shirt which was a combination that had always been one of Fiona's favorites. More important, perhaps, he had a well-weathered face, a face not tanned and darkened in the wind and sun like mine, for instance, but so weathered and pebbled, so grained in darkness and cold rain that it resembled stone. Gray stone. I knew I had never before seen the thin lips, narrow bright boyish eyes, high sandblasted cheekbones, pointed ears, black hair curling across his forehead and curling in a few odd ringlets in what appeared to be a beard newly grown. Yet I recognized his face immediately because its exact replica, an image of Saint Peter that was perfect except for the broken ears, had been chiseled along with the head of Saint Paul into the granite arch of the entrance to the squat church where one candle, I knew, was still burning. Saint Peter in stone. No wonder Fiona called his striking features to my attention. Any woman would have found Saint Peter attractive. And in the case of my wife, how could Fiona help but appreciate a face whose exact replica we had seen and admired during every one of our rambling visits to the squat church? On every one of our visits the stone face, with its strength and malice, had invariably caused Fiona to hold her breasts while standing perfectly still and gazing up at it. Now of course she was busily waving at the frightened child.

But then the tall figure with the saintly goatish face was grinning, not to himself, not at Fiona, but directly at me, and in that instant I recognized that we were friends already and, seeing the empty powdery blue sleeve bent double and fastened with a large safety pin just below the shoulder, realized that for some reason Fiona had failed to comment on his obvious deformity, which to me was the most interesting thing about him, and realized that it was in my power to lead them both to the exact spot where his missing arm was hidden.

"He's great, Fiona. But did you notice his arm?"

I would have liked to see her face at that moment, but she went on waving. And then it was too late. Because suddenly the hatless driver and stunted members of the fire brigade began to cooperate, made large gestures with hairy hands, splashed into the water, manipulated the ladders tied together with wire and thongs, found the escape hatch in the roof of the bus, pushed and pulled and cried *croak peonie* beneath the slow wheeling of the pigeons, cut loose the baggage on the roof and mingled together inside the bus and then again waist-deep in the canal, bumped and struggled together until at last the empty motorbus was abandoned altogether to the smell of time.

The eyes of the rescuers were concealed, of course, beneath the thick curving brims of leather helmets. And yet as by a begrudging and prearranged signal, and somehow understanding that the man and woman in the bus were as tall as the man and woman on the embankment, and that there was in fact some similarity between yellow suede coat, white pullover, blue jacket, and pea-green slacks (which was what the woman in the bus was wearing), each struggling member of the fire brigade deposited one by one his burden of dog, child, suitcase in my own waiting arms or at my feet. I was picked out of the crowd, so to speak, as the man with the authority to receive survivors.

"Oh, baby, you're doing beautifully," came Fiona's cold milky voice ringing with pleasure, and holding the dog by the long wet fur and folds of skin at its throat, holding one of the little girls by an elbow bundled into the sleeve of a sweater the color of her father's coat, noticing that the laces of all three children's blunt brown shoes were untied and dangling, and that the older girl had hair the color of ginger, and waiting now for the woman and the man himself to climb dripping to our embankment and repossess their dog, their girls, their wet luggage—during all these first moments of their rescue and their arrival I was grateful for the laughter in Fiona's voice, took a curious pleasure in the smell and feeling of the large quantity of canal water that my pullover and beige-colored trousers had already absorbed from the clothes of the children and the black hair of the dog.

I was squatting down on a knee and a foot, one of the smaller girls was climbing onto my back, the luggage was piling up around us. I saw the round-faced woman in Fiona's immediate embrace, watched the woman's one-armed husband pushing toward us unassisted and with leather cases dangling from straps held high in his single hand. But it was not for us to see the future, not for me to know that the large woman trembling in the arms of my wife was soon to be my own last mistress, while the man with the face of Saint Peter and who was now climbing the shaky ladder into our midst was soon to use his one good hand to explore the cool white skin of Fiona's life.

When at last he stood among us, grinning and dripping,

smelling of the canal and dangling the leather cases of all his cameras against the wet knees of what I saw were long-legged navy-blue bell-bottom trousers, and when Fiona dropped her arms, turned quickly with aimless hands and bright eyes that appeared not to see flying pigeons or squatting husband or distant embarrassed driver of the motorbus, and then laughed and took a step and suddenly kissed the gaunt stony cheek of this tall hero who had come to us over the same mountains once crossed by the barbarians, certainly I knew then that we were due for some kind of new adventure, Fiona and I. What else could it be?

AM I EMBRACING AIR? COULD THAT BE ALL? IS THAT WHAT it feels like to discover with absolute certainty that you yourself have simply disappeared from the filmy field? When Love withdraws her breath from your body, and as with the tip of a long green tail flicks the very spot where you stood or thought you stood in the upper right or lower left-hand corner of the endless tapestry, is that what it is like? Embracing air?

Fiona's mouth kissed dozens of aching mouths, including mine, and my own large mouth kissed at least an equal number of smaller mouths, including Fiona's, and though her lips were small, Fiona's mouth could in the proper light and proper mood become quite as hard and voracious as my own and nearly as large, and time after time we kissed so that bone struck bone and teeth lay against teeth, each of us struggling, maneuvering, to eat the other's mouth, to catch the other's jaw between the rows of his own hard teeth. Time after time I ate the darkness that Fiona pumped from her throbbing throat into her open mouth, time after time Fiona took from my own lips and tongue and teeth a taste much stronger than cigarettes or wine. For my part no flavor discovered in a kiss ever aroused my oral greed as did the special flavor I always found in Fiona's mouth, a special taste of mint tinged with that faint suggestion of decay which I drew each time from the very roots of her perfect teeth.

Is it then mere pompous lyricism to talk, to chew, to blow smoke rings, to breathe when I am no longer able to look at Fiona or talk with her or run my finger along the curve of her smallest rib or put my mouth to hers? Are memory and clairvoyance mere twin languorous drafts of rose-tinted air? Or to notice Rosella's raw hips beneath her mangy skirt and then not even to seize them for a moment in friendly hands, or to allow Rosella to sleep alone at the far end of my villa without so much as one clandestine visit from a man who was once master of the clandestine visit, or to do no more than smile at a few of Hugh's now-faded photographs of naked girls, or to explain to Rosella in a language she cannot understand exactly what pleasures await us when the veil of dormancy dissolves—are all these further instances of mere wind feathering endlessly through hands, fingers, empty arms? Should I be feeling some kind of loss, some hollow pain? Or am I dying? Already dead?

But it is hardly a fault to have lived my life, and still to live it, without knowing pain. And dormancy, memory, voyance, what more could I want? My dormancy is my hive, my honeypot, my sleeping castle, the golden stall in which the white bull lies quite alive and dreaming. For me the still air is thicker than leaves, and if memory gives me back the grape-tasting game and bursting sun, clairvoyance returns to me in a different way my wife, my last mistress, the little golden sheep who over her shoulder turns small bulging eyes in my direction. But not Hugh. He is gone for good. And Hugh is the man who died for love, not me.

And yet every man is vulnerable, no man is safe. If my world has flowered, still flowers, nonetheless it stands to reason that even the best of men and the most quiet and agreeable of lovers may earn his share of disapproval. There are those who in fact would like nothing better than to fill my large funnel-shaped white thighs with the fish hooks of their disapproval. There are those who would deny me all my nights in Fiona's bed if they could, would strip me of silken dressing gown and fling me into some greasy white-tiled pit of naked sex-offenders. For some, love itself is a crime.

I realize all this. I could hardly have lived so long among the roses without feeling the thorns, could hardly have enjoyed so much in privacy without seeing the scowls of the crowd. But it will take a dark mind to strip my vines, to destroy the last shreds of my tapestry, to choke off my song. It will take a lot to destroy Hugh's photographs or to gut the many bedrooms of the sleeping castle. I am a match, I hope, for the hatred of conventional enemies wherever they are.

THE SUN WAS SETTING, SINKING TO ITS PREDESTINED DEATH, and to the four of us, or at least to me, that enormous smoldering sun lay on the horizon like a dissolving orange suffused with blood. The tide was low, the smooth black oval stones beneath us were warm to the flesh, we could hear the distant sounds of the three girls playing with the dog behind the funeral cypresses. Fiona, wearing a pale lemon-colored bra and pale lemon-colored briefs for the beach, and I in my magenta trunks as sparse and thick and elastic as an athletic supporter, and Hugh in his long-sleeved cotton shirt and loose gray trunks like undershorts, and Catherine dressed in her faded madras halter and swimming skirt and shorts—together we sat with legs outstretched, soles of our feet touching or nearly touching, a four-pointed human starfish resting together in the last livid light of the day.

No one moved. Without calculation, almost without consciousness, Fiona lay propped on her elbows and with her head back, her eyes closed, her tense lips gently smiling. Even Catherine appeared to be sunk in a kind of worried slumber, aware somehow of the thick orange light on her knees. Prone bodies, silence hanging on the children's voices and scattered barking of their old black dog, the empty wine bottles turning to gold. All of us felt the inertia, suspension, tranquility, though I found myself tapping out a silent expectant rhythm with one of my big toes while

Hugh's narrow black eyes were alert, unresting, I noticed, and to me revealed only too clearly his private thoughts. But the small black oval stones we lay on were for us much better than sand. Our beach, as we called it, was a glassy volcanic bed that made us draw closer together to touch toes, to dream. With one hand I was carelessly crushing a few thin navy-blue sea shells, making a small pile of crushed shell on my naked navel. And yet it was the sun, the sun alone that filled all our thoughts and was turning the exposed skin of all four bodies the same deepening color. The lower the sun fell the more it glowed.

I felt someone's foot recoil from mine and then return. Even the tiny black ringlets in Hugh's beard were turning orange. I could hear the powdery shells collecting in the well of my belly and I realized that all four of us were together on a black volcanic beach in the hour when fiercely illumined goats stand still and huddle and the moon prepares to pour its milk on the fire.

"Cyril. We don't have to go back yet, do we?"

I glanced at Fiona, heard the matter-of-fact whisper and saw that her expression had not changed, that her lips had not moved. But rolling onto one hip, propping myself on one elbow, brushing away crushed shells with a hasty stroke of one hand, I saw also that there was movement in the curve of her throat and that the sun had saturated one of her broad white shoulders. And before I could answer, Fiona giggled. My sensible, stately, impatient, clear-bodied wife giggled, as if in a dream a small bird had alighted on her belly. Giggled for no reason apparently, she whose every impulsive gesture was informed with its own hidden sense, and at the sound Hugh became suddenly rigid, Catherine opened her eyes. I knew what to do.

In silence, while the sun flushed us most deeply and unrecognizably with orange light, I got to my knees beside Fiona, who did not move, and with a flick of my hand untied the silken strings of her pale lemon-colored halter, those thin silken cords knotted in a bow behind her bent neck and curving back, and then with a few more skillful movements removed altogether Fiona's little lemon-colored bra. Then I folded this the briefest of all Fiona's half-dozen bathing bras, stuck it for safekeeping inside one of my empty shoes, and flowed back slowly into my former position on the hot rocks.

Understandably perhaps, for the first few moments Catherine and even Hugh could not bear to look. I myself hardly dared to look. But then I heard a sound like a finger scratching inside Hugh's throat and our three heads turned furtively, shyly, violently or calmly in my wife's direction. And Fiona's eyes, I saw, were open. We said nothing, Fiona was looking straight at the sun and smiling. But had she wanted me to expose her breasts, I wondered, for Hugh's sake or mine? Or was the exposure purely my own idea and something that entered her consciousness and gave her pleasure only after I had touched her, untied the strings? I could not know. But I knew immediately that it was a good idea.

Fiona's breasts were not large. Yet in the sun's lurid effulgence they glistened, grew tight while the two nipples turned to liquid rings, bands, so that to me Fiona's two firm breasts suddenly became the bursting irises of a young

39

white owl's wide-open eyes, and when in the next moment she giggled again, again apparently without reason, those bright naked eyes, breasts, recorded the little spasms of pleasure that, otherwise unseen, were traveling down Fiona's chest and neck and arms.

"Baby, can't we just stay like this forever?"

We heard the words, we watched the very motion of Fiona's speech in her lips and breasts. In mouth and breasts my wife was singing, and despite the possibility of another unexpected giggle, which no doubt would be accompanied by another small eruption of rolling or bouncing in the lovely breasts as well as a slight twisting in the slope of the shoulders, despite all this or perhaps because of it the preciousness of what Fiona said maintained the silence, prevented the rest of us from talking. I could see the thin white edge of Fiona's teeth between the slightly parted lips, the voice was soft and clear, the naked orange breasts were unimaginably free, her eyes were partially open. Even in the silence she was singing, and the rest of us were listening, watching.

Then suddenly Hugh began to scratch viciously at himself beneath the loose gray shorts, and Catherine moved. With a brief flashing sensation of regret, it occurred to me that she was about to climb heavily, angrily to her feet and leave. She too could hear that in the distance the children were beginning to quarrel, beginning to tease the dog. But I was wrong, and she merely drew herself slowly out of her supine state, raised her back and lifted up her long heavy legs and sat upright with her thighs pressed together on the black rocks and her knees bent and her strong calves crossed at the ankles.

And then Hugh spoke. Stopped scratching himself and spoke, while Catherine's unreadable eyes met mine and I smiled, allowed my large right orange hand to lie comfortably where my upper thighs, which were about twice the girth of even Catherine's thighs, joined in special harmony the inverted apex of my own magenta briefs for the beach.

"That's it. All these years you've been castrating him!"

On this occasion it was hardly what I thought he would say. Was this the extent of the private thoughts I had been watching all this time in his black eyes? But then I laughed, because Hugh had been staring all this time at the bare breasts of my wife and because he was thin and because despite the ringlets of his beard and curls of black hair across his forehead was nonetheless wearing the long gray shapeless bathing trunks and the white cotton collarless shirt with the right sleeve pinned up with one of Catherine's large steel safety pins. Perhaps he did not enjoy the sight of Fiona as much as I did, or would not admit that he did. Nonetheless, that he could lie in my shadow and stare at my wife as he was in fact staring at her, and then pronounce what he had just pronounced, aroused in me new admiration for so much craft, for so much comic design.

"Cyril is virile, baby. He really is."

The absolute certainty of the soft voice which in timbre matched the curve of Fiona's throat, the pleasing brevity of the assertion, the mild sex-message of the accompanying giggle, which was more than the giggle of a mere girl, the fact that Fiona still had not moved but lay back on her elbows with one slender leg raised at the knee and her breasts falling imperceptibly to either side—at that moment I could not have loved Fiona more or felt more affection for my courageous, self-betraying Saint Peter, as I had come to call Hugh mentally whenever our quaternion reached special intensity or special joy.

Suspension, suffusion, peace for the four of us on that black beach. But it was all beginning to pass, I knew, and still I waited, now hearing the older girl shouting at the smaller girls behind the funeral cypresses. Shifting a little, growing mildly impatient myself, I waited, wondering if this momentary idyl would pass before the rose and golden metallic threads could begin to spin our separate anatomies forever into the sunset scene, would come to a sudden conclusion, incomplete, unbalanced. What was the matter with Hugh? Why was he not holding up his end?

I could understand Hugh's affected lack of gratitude, could enjoy his efforts to conceal his feelings on seeing Fiona without her bra. And of course Hugh could not possibly know that I was well aware of the fact that he had already seen Fiona's naked breasts, had already held her breasts in his good hand, so that in taking off her halter I knew full well that I was violating no confidence and was merely extending naturally the pleasures of a treat already quite familiar to the two of us. And I realized also that Hugh did not know that already I was as familiar with Catherine's naked breasts as he was with Fiona's, so that the baring of Catherine's breasts would be no surprise for me. Was he then thoughtless? Selfish? Without even the crudest idea of simple reciprocity? Certainly he must have known that it was up to him, not me, to unfasten Catherine's overly modest halter and take it off. What was holding him back? Could he not see that Catherine herself was puzzled, uncomfortable? Could he deliberately mean to embarrass his wife and to tamper with the obviously intended symmetry of our little scene on the beach? Hugh was unmusical, but I had hoped I could count on him for at least a few signs of romantic temperament. After all, how could any man love my wife and yet fail to appreciate simple harmonious arrangements of flesh, shadow, voice, hair, which were as much the result of Fiona's artistry as of mine. But perhaps I had been wrong. Perhaps Hugh had no eye for the sex-tableau.

I yawned, glanced at the finely muscled music of Fiona's breathing, began crushing another pile of shells. Back at the villas one of the smaller girls was now shrieking distantly in short monotonous bursts of pain.

And then, nearly too late, Catherine acted on her own behalf, brought herself to do what Hugh should have done, and out of feelings of exclusion or possibly pleasure or more likely irritable retaliation, managed to complete the picture that Hugh had almost destroyed. She frowned, tightened her lips, took a short breath and, crooking her elbows so that her bent arms became the rapidly moving wings of some large bird, reached behind her back and quickly, without help, unfastened her halter and pulled it off. It was an awkward, rapid, determined, self-sufficient gesture of compliance, and I was proud of her. And even though in that first moment of exposure she looked as if she wanted nothing more than to cross her arms and conceal beneath the flesh of her arms the flesh of her breasts, still she sat up straight and kept herself uncovered. I was proud of her.

And though I had already known what we would see

when she finally bared herself, could visualize to the last detail the surfaces of Catherine's nakedness, still it pleased me to see the round rising breasts and the nipples that resembled small dark rosebuds tightly furled, and to see all this, not at night in their villa, but here at sunset on the polished black stones born of the volcano's chaotic fire.

How long would we manage to preserve this balance of nudity? For how long would we be allowed to appreciate the fact that the nude breathing torsos of these two very different women simply enhanced each other? I could not know. But here, at least, was the possibility of well-being, and though Catherine sat with eyes averted and arms straight and the large halter half-wadded, clutched, in one large hand in her lap, still at that moment I found myself tingling with the realization that Hugh's wife had acted deliberately and in large part for me. And now, this instant, if Catherine had been able, say, to cup her breasts in her hands with Fiona's thoughtless exhilaration, might not the sight of Catherine be as stimulating as that of Fiona? Then again, wasn't the naturalness of Catherine's slight lingering discomfort exactly as stimulating as the naturalness of my own wife's erotic confidence? I smiled, I found that the ball of my right foot was pressed gently to the solid front of one of Catherine's knees, I heard Fiona giggling and saw that Hugh's blue-gray ankle was now trapped, so to speak, between both of Fiona's energetic feet, and again I began to hope that I had not overestimated Hugh after all.

But rolling onto my hands and knees, getting to my feet with a cheerful groan, lumbering to cut off the oldest girl who was running toward us out of the cypresses and shouting for Catherine, and stopping her and displaying friend-

44

liness and knowing that when I turned to wave I would see distant gestures of busy hands fastening big and little halters once again into place—still I could only smile and do a few dancing bear steps for the angry child, because no sex-tableau was ever entirely abortive and because ahead of us lay an unlimited supply of dying suns and crescent moons which Fiona, and Catherine too, would know how to use.

"Don't think I don't know what you're up to," whispered Meredith and shook off my hand. But after all, I told myself, her one poor sour note could never be any match for old Cyril's song.

YESTERDAY ROSELLA AND I WENT HUNTING FOR BLACK snails. And yesterday, for the first time, Rosella and I ate a meal together. Side by side on hands and knees, or squatting together, prowling about the walls of the villa, spreading the tall grass that grows in senseless clumps against the smoke-blackened walls of my crumbling villa, or poking one after the other in the flower beds nearly invisible now under thickets of crab grass, dead brambles, translucent yellow weeds that turn to powder at the slightest touch, or taking turns with a stick at the base of the little well house which is like a miniature chapel and in fact once wore a small flimsy hand-wrought Byzantine cross of iron on its conical stone roof—for some time Rosella has joined me in my pursuit of the snails, in silent accord has accepted the snail hunt as one of my simple activities safe enough, perhaps, to share. But then yesterday, filling the two hot bowls and with no change in her reluctant movements or empty face, pretending that our meal for two was a mere matter of course, Rosella sat across from me and ate her evening meal at the same time that I ate mine.

Because of the way the birds changed the pitch of their singing, or because of subtle light changes where I sat under the low hand-hewn beams, or because I could tell by the smoke's odor that the fire was out, and by the breath of air at my small lopsided window as well as the sounds that reached me from the dead gardens could tell that the day was fading, somehow I knew as usual that the time was right, that Rosella had put aside her broom of twigs, had emptied her buckets and left her scrub brushes out to dry, had once again come unstuck from the web of her crude and exhausting day. It was twilight and time to look for the silver trails. Rosella stood waiting for me beside the well house, and I was pleased to see the earthen pot in her arms, the worn-down wooden sandals on the naked feet, the thin earthen-colored dress worn with blunt indifference.

"Here you are again, Rosella. The girl by the well."

I smiled, Rosella merely shifted the chipped pot in her arms. Did she yearn for my hand, did she sometimes wish that I might join her in the squat church of the wooden arm? Did she admire my shabby black coat and vest and trousers, did she yearn sometimes to feel between her stubby insensitive fingers the golden watch chain that hung across all the breadth of my black vest? Was she beginning to need some physical gesture of affection? I thought she was.

46

I was close enough now to see the pocks in the fired flesh of the old pot and to see the bones in Rosella's shoulders and the crow's-feet at the corners of her youthful eyes. Her skin was swarthy, her nose was oddly aquiline, no doubt she was a long-descended daughter of the barbarians. But in her childhood had she also been tutored in the lore of the female saints? Is that where she got her indifference, her strength, the blunt crippled look in her dark eyes, from wooden pitchforks and the lives of the female saints?

There was moisture in one of her nostrils, her hands curved naturally to the roundness of the pot, a little dried blood was caked on one of her feet. For a moment I thought of Catherine, as I often do, and then wished that Fiona could see me boxed in by the funeral cypresses with Rosella whose head barely reached my chest and whose voice I hardly heard from one month to the next.

And with my knuckle tapping the earthen shape in her arms: "This evening, let's see if we can fill it right to the brim, Rosella."

Moments later I was once more able to enjoy the sound of heavy snails falling into the wide-mouthed pot. In the twilight we were side by side, Rosella and I, kneeling together at the edge of a small rectangle of pulpy leaves. The snails were plentiful and the sticky silver trails crept down dead stems, climbed over exposed roots, disappeared under black chunks of decomposing stone. Everywhere the snails were massing or making their blind osmotic paths about the villa, eating and destroying and unwinding their silver trails. They were the eyes of night, the crawling stones.

"Faster, Rosella," I murmured, "a little faster."

She seemed to understand, and shifted her knees further

apart, tightened her kneeling animalistic posture, tugged at a small jagged shard of buried tile and suddenly unearthed a pocket as large as the blade of a shovel and packed like a nest of mud with the sightless snails. In both hands she scooped them up and, while I steadied the pot, dropped them covered with flecks and strings of fresh mud into the warm hole of the pot. Then I laughed, reached into the pot with my large white hand, frayed cuff and golden cuff link (anniversary gift from Fiona), seized one of the snails and pulled it out quickly and smashed it against the cream-colored grainy side of the pot.

"That's what they look like, Rosella. Smell?"

She was backing up. Her haunches moved, her thighs began to work, again one of her sandals cracked against the pot, and suddenly one hand reached behind and tugged up the constricting skirt of her hemp-colored dress. Rosella, I saw, was moving backward. And smelling the gloom of the funeral cypresses, I laughed and, despite the rules, thrust out my hand so that in another moment my hand might have confronted her flesh and staved off the now partially exposed buttocks, though even my hand pushed hard against her buttocks could not have prevented us from tangling in what would have been a kind of accidental Arcadian embrace. I lost hold of the pot and it tipped over. Rosella looked at me, and in the clear rose-tinted twilight and amidst small noises of grass, brambles, stones all disturbed by our movements, I thought that Rosella's eyes reminded me of the bulging eyes of my little long-lost golden sheep. And then we stopped. Stopped, waited, listened, heard the ticking of the grass, the brushing sounds of a few small birds, the slow dripping of contaminated water and, from somewhere in the increasing shadows, footsteps.

"Someone's coming. Hear it?"

And then it was dark, and I smelled the flaking roof of the well house and stood up and brushed the burrs from the sleeve of my jacket, straightened my golden eyeglasses, pulled at the little points of my vest, and immediately saw the hunchback standing beneath the rotting arbor with a stone crock in his arms.

Leather coat, leather cap, rubber boots, shoulders as broad as mine, even in the deep green light from the funeral cypresses and with a cluster of dead grapes brushing his high muscular hump, still I could see that he was someone easily frightened. And yet he was staring not at me but at Rosella, seemed to expect not an assault from me but rather some kind of recognition from her. When he spoke as he then did, it became obvious that he was young. He took a breath, his lips moved, he spoke. And out of all that leathern bulk and deformity of a man who looked like a capped and muzzled bear came a voice that suggested only the softness and clarity of a young girl's voice poured from a shy pitcher. *Croak peonie*, he must have said, or *crespi fagag*. I could not be sure.

"Who is he, Rosella? Your brother? Cousin?"

I was right, of course, because Rosella said a few words not to me but to the deformed intruder who turned, put down his crock, and in the darkness and crushing shriveled grapes beneath his boots, disappeared around the corner of my long low-silhouetted villa. By now everything had succumbed to the light of the somber trees, to the silence, to the purple shadows of the cypresses. And in this silence,

49

this gloom, the crock was white and plainly visible. I took a step. I heard the slapping of the wooden flats, felt Rosella's shoulder brush my sleeve in passing, saw her little shadowy figure stooping down. And Rosella and the white crock were gone.

Night. Silence. Decayed and dormant stones, tiles, vines. Crude arbor. From my pocket I fished a cigarette, glanced up at the stars, inhaled. Turning to retrieve the pot of snails I paused, inhaled again, thought I detected in the wall of funeral cypresses that narrow but convenient passage through which I used to make my nightly way to Catherine.

No regrets.

In my mouth the smoke was the color of mustard, around my ears the curling hair was both gold and gray, overhead the night was thick with stars. So I had no regrets. I smelled the peppery darkness, retrieved the pot and left it where Rosella could dump the snails down the hole in the flat stone of our crude lavatory in the morning. Then I groped my way toward Rosella and the light of the olive-twig fire, the smell of smoke.

At first glance I thought the crock was packed with fur, because by the uneven light of Rosella's fire the soft brown substance rising somewhat higher than the square mouth of the crock rippled and gleamed softly, was alight with richness and flashing colors so that it suggested fur. But my fingers told me immediately that the crock was packed not with fur but birds. I could feel their concealed bodies smaller than the bodies of mice, could feel the fiercely contracted wings, the feet like flecks of wire, the little beaks that made me think of the sharp nibs of old-fashioned pens. I seized one by a brittle wing and held it to the light and recognized it immediately as some kind of sparrow. More than three or four dozen sparrows in a stone crock, and obviously Rosella intended to cook them all. And weighing the almost weightless bird in my palm I knew, suddenly, that the crock was a gift and that all the time we were hunting snails Rosella had known it would arrive, was perhaps instrumental in its arrival.

Had she asked that disfigured youth to shoot sparrows among the rocks and in the steep, sparsely wooded hills near the sanctuary? On her demand had he spent all day discharging his untrustworthy weapon at those swift targets? Had Catherine heard those very shots? And was all this for me? All this for the idle middle-aged man from over the mountains? Three or four dozen sparrows, I thought, were a good many.

We cooked them together, ate them together. For the first time I not only ate with Rosella but joined her in that damp cavelike room of stone and tile where, until now, Rosella had moved alone with a young woman's bored carelessness through all her days and nights of cooking. I joined her and removed my black coat and in frayed shirt sleeves and soiled vest sat beside my standing Rosella and helped her, pulled the feathers from my share of the sparrows, which was no easy job, and despite my size hovered as near as I could to her shoulder while inside the casserole she built up the layers: butter, thyme, sparrows, onions, butter, thyme, sparrows, onions, and so forth. She prepared a sauce and I scrubbed out the iron vessel. Hovering stolidly beside Rosella, I sniffed the now browning sparrows and fed the fire, felt the oil of the cooking birds on my own brow and on my cheeks, felt without a single touch each movement of Rosella's small bones, muscles, ligaments. I watched Rosella's fingers at work, fingers even now stained with the black earth of my garden. Sometime toward the end of these preparations I sighed a deep sigh and realized that next time I too would be able to tie the wings, chop off the miniature feet.

"The heads. I see we eat the heads, Rosella. And the beaks. For the full effect we must eat the entire bird. I understand."

Her example was not at first easy to follow. Beaks that were very much like little split black fingernails. Heads smaller than my thumb and without eyes. I noticed such details, calmly watched how Rosella ate each sparrow in a single bite, and realized that it would be difficult for even a seasoned sex-aesthetician to follow her example. But then I saw that Rosella's two front teeth overlapped each other, and at this observation, this further instance of poignant incongruity, I could hesitate no more. And there amidst heat, shadows like finger puppets, savory taste and savory thoughts, how wrong I was to have hesitated in the first place. Because thanks to Rosella's cooking, the sparrows, I found, were simply soft and crunchy too, as if the different textures of sweetness had been so combined that it was still necessary to chew a moment that very substance which had in fact already dissolved, melted, in the aching mouth.

"Rosella," I said, with my jaws working and elbows propped casually on the table, "magnificent!"

Across from each other at that ancient broad lopsided table we sat, and according to the rules there was no touching of knees, no ravaging of sticky lips. My hand did not find her thigh and, in rhythm to that long slow dripping meal, please her thigh with the unexpected strength and tenderness of its unhurried caress. None of this. No removal of shoes and sandals, no meeting of bare feet. No slipping down the dress or licking fingers.

Throughout the meal I was unable to tell what Rosella was thinking, throughout the meal she managed to keep her face expressionless and her eyes averted. To me it was poignant that still I had no desire to put one finger behind her ear or to take her little mouth in mine. And yet her lips were sticky and there were a few drops of gravy on my vest while my plate, at last, was empty. Had I gone too far? Had I somehow raised false hopes? Was that whole vast tapestry beyond villa, cypresses, village, crying out for my re-entry into the pink field? Was my very skin about to be fired again in the kiln that has no flame? At least the sparrows inside me were already singing a different song, and I was listening.

Y ESTERDAY I KISSED MY MIMOSA TREE. AT NOON, WALKING slowly toward the well house with my shoulders heavy and hands thrust into empty pockets, I noticed that overnight my mimosa tree had reached its prime, had attained the totality of its yellow massiveness, and a little more. Each of its green filaments was bright, each of its seeds had become a puffy yellow globe as large as the tip of my middle finger, and packed together they hung, drooped, in thick puffy clumps, clouds, each one three times the size of a cluster of fat grapes. I stopped, reconsidered, turned to the mimosa tree, and with nothing more than a mild and rational interest in this sudden burgeoning, approached the tree and found myself standing unusually close to its silent flowering. Actually, at that moment one of the yellow clumps was already brushing against my vest. I stood there thinking of the delicate structure of so much airy growth and admiring this particular depth of yellow. I was alone, the sun had warmed the tree, the tree was full throated, I began to smell its gentle scent. And then I raised my hands, displaying my thick black coat sleeves, my frayed white cuffs, my golden cuff links and golden ring, and slowly thrust my hands deep into the vulnerable yellow substance of the mimosa tree. Into my hands I gathered with all possible tenderness one of the hivelike masses of yellow balls. And keeping my eyes open, deliberately I lowered my face into that cupped resiliency, and felt the little fat yellow balls working their way behind my spectacles and yielding somehow against my lips. I stopped breathing, I waited, slowly I opened my mouth and arched my tongue, pushed forward my open mouth and rounded expectant tongue until my mouth was filled and against all the most sensitive membranes of tongue and oral cavity I felt the yellow fuzzy pressure of the flowering tree.

The kiss, for it was a passionate kiss, really, reminded me of the grape-tasting game, though of course we never allowed ourselves to use hands in the grape-tasting game. But also in the midst of the kiss I thought I heard Fiona's giggle, Catherine's sigh. And Rosella may have seen me kissing the mimosa tree. If so, will she today or tomorrow follow my example? I think not. Kissing the rich yellow fluff of the mimosa tree may always lie just a step beyond Rosella's abilities or inclinations. Yet kissing me, or her chances of kissing me, daily assume a still faint but ever-increasing tangibility. Perhaps I shall turn out to be Rosella's mimosa tree as well as her white beast. Who knows?

TOGETHER TWO HEAVENLY CREATURES SPREAD THEIR BLUE feathers for me on a rock wall overlooking sea and sky. I uncupped Fiona's breasts and Catherine lifted her own white breasts from the madras halter. The buttons on Catherine's white cotton pajama top were like eyes of pearl. Fiona caressed the wooden arm, I removed my spectacles, Hugh moaned. Between the two villas I strung the clothes-line high. Remember?

WITHOUT PAIN? PERHAPS NOT EXACTLY WITHOUT PAIN. After all, the artistic arbiter of all our lives—Love—is only too expert at depressing with one of her invisible fingers the lonely key, the sour note of pain, and most of us enjoy the occasional sound of pain, though it approaches agony. In fact, could any perfect marriage exist without hostile si-lences, without shadows, without sour notes? Obviously not. Throughout the many years of my sexually aesthetic union with Fiona, for instance, there were the momentary but nonetheless bitter whispered confrontations over use of the bed in the master bedroom, brief spurts of anger about a sudden loss of form on the violet tennis court. And there were also instances of deeper and more prolonged periods of threatened harmony, such as the nearly disastrous days of my love for a small young woman whose husband was one of the few men whose spirit and personality and entire body (his lips, his eyes, his fat chest, his beard) Fiona found intolerable. Revulsion in my wife was rare, this woman whose very quickness of breath could liberate the lover buried inside the flesh of almost any ordinary man in undershorts. But despite his strength and crippling desperation, the husband of the small young woman was clearly doomed. I pleaded for him. Fiona tried. We failed. There were tears, locked doors, a wedding ring slipped like a cigar band around a rolled-up handwritten note of accusation. We failed. Then luckily enough, Love herself changed the metallic scene, shifted to some sweeter pitch our melodies.

I am a man of feeling. And in our more than eighteen years of dreams and actuality, Fiona and I knew hours of miserable silence, knew the shock of intimacy momentarily spurned, attended funerals, held hands in the whiteness of other weddings, tasted departure and the last liquid kiss, tried to console each other for each pair of friends who, weaker or less fortunate than ourselves, went down in flames. Once in anger Fiona snatched from my hand the brief silken panties she had only moments before slipped down and removed. Once I was graceless enough to lead Fiona nude from our dimly lit living room under the quiet eyes of a naked man whose extended fingers were pressed together as if in prayer.

And more. The gradual discovery that most people detest a lover, no matter how modest. My unavoidable fist fight with an older wind-sucking man over the question of virginity in young girls. Fiona weeping through the wood with the sun running wild over her lovely buttocks. Hugh's neck in his noose. All this and more we knew, all this we suffered.

Much of it must be described as pain, or at least as degrees of pain. But when I saw Fiona's long fingers reaching inside somebody else's heavily starched white shirt, or when I heard her voice receding, or when I listened with interest to one of her analytical and yet excited accounts of a night of love away from me, or smelled cigar smoke on her belly, or (to shift perspective) on all those occasions when I found myself alone for the last time with a weeping woman, when I tore myself away from the small sheep's golden curls and gave back keys, turned off certain bedroom lights forever, understood that this small voice or that would never again lie coiled in my golden ear and that never again would I know this girl's saliva, that woman's passionate secretions, when an unhappy negative magic was actually transforming a real mistress into a mental mistress —was all this at least my true pain, my real agony?

Not at all. The nausea, the red eyes, the lips white in blind grief and silent hate, these may have been the externals of a pain that belonged to Hugh but never once to me. Hugh's pain perhaps. Not mine. It is simply not in my character, my receptive spirit, to suffer sexual possessiveness, the shock of aesthetic greed, the bile that greases most matrimonial bonds, the rage and fear that shrivels your ordinary man at the first hint of the obvious multiplicity of love. Once Hugh told me that some small question of sex or the mere beginnings of jealousy often produced in him the sensation that he was drawing fire into his large intestine through a straw. But this pain, at least, is a pain I have never known. Not for me the red threads around the neck, the pillow in the open mouth, the ruptured days, the nights of shouting, the nights of trembling on the toilet. Jealousy, for me, does not exist, while anything that lies in the palm of love is good.

Of course in his own way Hugh was also a sex-singer of sorts. But Hugh was tormented, tempestuous, unreasonable. He was capable of greed and shame and jealousy. When at last he allowed the true artistic nature of our design to seep into consciousness, for instance, he persecuted himself and begrudged me Catherine, tried to deny me Catherine at a time when I knew full well that, thanks to my unseen helping hand, he himself was finally about to lurch down his own peculiar road with Fiona. And yet Hugh was also a sex-singer of sorts. But in Hugh's dry mouth our lovely song became a shriek.

"THERE SHE IS!"

Hugh clutched my arm with that hand that served as two, whispering and pointing his flipper into a nearby field: "There she is. See her? Perfect, perfect!"

His whisper was as dark and sparkling as the light in the black center of his narrow eyes. Hearing his curiously eager words and the three small black cameras knocking together on the ends of their straps, and seeing the white sun and sandy hills and the sweat that was already seeping from under the alpine pack Hugh carried high on his shoulders, of course I felt that his black sylvan whisper and all this hot rich ceramic desolation augured well for this our first photographic expedition together. And in sympathy if not complete understanding, my own whisper became as deep and eager as Hugh's.

"Perfect," I said, "let's hunt her down."

For a moment his fingers squeezed my arm in a fierce rippling peristaltic motion, and then his hand, that serpent's head, drifted down to one of the cameras and rested. Together we stared at the field, I with one hand in a convenient pocket, Hugh with his curly black hair uncombed as usual and the long black sailor pants low on his hips. The mattock, wielded by our quarry in a nearby field, continued to rise and fall, to flash in that hot clear air, to ping on an occasional stone. The crumbling cottage, the crumbling stone lean-to, the haystack shrunken and propped in position with pieces of fossilized wood, the small well without visible rope or chain or bucket—at a glance the desolation of the farm was obvious, and already I knew that so much desolation aroused in Hugh at least a shade of my own crisp appreciation. It was all complete, down to the usual upright skeleton of a dog affixed to the tall stake driven through the center of the haystack. And shading my eyes with one dry hand and nudging Hugh, gesturing toward the white bones strung intact to the pole, I could not help

...ing at this poignant evidence of their archaic ways, could not help thinking that the bones of the dead dog might serve some greater purpose than the bones of the child Fiona had discovered that distant day in the church.

And nodding toward the field that looked like fired putty: "The haystack would make a pretty good picture. Don't you think?"

He waited. "Hold on now," he whispered. "When she's warmed up a little, I'll wave."

Already I was beginning to see the afternoon through the eye of one of Hugh's cameras. Sitting on a naturally sculpted boulder in the bend of our dirt road, smoking and clasping my knee, and with a certain mild intensity watching Catherine's one-armed husband cross the field and in long cheerful strides approach the stooping figure, suddenly I began to smile at that total incongruity which must lie, I thought, at the center of what Hugh had several times referred to as his field trips into the old world of sex. At best a photograph could result in small satisfaction, I thought. Yet now even this small satisfaction was beginning to take shape in my mind, and for Hugh's sake I welcomed it, breathed deeply of the scent of pepper on the hot air, made fish lips for myself and through them expelled a few thoughtful puffs of smoke, considered the artfulness my one-armed friend might yet display.

Certainly Hugh was artful even now. Watching them from my place of comfort on the large hot boulder, I could see that he was talking, though he could no more speak *croak peonie* than I could, was demonstrating his cameras and displaying the contents of his alpine sack, which by now he had unslung from the enormous bony construction of his shoulders. Already the mattock lay abandoned in the deep brown furrow, already the tall man and short girl were standing face to face, obviously Hugh was trying to use his pinned-up flipper to fence his way through the darkness and sullenness of her suspicion. In the distance and in the shade of my hand they faced each other, and already I knew that today the lone girl would farm no more.

Hugh's head was nodding. Once he squatted and reached his single all-purpose hand into the furrow and then extended that dark hand palm up to the girl. What lay cupped in the palm of his unquenchable hand? Was he admiring the soil? Was he admiring some scrap of root, some fibrous hooflike bulb that the girl had been attempting to cultivate with patience and the dull hand-crafted mattock? To myself I laughed at Hugh's ingenuity, energy, determination to win the lone figure in the field for the probing unblushing gaze of his high-powered cameras.

I changed hands, squinted at Hugh's distant, persuasive, perhaps even poetic use of sign language. The heat was intense, I realized, and yet my skin was dry.

And then all the glazed ceramic substance of that colorful and nearly lifeless panorama trembled, shivered, cracked and splintered into new and suddenly moving fragments of light, color, shards of earth, and side by side Hugh and his new photographic subject turned, began to walk together in the direction of the crumbling barn. Hugh's one long powerful arm was in the air and waving.

We stood in the earthen darkness of that barn, the three of us, and I saw immediately that two urine-colored sheep were trembling together in one heavily cobwebbed corner.

"My latest model is going to pose. These sullen types always end up compliant."

"We're in luck," I said. "She looks beautifully indifferent. Anything I can do to help?"

Unleashing one of his small black cameras, Hugh frowned at the setting of its highly polished and unmerciful lens.

"In a minute. Right now just smile at her. Make her feel at ease."

I had only to glance at the girl to see that she was in fact quite unafraid of Hugh, of me, of even the cold and completely foreign complexity of the cameras hanging in their black cases around Hugh's neck. At once I saw that she was young, untutored, uninterested in anything except the clumsy mattock and challenge of the ceramic field. The dull rubber boots cut off at her bare knees, the dry knees that appeared to have been scoured with sand, the colorless apron tied around a long burlap skirt sewn no doubt by an old woman, and the leather coat—at once I saw that so many unappealing articles of dress might well conceal a body that would prove to be in absolute contrast to the clothes themselves. But would this girl actually pose for Hugh without her rubber boots and burlap skirt and stocky leather coat? I was unconvinced. Her mouth was small, her eyebrows were gently drawn. And yet her face was the color of green olives and made me suspect that the composition of her blood might have been determined at least in part by one of the barbaric strains. Perhaps she was strong. Perhaps her indifference was not at all the same as compliance. Perhaps the old woman who had sewn the skirt had also taught her some outlandish and hence all the more crippling version of a moral code—though the girl's small eyes were dark, and I had faith in Hugh.

I smiled at Hugh's latest model. She did not smile back. But her eyes remained on mine and I began to wonder if she was aware of my large and closely shaven face, my slice of pure gold hair. And the barn was filled with a warm aura of suspension. There were the shadows, the dust, the floor that was a soft black pebbled carpet of sheep droppings, the smells and light that made me think of the inside of a dying rose. Hugh was squatting while the girl waited and the sheep peered over their shoulders at the three of us.

"*Peasant Nudes,*" Hugh whispered, and simultaneously the girl and I glanced down at his camera which was now clicking. "That's what I'm going to call my collection. *Peasant Nudes.*"

He was taking photographs, for some time now had been taking photographs. Oddly squatting with one knee sharply bent and one long leg stretched out in a nearly horizontal position, eyes and nose buried inside the back of his camera, in this way he was crouching, inching to and fro at the girl's feet, aiming up at us the enormous wide-open lens of that clicking camera.

"That's it. That's perfect. Now let's just shove her over against the beam."

Coming between us, pushing and inching with his dark blue contorted legs, suddenly rising to both knees so that the girl drew back, and clicking the shutter release and rewind lever and hissing eagerly between his lips which had become little more than a tight shadow, slowly Hugh approached us on his knees and then, with little more than his own intensity and the aim of the camera, moved her, repositioned the small dark head against the dark worm-eaten flank of an upright beam.

"Easy. Easy. That's perfect. See how she's holding her head jammed against that old beam? Perfect. Most of the faces of these peasant nudes are just fat and happy. They're all mothers, with or without children. But this one," inching his knees across the carpet of sheep droppings, doing his one-handed sleight-of-hand tricks with two cameras and what I supposed was a light meter, "this face is skintight with the beauty of illiteracy. That's what will show up in the pictures. Wait and see. The sullen face of an illiterate virgin."

I waited, then heard my own low whisper: "I've been thinking the same thing. That she's a virgin."

"She's got a few little brown hairs on her chin. She couldn't be better."

Yet now I was watching not the girl but Hugh. And Hugh remained on his knees, continued to walk about on his knees. His shoulders were struggling against the sudden unreasonable dictates of his dream, were working against impossible odds to maintain his balance. He was sweating. His thin cotton shirt had come free at the waist. But his arms, or rather that lurid combination of arm and partial arm, most held my attention. And in passing I noticed that the girl's small dark expressionless eyes were fixed, like mine, on the excited and suddenly gesticulating remnant of his ruined arm.

"Make her smile! Come on, do something. Make her smile. Quick."

While I was still contemplating the odd magic that Hugh somehow extracted from his injured arm, Hugh himself unaccountably changed position, bolted upright from his knees to his feet and thrust the camera into the girl's face so that for one instant the poor lips parted in what might have been a silent laugh. I caught a glimpse of her tongue and the small overlapping front teeth, and heard the click of the camera, felt Hugh wheeling in my direction. He let go of the camera, expelled his breath in a single relieved heave of his expanded chest, ducked his head and, with the flat lower side of his twitching stump, wiped the perspiration from his forehead and thin gray face.

"Time to change tactics," he said, and with one brutal thrust of his hand ripped a small flesh-colored wineskin from the alpine pack, held the wineskin at an angle of shocking self-confidence before his upturned face and shot a steady thin dark jet into his waiting mouth.

"Want some, boy? It's hot work."

I declined and hoisted myself to a seat on the ancient cart and crossed my knees, braced myself with both arms and hands. Again Hugh thrust up the bag and squeezed it, prolonged his exhibitionistic drinking as if he were an indelicate disheveled god in the act of forcing some invisible monster to send down its urine.

"Now, boy. To business."

And suddenly the wineskin lay in the rancid hay, the third camera was in his claw, he was close to the girl. Once again his stone cheeks and little pointed beard were wet with the perspiration of his art photographer's single-minded desire. He did not move. Yet his stump, though held tightly to the side of his body, was impatient to wag, to flex, to rise into action, and his eyes were sly but also vacant. He seemed to be listening to the girl's silent life rather than staring at the visible shape of it. The girl continued to stare up at Hugh. The thin sheep had managed to turn and now were facing us and once more were rubbing together their crusted woolly coats. The girl was alert.

Then Hugh sprang back a step, let go of the camera, smiled with absurdly pretended helplessness, with his hand made sweeping motions from the girl's head against the beam to her booted feet on the dung. Did she understand, he seemed to be asking, could she share his amusement at his own discovery of what was wrong? Slowly, with a mild tightening of the lips, she glanced down the length of her body. She saw nothing wrong.

So he held up the camera, turned it slowly in front of her face, in front of her narrow eyes, displaying and silently extolling its value, its delicacy, its enormous power, suggesting for all I knew that this one small instrument was more important than a simple illiterate young woman or even an entire farm. And then once again he dropped the camera. But now, suddenly, he was stern, insistent, and with one terrible extended finger he pointed at her pathetic boots, her clumsy coat, and slowly moved both hand and finger back and forth, at the same time using tongue and teeth to produce a cadenced clicking sound of austere disapproval and even, perhaps, of anger.

"No boots, no coat," he said, rolling from side to side the enormous hand and rigid forefinger. "No boots, no coat."

Again he pointed, again he sucked tongue to teeth, filling the barn with that loud unmistakable sound of exaggerated negation, and then with amusing yet somehow admirable restraint he actually pantomimed the removal of his own

66

slick boots and the removal of an imaginary cumbersome sheepskin coat. She watched. She listened.

And then he transposed himself from the girl to the alpine pack and knelt and thrust his hand inside the pack. The girl, without a glance at Hugh, slowly unfastened her scarred leather coat and removed it, leaned against the ox-cart and slowly pulled off first one worn-out rubber boot and then the other. Hugh's back was turned. But I was watching, waiting, and was close enough to take from her the discarded coat, close enough to wait until she dropped the boots and then to indicate with gentle fingers the familiar apron and the billowing and slackening skirt which, after only a brief moment of further incomprehension, she also took off and gave me.

Perhaps I should have known, as Hugh had known, that without the coat and skirt and boots she would be nude. Should have known, perhaps, and yet had not, so that standing now with the apron, coat and skirt still warm in my arms, I was both pleased and surprised at her apparent indifference to her own nakedness, and was amused to think that for this naked girl the world of underclothing was a world unknown.

Did I hear the camera? Had Hugh returned again to his work? Perhaps, perhaps. But I too could become absorbed in the act of assessment, appreciation, and now it seemed to me that the mild sag in the breasts of this girl might in her case be an aesthetic attribute. Through my polished gold-rimmed spectacles I stared at the nude girl, and it occurred to me that I was at last acquiring a more personal understanding of Hugh's photographic collection. I realized that never before had I seen a young female body quite so aesthetically self-defeating as this one. I stared and smiled. She glanced at me. She scratched her right flank.

Yes, self-defeating, as perhaps are the bodies of most girls whose origins lie in historical darkness beyond the mountains. The breasts, for instance, had never given suck and yet already they sagged. And the thickness of the fat at the waist seemed to pull against the hardness of the belly, the muscles in the calves detracted from the solid but symmetrical thighs, the narrow but slumping shoulders somehow maimed the aesthetic reality of the full and rounded buttocks. Self-defeating, I thought, but harmonious too.

Unaccountably she took hold of one of her breasts, appeared to squeeze it, then dropped her hand. And with this gesture I found that I was witness not only to the girl's patient nudity but also to that leave-taking scene which perhaps only an hour before Hugh had disdained to photograph. In the acrid and rose-tinted darkness, and transparently superimposed on the olive and white reality of the undressed girl, clearly I saw Hugh's wife and mine standing within arm's length of each other beneath the clothesline on Hugh's side of the funeral cypresses and waving, watching us depart, and saw the dog in mid-air, the two fat smaller children holding hands but also waving at their lanky father, saw Meredith with her back to us and no doubt scowling at Catherine's white cotton pajamas on the clothesline, and beyond it all the rocks and bright sun and silhouetted wreckage of the small coastal fort. How they complemented each other, this girl we had conducted into a near-empty barn and this prior vision, our suddenly present bird song of domesticity embedded in the flank of collapsing time. Deliberately I shut my eyes, as if the better to taste some offered drink, and thought of the wine I planned to share with Catherine when the night was again ours.

"Come on, Cyril, give her the rake. Let's try the rake. And then you can give her the pants."

At the sound of his choking voice the tableau of domestic multiplicity dissolved in an instant. And with the girl breathing methodically within arm's length of my softly sweatered chest and now and again shifting the position of her feet or glancing into the darkness overhead, it was no longer possible to separate the photographs and the waiting girl. While smelling the girl I could not help looking at Hugh and saw him sprawled on his back with head and shoulders propped against the alpine pack and the camera once more substituting its cyclopian lens for his eyes and nose. Above the sound of Hugh's voice and the girl's breathing I heard the clearly and inexorably rapid sounds of the camera and knew that I had been hearing it all this time.

"Look," I whispered, knowing that prone on the dung he could not possibly have seen what I had just seen, "look there. She's grazed a cobweb. My god, her breasts tangled in a broken cobweb. Can you see it?"

And writhing, jerking the camera to and from his face, lying on his back and with his sharp heels and single elbow propelling himself about in crablike motions for the sake of angle, light, depth, expression: "Magnificent ... It'll all show up in the enlargements ... I've spent more than a year on my collection, my catalogue of natural art photographs, my peasant nudes... My unmarried girls of barren countries ... Each one's better than the last ... I've got them sitting in straw, standing in the black and empty door-

ways of ruined barns . . . And all nude or nearly nude . . .
My peasant specimens . . . Each one gets a cheap little
gift . . ."

He laughed, gave me a long look over the swiftly lowered
camera, and then I stood up to my knees in the white
pulpy straw in order to reach down the wooden rake,
dragged a bottomless iron bucket from under the straw,
and hauled from beneath the oxcart a great leather skein
of primitive mildewed harness. And thanks to my own patient industry and quickening interest, and also to Hugh's
sweating inventiveness, we managed that day to photograph
our smallish naked girl holding the rake, holding the bucket,
managed to photograph her with the entire length and
weight of the crusty black leather harness draped over one
narrow shoulder so that, front and back, it hung down
stiffly as far as the bare feet.

"The pants," he whispered. "Give her the pants."

The girl watched my every move, the small red eyes of
the sheep were filled with ruby-colored supplication. And
of course I found the cotton underpants lying in a heap
beside the alpine pack. I picked them up, turned to the girl,
and between thumb and first finger of both hands held out
the underpants in a cheerful and magnanimous display. Her
eyes tightened, the camera clicked.

But what was wrong?

Silence. The clicking had stopped, the agonized camera
was silent. And then Hugh moaned.

"What's wrong?" I whispered. "For God's sake, what's
the matter?"

At a glance it became apparent to me that Hugh lay
there in the grip of something serious. He was not moaning

in the throes of a pseudosexual climax resulting, say, from the many photographs he had taken of a girl who was, after all, young, naked ,and a stranger to us both. The hunching shoulders, the forgotten camera, the single hand driven against the center of his bony chest, the apparent sapping of that little color usually evident in the long thin granite face, the fact that he was frowning and that his usually crafty eyes were suddenly wide open and staring at what I was sure was nothing—all this told me that Catherine's husband was sprawled motionless before me not in the aura of trivial physiological reaction, but in pain. He appeared to be thinking about some deeply unpleasant subject, the hand was trying to dig its way inside his chest.

I knelt beside him, I was concerned. But my life had not attuned me to medical emergencies and now, kneeling at Hugh's side, large but at the same time trim with an excellent health I was unable to share, I did not know whether to touch him, to seize his gigantic deformed shoulders in my own enormous gentle hands, or leave him alone. Or should I shoot into his dry mouth a jet of the dark wine? Raise him to a sitting position? Go for help? Carry him in my two arms back to our wives?

"Heart attack," I whispered. "Is it a heart attack?"

He moaned, licked the small wispy wings of his mustache with the tip of his tongue, finally glanced up at me. "Hand of death inside my chest, that's all. But it doesn't last . . ."

He winked, I felt relieved, already the shadows were massing in interesting patterns once more down the length of his rock-colored grainy face. He sighed, pushed himself up with his good arm. And yet for all my relief, and even as I was helping myself to a long curving drink from the wineskin, I could not help thinking that my preoccupied friend was dangerously ill and that this kind of collapse, along with his collection of "peasant nudes," probably did not bode well for Fiona. If mere photographs had led in some devious way to this kind of prostration, what would happen to him when Fiona finally managed to gather him into her lovely arms? And did Fiona know already what she was up against? It would be my lot, I knew, to warn her.

When, blinded and laughing, Hugh and I stumbled out of the barn together, Hugh's good arm resting powerfully and in unadmitted necessity on my own broad shoulders, and the straps of all three cameras and the alpine pack held firmly in my own left hand, I noticed that the girl was once more fully clothed and at work in the field. I knew that I would see her again, but also knew more immediately that in only a matter of minutes Hugh's black flapping dog would race out yapping to welcome us back to villas, children, wives already involved in the pursuit of nudity, passion, love.

But when I finally did return alone to the little ceramic farm and to Rosella (for of course it was she), I returned only to procure for myself a silent companion willing to cook my meals and clean my cold villa. Thanks to Hugh, Rosella became mine, so to speak, along with the best of the photographs. And Hugh? Better for Hugh had he died at a blow of his black fist or whatever it was. Much better.

IN THE MIDDAY BRIGHTNESS, LYING NEAR OUR LITTLE WELL house on an old settee over which she had tossed one of her white percale sheets, and with her feet bare and her torso also bare, dressed only in her sky-blue slacks that she pulled on like a pair of dancing tights, and looking up at me with one long finger marking her place in the slender book and her other hand thrust into the open slacks—in this attitude she appealed to me with somber eyes, low voice, unhappy smile: "Baby, he says I'm Circe all over again and that he's the only man left in the world who can resist my charms. What'll I do?"

"I warned you a long time ago. Remember?"

"I remember."

Hands in pockets, standing over her, smiling down at Fiona stretched out in one of her rare half-hours devoted to a kind of personal cessation that came as close as she was capable of coming to inertia, suddenly and with my lips so much thicker than hers I made a few silent kisses and sat down on the edge of the settee so that our hips rolled together and I could smell her breath. On the other side of the cypresses all was even more quiet than usual at this time of day, and I wondered what Hugh had done to muzzle the dog, the twins, the constantly accusing and complaining Meredith. I heard the little desolate rustling sound of the book landing beside the settee.

"Cyril is virile. Remember when I told him, baby?"

I nodded, slowly removed my eyeglasses and folded them, stuck them under the settee for safekeeping.

"And it's so true. Oh, it's so true."

One of her rare half-hours of self-surrender. And yet the casualness of bare feet and partially unzipped slacks, the personal disregard expressed in the naked breasts, stomach, arms, the thoughtless and candid position of the hand thrust into the little blue open mouth of the slacks—all of this was rare and yet characteristic too, almost as characteristic as the familiar sight of Fionda smothering or sculpting her breasts in hands whose supple grip and long white fingers never failed to excite my admiration.

"You're wearing your magic pants again," I whispered, and her body rippled against me. She bent her outside leg at the knee and allowed her tight blue knee, bent leg, to list away from me slightly in the direction taken by the now disregarded book. With two long fingers of her free hand she began to stroke the white naked heel that she had just drawn into sensitive proximity to those hard blue buttocks which at the moment I could not see but only imagine. She pursed her lips and, despite the still considerable space between us, began to blow a deliberate breath up toward my weathered bland expectant face.

"And you're wearing your magic pants too, baby, aren't you," she said in that willowy voice which, no matter how soft, suggestive or dreamlike, never allowed for contradiction.

"Sure," I murmured. "Of course I am."

"Maybe I'll steal your magic pants. For him. OK?"

The shadow of the thin Byzantine cross of rusted iron on top of the conical well house now lay directly in the center

74

of her naked chest, and it amused me to think that sometime within the next half-hour the cross would lie not on
Fiona's chest but in the middle of my broad back. All
around us the little orange marguerites had never been
more profuse, more deeply orange, more innocent.

I patted her raised knee and leaned down, untied my
fresh white *espadrilles* and pulled them off. When I
straightened I saw the lower lip caught gently between her
teeth and the long first finger of her left hand tracing firm
lines up and down the inside of her shining thigh. I laughed.
Because she was right, of course, and I knew as well as she
did that my own elasticized underpants and Fiona's sky-blue
slacks were in fact magical, as she had said. My shorts, for
instance, were like the bulging marble skin of a headless
god. But Fiona's sky-blue slacks, which she never wore except when alone, or with me, or with some privileged lover,
certainly that garment clinging low on her hips and riding
high on her ankles was matched for magic only by Fiona's
own total and angular nudity. The little masculine gold-
plated zipper in front, the slanted pockets, the blue web-
bing that left an attractive pink welt around her squarish
hips and lower belly and the soft eyes of her buttocks were
all the true signs of a woman's sex-suit, Fiona said. And in
her moods of self-surrender, when she felt like wearing the
blue slacks and nothing more, these were the details that
enabled her to lie reasonably still and smile and enjoy the
magical vacancy at her finger tips. And at the moment, the
zipper was halfway down and the welt was pink.

"I want to see your magic pants. Right now."

I obeyed, of course, and with languor and pleasure stood
up beside my prostrate wife and, smiling down into her

75

open eyes, which made me think of two doves frozen in the hard light of expectation, slowly pulled off my shirt and trousers and, glancing at the empty heavens, for a moment enjoyed the statuesque weight of myself contained and molded, so to speak, in my brief but extra-large white magical underpants. I could feel that my broad sloping shoulders were a little soft. Some tiny living creature splashed in the depths of the nearby well.

"Come on," she whispered. "Submit."

I sat down again slowly and carefully. With her free hand, the hand with which she had been stroking her upraised thigh, she now suddenly began pulling at some of the long soft brown hairs on my own mammoth thigh. Then her hand slipped, a finger grazed the broad sloping front of my elasticized white shorts, and in mid-air the hand began to tremble while her breathing, suddenly, changed pitch.

"Kiss me, Cyril. Kiss me."

Even while smelling the sweetness of Fiona's breath and tasting the taste of her mouth, sucking on the marrow of Fiona's life, and biting her teeth, her small lips, her tongue, and while feeling the sun sealing us once more together, it occurred to me that this particular kiss was unusually cannibalistic, even for us. It is not easy to force a pair of heavy lips into an expression of mock disapproval while involved in such a kiss, and so when I became aware that our time was dissolving, and that we were indeed struggling to devour each other's mouths, jaws, cheeks, I simply raised my head, pulled loose, stopped, listened. As usual Fiona's preliminary humming was food for us both.

"Cyril," she whispered, "Cyril . . ."

Her free hand gripped the back of my head, she held my head exactly where she wanted it and nuzzled my face and stared at me with her eyes that were like dying doves. With all the care I could summon I rested my right hand on the wrist of the hand that was driven so beautifully into the tight blue pit of the open slacks. Slowly I propelled my own hand down until it very nearly covered hers, and for a moment I thought that even Fiona had become insensible beneath the pressure of her hand and mine. But then it became evident that Fiona, my ageless tree, was still willowy, rational, self-possessed, and I was proud of her. Because now with considerable strength and slow determination, she began to inch her hand from under mine.

"Wait, baby. Wait a minute. Meredith isn't watching us again, is she? I don't want her watching us through the cypresses. OK?"

"Of course she's not watching us," I whispered, though I knew that Fiona did not intend me to turn now and study the dark green wall of cypresses for the little flashing white signs of Meredith's face. I merely answered Fiona's question as she wanted me to and pressed on.

Fiona's hand came loose, my own impossibly large weathered hand was stuffed once more inside my wife's unzipped pants.

"Baby . . . oh baby . . ."

I forced my hand down and suddenly, as if to achieve nothing less than absolute display of her presence of mind, Fiona tilted up her pelvic area to meet me, and in my wet palm I held her eagerness and felt the center of her life beneath the brief pattern of hair like sandy down. On my part it took some presence of mind, finally, to disengage my

77

hand, pull down her sky-blue pants, toss them aside with my own white marble shorts among all the bright orange marguerites.

And later, much later, both nude, she on her stomach on the flimsy rattan settee and I seated on the ground with knees drawn up and cigarette lighted and heavy shoulders drifting to the slow massage of her strong hand: "Why can't they all be like you, baby? Why?"

T HEY HAVE GIVEN HER RABBITS. YESTERDAY I FOUND CATHerine not wrapped in her blanket on the silent balcony as usual but rather sitting on her heels before the cage of rabbits. It was the moment of transformation, the beginning of Catherine's cure, the first hopeful sign of metamorphosis cast in the powdery blue light from the reflecting tiles. My guide, the small fat woman in dark blue apron and wooden sandals, led me to the balcony and pointed at the blanket, the empty makeshift lounging chair. Her little round face and upraised pudgy arm were bright with unconcealed pleasure, as she watched my own responses to the obvious fact that something had changed in Catherine's life and mine. Then she pointed in a different direction, beckoned me on to a fragment of whitewashed walls, warm cobblestones, empty sky, the low cage raised on a slight altar of stones and pink succulents. Again the matron pointed and of course I knew before looking that the large woman sitting on her heels and peering without sound into the rabbits' cage was Catherine.

She was unaware of the little fat woman and myself now standing side by side behind her, was obviously unaware of her own dark jersey and faded maroon-colored shorts and the strand of hair hanging from the bun she had fastened indifferently at the back of her head. She was resting with her hands on her bare knees and leaning heavily forward into the darkness of the wooden cage and sweet smell of the shadowy rabbits. The jersey, I noticed, had pulled loose from the elasticized waistband of the cotton shorts, and in a sudden return of poignancy I found my consciousness brimming with the sight of this brief once familiar strip of nakedness.

I smiled, thinking of my now ruined bicycle, my hot climbs to the sanctuary, my playful smoke rings and patient monologues, all the ingredients of my timeless fidelity which had accomplished nothing, after all, had not moved Catherine to a single word or even to tears. But thanks to what I could only assume to be the sudden emergence of primitive intuition in the little fat untutored woman at my side, and to the curative powers of two large sable-colored rabbits, now Catherine was kneeling with open eyes and heavy girlish concentration and was slowly reaching toward the rusty hook on the little door of the cage. The life I had failed to arouse was now being restored by two soft mindless animals and a woman who was perhaps unfamiliar with even the *crespi fagag* alternative in her own language. The cure was obvious, I told myself, since for certain temperaments the presence of gentle animals is magical. Yet I myself could not have thought of it. I watched Catherine's fingers touch the hook, heard the twitching and chewing sounds of the rabbits.

Yes, I thought, Catherine's large amber eyes must now be meeting the fearless but vulnerable eyes of one of the rabbits. Catherine lifted her upper body away from the naked heels, waited a moment, and unhooked the sagging wire-covered door of the cage and swung it open. Her arms were moving, a rip in the side of the maroon-colored shorts still betrayed some small long-forgotten carelessness, the jersey rose another few inches on her bare back, the sudden new smell from the cage might have burst from the slit belly of a golden faun brought down by a loving archer.

I felt the tugging at my sleeve and saw the large docile rabbit in Catherine's arms. The sable-colored head was on her shoulder, one of the long soft ears was brushing against her neck. I nodded and retreated silently without disturbing this brief portion of my old tapestry that would now undulate forever, I thought, with gentle yet indestructible life.

Had she known I was there? Had she in fact cradled in her arms the warm trusting rabbit for my benefit as well as her own? Might she have heard my breathing, seen my shadow, and busied herself with these simple mysteries for the sake of the large perspiring middle-aged man who was the only lover she had ever known? The plain shorts, the kneeling position, the silken animals—were these fresh omens, the unmistakable signs that Catherine had finally changed her mind and retracted her vow of speechlessness? Yes, I thought, unmistakable. And striding down the caramel-colored hillside path with its purple rocks and white streaks of dust, and far below, the vista of the slick dark village and empty sea, walking more quickly and hearing my own hot dusty footfalls, the heavy irregular sounds of my lonely but powerful descent, at that moment I knew at last that it was only a question of time and that my final visit to the sanctuary was drawing near. If Catherine had begun her metamorphosis and could play with the rabbits, she could also return to my villa among the funeral cypresses and share with me the still music of what I had already come to think of as our condition of sexless matrimony.

After that, who knows?

Twilight was always my favorite hour. and so it remains. At twilight I stroll, I smoke, I hum to myself, I inspect my lemon trees which are at their peak of bearing, and inspect my arbor thick now with hanging tendrils of grapes no larger than small warts or the heads of pins, mere intimations of all the bunches of fat clear green grapes to come. I stroll among my trees and under the arbor and then say good night to Rosella and sink into the darkness, sleep alone. And my nights are never sleepless. My concentration is quiet and slow paced, after all, and filled with purpose. My large hand never shakes. The headless god? Perhaps. I eat my lemons as other men eat oranges. In my slow mouth the lemon pulled by Rosella from one of my twisted trees and thoughtfully sliced by me with my faded gold-plated pocketknife is sweet. I think, I chew, I suck my cheeks. My mouth hardly puckers. I sleep in peace.

Catherine will have to learn to do the same.

W HAT WAS HE DOING? SUNBATHING? OR WAS HE LYING in naked embrace with my equally naked wife at last? He was there, I knew, a prone white emaciated figure just visible through a low, dark green fringe of crab grass agitated by a sultry midday wind, a long low sheet of green flame burning at the edge of the bed of black rocks about twenty feet from where I stood in the shadows cast by the thick growth of pine. Hands in pockets, freshly bathed, wearing my yellow shirt in the hopes of meeting Fiona on this dark seaside path, a path she often took alone, here I stood in the darkness on a blanket of dead pine needles, stroking my chin and wondering if I had indeed discovered Fiona but worn the yellow shirt in vain.

With my usual presence of mind I had awakened from my dreamless midafternoon sleep, had rolled over, found Fiona missing, had assumed that I would meet her on the ocean path. And fresh from immersion and scrubbing in the clear water of my ancient stone bathing tank, scented, externalizing my mood in the special color of my bright shirt, slowly I had strolled past the second villa, had paused to listen, had drifted on, assuming that Hugh and Catherine and all their distracting daughters lay just beyond those tight shutters and thick white walls drugged in the heat. On both counts had I been wrong? Taking a soft step forward and catching another glimpse of his naked movements out there in the crab grass, it appeared that I had indeed been wrong. But those movements, of course, were what Fiona wanted, so that my trivial mistakes were righted, so to speak, by the richness of the vision and what I took to be the abrupt fulfillment of Fiona's latest dream.

He was facing south, and the horizontal position and the density and frenzy of the low wind-whipped screen of nearly black grass made his long white body appear longer than it actually was. I watched, pulled at my chin, took a few more slow steps that placed me definitely beyond the safety of the trees and into his aura of bright colorless sun and the hot wind that clashed in the ears. Beneath my thonged and silver-studded sandals, the blanket of dead pine needles had given way to a strip of unclean gray sand. I could not hear the ocean but saw that it was thrashing with unusual and irregular fury up and down the length of our desolate private beach of black stones.

Just as I had decided to return to the dark and echoing shelter of the pine trees, leaving the two of them to enjoy in peace whatever they had found together in that exposed and inhospitable spot amidst wind and sun, speculating to myself about the kind of passion that had driven them to strip off their clothes in all this shattering light and noise, suddenly it occurred to me that I could see nothing of Fiona's brown arms and passionate hands which, even from this distance, should have been visible clasping Hugh's thin white naked back or stony buttocks. I hesitated, turned again into the wind that now seemed to beat the motionless sunlight into my face, my hair, the depths of my yellow shirt. I took another look and, filled with a kind of voiceless compassion as well as a curiosity I had not known before, knew that Fiona's invisibility was no longer a problem and that I could not retreat. Because Hugh was alone, I was convinced of it, and I could not abandon him there to sunstroke or aching muscles, certainly could not allow the reason for his lonely presence there on the empty beach to go unexplored.

But what was he doing? Sunbathing? Embarking on some kind of freakish photographic experiment? Reading one of his faded erotic periodicals hidden from my sight in the crab grass? What?

And then I stopped, leaning into the wind with legs apart, hands in pockets, head lowered, stood there frowning and trying to resist the temptation to lean down and shake him by the shoulder. He lay at my sandaled feet like a corpse, a long fish-colored corpse, or like some fallen stone figure sandblasted, so to speak, by centuries of cruel weather. Yes, an emaciated and mutilated corpse or statue, except that he in his oblivion was moving, while I, despite the compassionate concentration of all my analytical powers and alerted senses, had become immobile, only the immobile witness to this most florid and pathetic expression of Hugh's reticence.

Because he lay there on his stomach embracing not Fiona but only his clothes, the twisted black long-legged sailor pants, soiled jersey and white shorts. No magazine, no camera, no living partner. Only the white shorts beneath his head and the pants and shirt bunched and almost out of sight now beneath his chest, his hidden loins, his rigid outstretched white legs of the Christ.

The motion in the pitted gray-white buttocks was intensifying, the shoulders were beginning to heave, the black grass was beating against his long meager thighs, the tight black curls on the back of his head were blowing, springing loose, were becoming drenched with black light. Was he moaning? Did he believe himself to be lying at midnight among our percale sheets a half mile away at my villa instead of sprawled out here in the grass with a few uninteresting broken sea shells and some large black ants that would soon be scurrying in aimless circles on his heaving back? I could not be sure.

Yet waiting, towering above him, watching the naked flickering gestures of his lonely one-sided prostration, I could only nod because suddenly I recognized that I had already lived whatever dream Hugh might be dreaming but also that without my presence Hugh's agony did not exist. And yet, if he mistook rough cloth and patches of sand for Fiona's life, flesh, firmness, did not the final agony of this discrepancy belong to Fiona, though she remained unaware of it, rather than to Hugh or to me? I thought so. But Fiona could take care of herself, of course. She always had.

Without a moment's hesitation I decided to spare Fiona this sight of Hugh dreaming away their intimacy in the crab grass. Without hesitation I turned away from the now tightening and trembling white figure and waved, shouted back some cheerful greeting to the yet invisible woman (Fiona, my wife) who was now calling to me from within the gentle darkness of the long grove of pines. I reached her in time to keep her from stumbling on our sleeping and naked Saint Peter at the height of his pleasure.

"What on earth were you doing out there on the beach, baby? I've been looking for you." We laughed, touched lips, I felt her fingers inside my yellow shirt after all.

"COME ON, BOY, HOW ABOUT SOME INDIAN WRESTLING? What do you say?"

Why did I submit finally to the strained voice, the forced jocularity, the challenge only too evident in his eyes and little black pointed beard? There in the grape arbor, bathed in darkness and the light of Fiona's candles, why did our two wives and even the children urge us on? When the two youngest girls began to clap their fat little star-shaped hands and even Meredith drew near and smiled her poignant introverted smile of spite and satisfaction at the contest she had already visualized as won inevitably and maliciously by her one-armed father, was there still not some way I might have evaded the ugly consequences of this abysmally classic situation?

"Go on, baby, be a good sport."

But as soon as I felt his hand in mine, I knew that in this case I should not have listened, should not have allowed myself to inflict such pain on a man who was obviously determined to fill our idyllic days and nights with all the obscure tensions of his own unnecessary misery and impending doom.

He began to squeeze, his hand was a claw. As if in some

86

ancient combat his upraised arm was dripping with raw meat and bloody bone, at any moment he might open his mouth and shriek. And in the midst of it I reminded myself that Fiona knew full well that the physical exercise I had undertaken throughout our married life surely guaranteed the muscle development of my thick arms. We were both at fault.

I TOO HAVE BEGUN TO HOLD THE LARGER OF THE TWO rabbits against my chest and in my lap. Silently we pass it back and forth, Catherine and I, pass it dangling from her arms to mine and from mine to hers. The pink succulents, the unhooked door of the cage, the powerful gently explosive smell of droppings and digested grass, the blue tiles turning into frosted metallic threads in the light of dawn— in all this it is apparent that both of the rabbits are female and that Catherine and I are equally attracted only to the larger, which has clear red eyes, crude musical notations on its long front legs (silent companion, I realize, to Love's swooping birds) and big paws that sometimes find slow footing on my watch chain. I stroke the rabbit, glance at Catherine, smile. She looks away and brushes a piece of straw from the lip of the cage. But sooner or later she reaches out her arms and I hook my thumbs under the forelegs of the rabbit, whose trust is airy and limitless, and whose bones feel as if they are immersed in a limpid shape composed entirely of warm water, and lift, watch the amazing distension of the silken spine and totally relaxed rear legs, then swing her over to Catherine's waiting hands.

An excellent basis for sexless matrimony, I tell myself. It will not be long.

F ACE DOWN ON THE BLANKET, SMILING AT THE MUFFLED sound of my careless yet also stentorious whisper: "I am not opposed to domesticity," I heard myself saying, "not at all."

No wind, no spray, no evidence of dead sea birds, no dissolving sun, nothing to distract us from this hour of attentiveness on the beach of black stones. It was another left-hand right-hand day, as I had come to call them, another one of those days when the four of us, and even the dog and the children, fit together like the shapely pieces of a perfectly understandable puzzle. Catherine on her side, Hugh on his knees, Fiona flat on her back and I face down on my stomach—we were holding each other in place, so to speak, on Fiona's blanket and talking softly, listening. A few yards away the twins were silent for once, held in check by the magnetism of the old sleeping dog, while Meredith was standing ankle-deep in the water and waiting, I thought, to be embarrassed. In the silence that met my unpremeditated remark I covered Catherine's hand with mine and squeezed it, wondered how long we could fend off the inevitable nemesis.

"What a beautiful thing to say, baby. Good for you."

Silence, more wine-flavored silence, and smiling into the hot blanket I saw distinctly our rigidly approaching nemesis (a small goat prancing out of a sacred wood) and knew that, despite the grip of my hand, Catherine was beginning to roll again under the weight of her fourteen years of motherhood.

"You didn't have children. That's all."

Fiona's turn, I thought, and wondered whether Catherine was actually aware of my tender grip or had in fact forgotten me, lost sight of me in the midst of thinking about Hugh's little black pointed beard and her three deliveries. Though it was I, after all, who was once more touching flame to the idea of the family and lighting anew the possibilities of sex in the domestic landscape.

"Oh, but we decided against children long ago. And now it's too late anyway. Thank God. But we love your children, Catherine. Don't we, Cyril?"

I raised my head and nodded, then shifted my weight and lowered my head again so that my weathered cheek smothered beneath it Catherine's fingers and now upturned palm. In nose and mouth and stomach I made the wordless contented sounds of an agreeable man settling down to sleep on a hot beach blanket, though in point of fact I had never been more crisp with attentiveness and lay listening to the epic inside Catherine's lower abdomen. I was waiting for the parents to become lovers and the lovers parents.

"What's the matter, Eveline? Come over here to your old dad."

The little fists were in the eyes, the lips were turned down, the small fat body was naked except for the gray cotton panties riding well below the navel, the brown hair was filled with burrs which only moments before had been clinging to the black fur of the dog. Without moving or opening my eyes I saw it all, the upright and sunburned child midway between our blanket and the sleeping dog and stumbling toward us silently, unerringly, while Catherine frowned and Fiona caressed herself. I dozed on, watching, waiting, enjoying behind my patina of sun the sight of Hugh's pebbly tight smile and the eyes that were glancing now at Eveline, now at Catherine and me, now at Fiona. It amused me to know that little Eveline was to be the lever with which her father would pry Catherine's warm pillowing hand from beneath my cheek. How like him, I thought, to begrudge me Catherine's hand in the middle of the afternoon and abandon her body to me throughout the night.

"Maybe she just needs to urinate," Hugh said. "Could that be it?"

And then the soft toneless maternal voice beginning to withdraw at last from motherhood: "Of course she does. But it's your turn, Hugh. I'm sun-bathing."

Once more I was proud of Catherine, who had managed to add another still note to our silence. Already Meredith was blushing at the edge of the sea. I waited for the prolonged and uneasy sound of Fiona's giggling. And then the little invisible white goat landed among us and I rolled toward Catherine, who did not move, and propped myself on one elbow in time to see Hugh sit heavily and deliberately on Catherine's haunch, as if on a convenient stone, and hold the baffled child between his knees and with his one hand pull down her panties swiftly, expertly. He was whistling and aiming his small fat daughter in the direction of the still sea where Meredith stood listening, blushing, shriveling.

"Get off me, Hugh."

"Hang on there. She's nearly done."

Would she throw him off? With a single heave would she dislodge him from his all-too-comfortable seat on her upraised hip? In some way would she appeal to me for help? But even as I wondered how long Hugh would be able to sustain this admittedly ingenious stroke of trivial revenge, wobbling happily on his wife's prostrate body, I saw that Catherine's eyes were open and that the small amber-colored pupils were fixed on my own in a long silent expression of love or indignation. I returned her secret stare and with slow pleasure began to realize that Catherine had chosen this moment to think of me and was quite oblivious to the weight on her hip.

Yet Hugh himself was thinking not of the naked sunburned child squatting between his angular protective legs, not of Fiona, though now I heard the prolonged and uneasy sound of Fiona's giggling, but was thinking rather of the woman he was sitting on, because even while I watched the arm and hand that Catherine could not possibly see (long arm and large versatile hand still fresh from the parental ritual of pulling down little Eveline's pants and holding her, caring for her), Hugh swung back his arm, reached down, and without changing his position or turning his head, fumbled briefly until his hand leapt suddenly like the small invisible white goat and, in a gesture of love or viciousness, closed on Catherine's heavy breast inside the madras halter. Did he know that I was watching? Or more likely, had he again managed to forget my presence and the immediate fact that I was now lolling only inches away from this reclining person who even at this moment was perhaps more my partner than his? Why could he not respect Catherine's conventional but nonetheless powerful intimacy? When would he ever respond to my omniscience and Fiona's style? But of course the wedding ring worn bizarrely, fiercely, on the third finger of Hugh's right hand told me that I must never allow myself to be unduly critical of Hugh. Even that monstrous hand of his wore its sign of love.

And then the nemesis of our brief respose became exactly the unpredictable display of cause and effect that I had anticipated, and Catherine struck away Hugh's desperate hand, Hugh jumped to his feet. Fiona caught Hugh's nearest thigh in her already waiting arms and squeezed slowly and yet for only an instant. There was no need to look and reassure myself that behind us Hugh was lapsing again into arrogance, was standing with his eyes shut, his stump upraised, his thin bare legs rigidly apart, his fingers driven into Fiona's hair even while Fiona's eager cheek lay pressed to his thigh. Would he never learn? I adjusted the faded strap of the halter, pushed my warm face into Catherine's face and clothed her suddenly naked mouth with mine.

"Look, baby. A little goat!"

But was it possible? Had I heard her bright words correctly? Had Fiona actually spoken somewhere outside the no doubt pedestrian aura of the muttered sounds of contentment I must have been making while kissing Catherine? Was it dream, change, coincidence, or was my state of mind a menagerie of desire from which real animals

might spring? Could it be that one of my speechless creatures of joy and sentiment had torn itself loose from the
tapestry that only I could see? Was it now bearing down
upon us with blue eyes and the wind in its hair? Was the
little goat that had danced among us in my mind now going to leave its little hoofprints in the center of Fiona's
blanket or come rushing and butting between our legs? It
did not seem possible. But of course it was.

"Oh, baby, look, he's wonderful!"

We separated, climbed to our feet, stood apart, all four
of us, and together stared in the direction indicated by
Fiona's outstretched arm and waving hand. And of course
Fiona's excitement was justified and the goat was real. But
he was not white, as I had thought, but cream-colored, a
small long-legged creamy animal splashed on the forelegs
and masked around his eyes with brown. At first glance he
was in the air, hung suspended at the height of his second
leap from the gloomy pines, and even from where we stood
we could see his bright blue eyes and the nubile horns embedded in soft down. At least I had been right about the
color of his eyes, I thought, and smiled.

Then he sprang, leapt, danced his soaring stiff-legged
dance. And while Hugh romped with the goat and I squatted beside the distasteful Eveline, comforting her and helping her climb back into the discarded pants, I glanced up
and saw that Meredith had stripped off her modest trunks
and halter at last and with both thin arms raised above her
head was leaping up and down in the black water. She had
kept her back to us and now her thin body was slick and
brown, her little white porcelain buttocks were winking at
me through the sheaves of spray.

"Meredith," Catherine called over her shoulder, "come look at the baby goat."

But their oldest daughter danced on and it occurred to me that after all there was hope for Meredith and even for Hugh. And Fiona was still sharing my thoughts because suddenly there she was, kneeling where I squatted with the child, and Fiona's whisper was filled with pleasure, confidence, elation, the smell of jasmine.

"Isn't he wonderful? I want him for my own, I really do."

"Goat or man?"

"The man, baby. The man."

LAST NIGHT (ONLY LAST NIGHT) I LAY UNACCOUNTABLY awake on my narrow iron bed in my small vaulted room and listened to Rosella snoring in the darkness at the other end of the villa. I was amused at the sound and in passing decided that it could only be the latent old peasant woman already snoring inside Rosella and that the sound was no doubt comforting to their partially domesticated animals. But what of myself? Why was I, who was always a heavy sleeper, now lying awake?

Slowly I raised my arms and clasped my large dry weathered hands behind my head. I had not been dreaming, there was no wind in the cypresses, the noises from Rosella's little open mouth were distant, faint, and could not have awakened me. Why then my open eyes, my slow ordered speculations? What had become of my ponderous capacity for peaceful sleep? After all, I thought then with amusement and mild nostalgia, Fiona used to resort to little kicks and punches to wake me out of total darkness, used to thrust a lighted cigarette between my still sleeping lips, used to tug at my hair and pound my chest, in mock fury fight my pajama buttons before I managed to open my eyes and speak a few thick golden words of reassurance and with my own fingers pull what she used to call the rip cord of my pajama bottoms. How different I was from Fiona, how different I was from Hugh who claimed that he spent all the nights of his life in sleepless writhing.

The bedstead trembled, I could hear its rust flaking onto the stone floor. At that moment I knew that even if I raised myself on one elbow and glanced at the window I would not be able to distinguish the blackness of the funeral cypresses from the blackness of the night. Lying in the very darkness in which Hugh and Fiona had suffered both together and separately, I admitted to myself that even while laving my memories of them in silent thought I could not blame my wakefulness on Fiona's long leaps through the night or on Hugh's torment. But was it even a question of blame? I thought not. And suddenly I knew with a kind of certainty that whatever in fact accounted for my wakefulness it was somehow pleasant—immediate, obvious, pleasant. Something had happened, something had changed, and I knew that in the thick neutral night of my middle age I had only to think, to wait another few moments in order to know why I was awake in this darkness of measured expectancy.

I listened, I concentrated all my receptivity on the nearly invisible crude contours of my low stone vaulted ceiling. Beyond the wall of funeral cypresses the black inhospitable sea was unaccountably silent. Out there beyond the other darkened villa my pair of little owls was sleeping. My solid bed was just large enough for one, its lumpy mildewed mattress was a denial of love, my weight was extracting some kind of faint lonely music from its rows of archaic rusty springs. And then I realized that I had lain awake once before in exactly this same state of suspended lucidity. Rarely a dreamer, blind forever to the possibilities of insomnia, nonethless I had somewhere, sometime spent another night lying awake in the presence of some unidentifiable delight. But where? When? The narrow bed, the springs, my unrumpled pajamas, the absence of sheet or blanket—all these, I thought, were clues.

In the darkness I made fish lips, frowned. Why was I, with my memory, my self-understanding, my ability to expose the logic sewn into the seams of almost all of our precious sequences of love and friendship, now at a loss to locate two separate but similar sources of warmth, surprise, pleasure? What bed could I be trying to recall? What night?

The marriage bed, of course, the couch of love, the first formal gift of conjugal darkness. For a moment I felt a sensation of relief and shades of triumph, and told myself once more that Psyche was on my side and that given time and thought I could always count on myself for answers. At least I was now recalling exactly what I had been attempting to recall: the sight of the mid-thigh silver wedding dress, the white stockings, the hot medicinal taste of the brandy I drank rather foolishly perhaps from her silver shoe, the late moment when finally I unzipped the metallic

dress and helped her strip off the stockings and then ca
her nude to the edge of the warm dark fountain amidst the
appreciative sounds of our most loyal friends.

*Don't bother being a husband, baby. Just be a sex-singer.
OK?*

Were those her words, her magic words? Again I heard
them, again the stark ceremonial details returned, though
lying there in the center of my night of analytical revery,
I was amused to realize that as a matter of fact I could not
remember the last time I had thought about this occasion,
the exact identification of which would remain forever
buried on the inside surface of the ring that served as its
reminder. Then why now?

The answer was mine even before this last question was
fully formulated, because suddenly and with total relief I
remembered living through precisely this same perplexing
night once before when, several hours after I had carried
Fiona to the fountain, I rolled onto my back and discovered that I was awake and that my mind was as clear as
usual but that something had changed, and that whatever
had awakened me was immediate, obvious, yet in this instant unidentifiable. But I had overcome Psyche's little
dramatic ruse and had thought my way backward to the
sudden fact of marriage and forward to the gift of Fiona, to
the sudden recognition that I was lying in the conjugal
darkness with my wife. And now Catherine, of course. My
logical associations abruptly flowered, giving me not Fiona
but Catherine, not the fact of marriage but the promise of
sexless matrimony, not the bottle of champagne embedded
in a basket of flowers but the rabbit waiting out this sleepless night in his new cage between the well house and the

97

overgrown remains of my ruined bicycle. Not the couch of love but my single bed. Not wife but former mistress on her narrow iron bed like mine in the small white room next to mine. The waving matron, Rosella's sullen greeting, my decision against touching Catherine's elbow in the door to her room, Catherine staring at the empty villa through the funeral cypresses—lying there in the darkness I at last reviewed all the details of Catherine's sunset arrival and thought that the two nights were oddly similar and that I was now as grateful to Catherine for coming to share my speculations on the painted bones of Love as I had once been to Fiona for feasting with me on the marrow.

On the night I had remembered Fiona in a shower of mental fireworks, so to speak, I had fallen again into the peace of my brandy-soaked sleep immediately. And now, remembering Catherine and knowing that I had only to grope my way along a few feet of whitewashed stone to confirm that this was in fact the first night of Catherine's muted presence on the other side of my crude bedroom wall, I did the same and relaxed my feet, withdrew both hands from behind my head, rolled over and immediately fell into the bemused contentment of deep sleep.

THE NIGHT WAS GOING TO BE A LONG ONE, I DECIDED, AND began to feel that the kiss Fiona had impetuously planted on the cheek of our one-armed hero was infusing the darkness with even greater expectancy than Fiona herself had hoped for. The strangers were saved, the old motorbus was only hours into its first invasion by the curious water rats and but a few hours into what would surely be its long life of deterioration in the black canal, the unattractive children were sleeping at last, the adventure was more clearly defined and further along than I had thought it would be by the middle of what was only our first night together. The darkness was like a warm liquid poured from the throat of an enormous bird, and above our heads and within easy reach of our mouths vast clusters of stars and tumultuous bunches of black grapes were merging. Each grape contained its bright star, each star its grape. My mouth was brazen with the long slow taste of white wine.

"Cyril, baby, are you all right?"

"Sure," I called softly toward the two figures momentarily visible among the lemon trees, "we're fine."

But already they had moved away from us once more, already the clear voice had lapsed again into a laughing, preoccupied frosty whisper, again we heard the playful confusion of footsteps and then the silence that told me that Fiona's happiness was dripping between the lemon trees again like dew. The surprise of the second kiss was drawing near, I thought. Or was it the third?

In the darkness I groped for another bottle, pulled the cork and filled our two small invisible glasses. The stone bench we sat on was chalky and warm, overhead the grape arbor was a sagging foot-thick blanket of hanging grapes and climbing roses. I sipped, listened to the breathing of the large woman seated within easy reach of my hip, my knee, the toe of my bone-white tennis shoe. I cleared my throat and smiled to think that it was like Fiona, exactly like Fiona, to set the first stage of her impending adventure in nothing less than a small lemon grove where she could run at will, and exactly like myself to settle for an unobtrusive niche in a grape arbor. Fiona always spent first nights giving literal chase to her dreams, whereas I, of course, preferred to muse on approaching possibilities and to wait, to listen, to sit out the preliminaries in quiet thought. Again I cleared my throat and glanced at the woman beside me who, in the darkness, was audible rather than visible, a large soft black-and-white image blurred at the edges and rustling with bodily sounds that expressed not meaning but presence. She was breathing, swallowing, twisting to peer over her shoulder. Was she sighing also? Perhaps. I waited and knew that like the stone bench I too was warm to the touch, seemed to be giving off broad waves of pleasing heat.

"You're not shivering, are you," I said, stirring the embers, allowing my voice to drift again toward lower, more reassuring registers. "My wife thinks you must be exhausted. She's worried about you."

Beyond the arbor and through the funeral cypresses I could see traces of the light from the old kerosene lantern they had left burning for their children. Beside me the woman was sitting quietly in remoteness, loneliness, indecision. A lemon struck the ground behind us and I thought I caught sight of Fiona's white hand waving at me from a slit in the darkness.

I sipped my wine and thought that the shoulder of the woman beside me was broad, soft, unknown. Unknown yet oddly familiar too. A warm shoulder, I thought, that was growing cool. Would the woman beside me manage unwittingly to earn my attention and find out for herself that she needed it? Had Love determined that this woman's shadow was to cross the white path of my capability? Or were we to separate forever at our very moment of meeting? At least these questions presented themselves. At least we could continue turning the pages together for a while longer.

"My wife admires your courage," I murmured. "Fiona's character judgments are always right."

The grape arbor and lemon grove were complementary, of course, and now our momentary silence in the arbor was equaled, exceeded by the silence that was again saturating the grove of twisted trees. I listened, began to dip my hand toward the wicker wine basket somewhere at my feet. It was a question of pantomime as opposed to orchestration, I thought, and waited patiently while out there the second or perhaps third kiss grew into a reality of held breaths. The very fact that we heard nothing determined the kiss. Did my companion know what was happening? Was she also able to enjoy the invisible kiss which we, seated open-eyed as we were in the darkness, might have been dreaming? But perhaps for now her appreciation of that kiss was too much to ask, because suddenly I knew that she was looking at me directly, silently, while I continued to stare down at the moldy cork I could not see. And then her husband laughed once and stumbled, called out Fiona's name, again was looping his way among the trees.

"We've been married a long time," she said, and her words were like the wine from the bottle—slow, inflection-less, filled with a taste that pleased the mind as well as tongue. I approved of what she had said, heard the soft breath that sustained the sentence, began to see the sweat and soiled years heaped up in the vague shadowy sockets of her eyes. Dull words, and yet enjoyable precisely because the three exhausted children and the now preoccupied one-armed husband could not be deduced from them. Her words alone, and they allowed me to choose between implied security or resignation or, finally, indignation at what she might have taken to be the first signs of betrayal. I put the wine into her fingers and made my choice.

"Married a long time?" I repeated slowly, turning her few words into mine and at the same time giving them back to her like low notes on a flute. "Fiona and I have also been married a long time. As a matter of fact, Fiona is a kind of priestess of marriage. Her most remarkable quality, I think, is suppleness. But it's late. Are you sure you want to sit out here like this?"

"I like your voice in the darkness."

"OK," I said, preparing to shape my words carefully, resonantly, and putting down my half-empty glass between us, "but what about your husband? He's probably worried about you, like Fiona and me. Wouldn't it be better if you were in there sleeping with the children?"

"You needn't worry. None of you."

I waited, and beneath my two hands now clasped around one heavy knee, the camel-colored cloth of my trousers felt like combed linen while the knee itself felt like some living prehistoric bone full of solidity, aesthetic richness, latent athleticism. Imperceptibly I rocked on the warm stone and again glanced briefly at the embryonic stars in the grapes.

102

"We can hardly see each other. We don't know each other. I'm a lot older than you think."

She appeared to be listening, sitting and waiting with her hands in her lap and her fresh glass of wine untasted, listening and waiting with eyes now averted and her large distant body filled with thought. But just when it occurred to me that she had drifted into some new private solitude or had merely decided not to answer, she spoke, and between the slow golden roll of my own last words and the sudden inspired appearance of Fiona, whose hopes were rising, I heard her brief declaration and found myself wanting to retrieve the subdued and levelheaded sound of her voice from the grapes, the black leaves, the dark night.

"I'm forty-three."

Was she more aware of herself than I had thought? Was she trying to change the subject or to confide in me? At least her statement of age deserved my attention, deserved the two of us sitting side by side. But then the air shook, the arbor shook, the scent of Fiona's bath soap and jasmine sweetened the night, and my own investigative mood and Fiona's springing bow collided, coalesced.

"Baby, you're sharing secrets!"

"We're just talking," I murmured. "Join us?"

"I couldn't sit still. Not tonight."

She had come from nowhere, as she often did, and was breathing quickly. Once again I observed that Fiona's obviously substantial bone structure was no impediment to her grace or to her abrupt and totally unexpected late-hour turns of mind. I nodded and allowed my face to reflect a faintly deeper shade of my composure, pleasure, good humor. Fiona shifted her feet, glanced around the arbor with what I knew to be girlish delight and womanly detachment, leaned close to me and apparently without thinking slipped the bows of my spectacles from behind my ears and just as quickly slipped them into place again. Her feet were bare. And then she was suddenly on her knees and holding my companion tightly about the waist while I, rocking and humming to myself in silent song, could not help marveling a little more at Fiona's transformational powers and sensual flights. I smelled Fiona's jasmine and perspiration and waited, with growing possessiveness stared at the solid and yet agitated shapes of the one woman seated and the other kneeling in the blackness of the night. My companion seemed neither to resist nor welcome my wife's embrace. But I thought she might be imperceptibly relaxing, if anything, into Fiona's arms.

"I'm glad you're here. I want you here. You and Hugh."

The voice I never tired of hearing was both muffled and clear, soft and strident. There was love in her voice and yet she was speaking quickly and in another moment would leap to her feet, I knew, and disappear.

"Easy, Fiona," I murmured. "Calm down."

"Oh, Cyril, don't be stuffy."

I laughed, made my musing face in the darkness, lowered my voice. "At least Catherine doesn't think I'm stuffy. Catherine and I were having a nice conversation until you came along."

"Sharing secrets, baby. I know. Drinking wine."

But again Fiona eclipsed the warm comforting sounds deep in my chest and before I could speak raised her face, reached up, seized the other woman's large hardly distinguishable head in both hands, waited, then dropped her arms. The gesture, I understood, was another intimation of a kiss between women, the kind of gesture Fiona allowed herself when she could not bear to merely kiss someone's cheek but when passionate kissing was nonetheless inappropriate. I was unable to see either woman's eyes, and yet I knew that they were looking at each other and that Fiona's eyes were probably moist and luminous.

"Cyril's different from other men. Do you like him? Do you like my Cyril?"

"Of course she likes me."

"Baby, you ruin everything."

But I was ready this time, and before she was able to relinquish my companion and regain her feet, slowly and deliberately I placed my hand on Fiona's hip and confirmed to my own satisfaction that the elastic of her panties was still to be felt beneath the gauzy nylon of the short dress. I had merely grazed her lower hip with the tips of my fingers, and of course the panties were not of any great importance. But Fiona always perceived my motives, no matter how subtle, and now standing in the darkness she had understood immediately the nature of the curiosity that lay like a shadow behind the delicate, nearly instinctive movements of my right hand.

"OK," she said, and for a moment became a flurry of swift purpose. "You asked for it. There they are."

I laughed, leaned down and with my palm covered the small white perforated piece of intimate apparel where it had landed on the toe of my white tennis shoe, then stuffed it easily into my right-hand trouser pocket. Catherine had not comprehended this domestic incident, I thought, and

Fiona was gone. I wondered if she had satisfied her own curiosity while pouting at mine.

"Where were we," I said and waited, adjusted the bows of the spectacles properly behind my ears, casually ran my fingers through my briefly disarrayed waves of hair, crossed my knees, struck up one of my slow-burning oval cigarettes. My wife and the one-armed stranger were everywhere and nowhere, the dark night was growing longer, deeper.

"Quiet, you two," I called agreeably in the direction of the invisible well house, "you'll wake the children."

And then again drifting, so to speak, to my partner: "We were talking," I murmured, "what about?"

"Ourselves."

"Exactly. Telling each other heart-stoppers, as Fiona would say."

"You're laughing at me."

"Of course I'm not."

"I don't want to run around all night in the darkness."

"Nor do I."

Pausing, moving one of her empty hands to the cool breadth of an upper arm, she spoke slowly out of the black shadows: "She said you're different from other men. What did she mean?"

I waited, and then another length of golden thread went toward its mark in the darkness: "The real secret is that she likes to pinch my bottom. That's all. But trust us," I added. "Trust Fiona and me."

And then quietly and without shrugging her shoulders: "Why not?"

I exhaled, nodded, began to feel at last that though we had not changed positions or touched each other even acci-

dently, nonetheless there was the decided possibility
my massive oral cavity and the vast dark sockets of her
invisible eyes were now groping toward each other in some
sort of sympathetic identification, some warm analogy of
bone and shadow. "I've told you a secret," I said. "Now
tell me one."

"All right."

Did she take a breath? Was she turning her head in my
direction? Had I heard the first welcome shades of laughter
in her voice? I shifted knees, waited. And then she spoke
softly, matter-of-factly: "Your wife really meant you're the
perfect man. I didn't have to ask what she meant. I knew."

"Another heart-stopper," I said as softly as I could, and
heard the sweetness thickening. "Thanks for the heart-
stopper. But how did you know?"

"I knew."

A fresh surprise, more pauses, the low sound of her
accent poised between invitation and resignation, a suggestion of despondency balancing the brief hint of pleasure.
Could she have meant what she had said? Seen what she
had claimed to see? At the very moment of wading from
the absurd and dangerous canal had some vague recognition
of the headless god lolling in the guise of my composure
overcome her mortification and fear for her children? I
could not be sure. But at least we were turning the pages
at a swifter pace. And was I about to subject us to the test
of the children? Perhaps. Perhaps not. Carefully I reached
through our small wall of darkness and filled her glass.

"So you think you see me as Fiona sees me," I said, and
laughed. "The perfect man."

"Yes. But it doesn't have much to do with me."

"Not even now?"

"Not yet."

"There you go again. More disappointment."

"Why should I be disappointed?"

"Of course Fiona exaggerates. I'm a lot more ordinary than she'd like you to believe."

"You asked for a secret. I told you."

"Good. Let's have another."

"No. It's your turn. What's in your pocket? What did she give you a moment ago?"

Wrong, I thought, I had been admirably wrong, and I allowed myself to shape one gigantic, tremorless ring of smoke and then set it free and watched it swell, widen, disintegrate heavily in our night of the untasted grapes. Apparently she had witnessed something of Fiona's playful exchange after all, had been aroused by being in the presence of Fiona's swift act of partially denuding herself. But did I wish to hazard a discussion of Fiona's simple and private gesture, or resort to it? Might I not better keep at least this relatively insignificant example of Fiona's sexlanguage to myself? Was the risk too great, the ploy too easy? I made my choice.

"Just Fiona's panties," I said under my breath. "They're not important."

"Why did she take them off?"

"Who knows? Do you really care?"

"I'm not sure."

"Trust me."

"You remind me of my father."

"Listen," I said then, as if our heads were inches apart, "listen a moment." I waited, holding out my hand for silence and knowing that it was in fact time to act, and then carefully I uncrossed my legs and stood up so that the hard cool globules of the lowest grapes spilled onto the top of my head and brushed my ears. I was relaxed. I was crowned with fruit. And then under my breath: "Listen. I knew they'd wake the children. Let's go."

"I don't hear anything."

"We'd better look."

She moved, she too must have felt the passing weight of the grapes. I led the way, she followed. I heard the sound of her breathing, strolled on. At the far side of the funeral cypresses I glanced at the dying eye of my cigarette and waited while the trailing woman slowly extricated herself from the thorns and brittle twigs that lined the opening through the tall black cypresses. Beneath the clothesline that I had rigged at dusk we paused among the silhouetted trousers, dress, miniature dresses, stockings, all greater than life size and still dripping with the waters of the black canal. As we approached the villa that Fiona had opened up for them, I noted the high silver grass, the broken tiles, the listing shutters stuffed with rags and impacted with the earthen ceramics of transient wasps, the small gothic niche near the doorway where birds had raised their young and no candle burned, no icon glowed. And entering the cold corridor, I in the lead and she following, I smiled at the sound of the snoring dog and at the feeling of wet stone beneath my hand and the smell of the old kerosene lantern that was smoking in one of the cell-like rooms ahead of us. Once again I knew that a ruined villa was even more appropriate to passion than was a silent grape arbor filled with stars.

"Come on," I whispered, "let's look at them."

And then I was holding high the lantern by its rusty wire loop and we were standing shoulder to shoulder and peering down at the two large and almost identical heads lying side by side in the smoky orange light at our feet. The faces were square, the curls were tight and dark, the lips were thick. Could these be the faces of small girls? I could understand their size (the mother was large, the father now silently romping with my wife was large) but it was difficult to account for their expressions of sexless power.

"That's Dolores," I heard my companion whispering, "that's Eveline."

Dolores, Eveline. Together we studied the sleepers, Catherine and I, and even these children were beginning to make a difference, were already strengthening nameless bonds between us, as I had thought they might.

"And somewhere over there," she whispered, so that I lifted the lantern and swung it loosely in the direction she appeared to be pointing toward with her restrained and contented voice, "is Meredith."

Together we felt our way among the piles of clothing, piles of blankets provided by Fiona, suddenly bulky articles of luggage (opened and ransacked or still locked, bound tight with archaic leather straps, but each piece smelling of the polluted water), until our slow elbow-knocking search at last revealed the girl called Meredith curled in naked sleep on a hasty pallet of Fiona's pink sheets spread on the cold stones on the floor.

"She doesn't like me," I whispered, and leaning closer saw that one of her thin fingers was in her mouth.

"Of course she does."

"Fiona always wins the confidence of children. No such luck for me."

And slowly, again attempting to point through the darkness with her whispering voice: "We're going to sleep in there. Hugh and I."

We waited, she made no further comment. It looked to me as if Meredith wanted to cry out in frail anger, but thanks to the sleep of children was unable to move, to make even the smallest sound. The hair across her brow was wet, one little sharply pointed ear was white.

"They're all safe," I said. "No nightmares."

"No. They won't wake up."

"Fiona and that noisy husband of yours may do their best," I whispered as if I myself were rolling over casually on a soft bed in the darkness. "But I'm glad we looked."

"So am I."

Already I was groping behind me with my free hand while probing forward with the hot lantern toward the room they had chosen for themselves. Already we were moving forward together into the darkness empty and silent except for the dismal snoring of their old dog. Even by then I knew that the poor wretched animal was deaf, and both of us knew that otherwise the room was empty and that there was no longer any danger of stepping on an unsuspecting child. And yet our breathing was becoming shallow, in unspoken accord we were wary, both of us, of stumbling against an alpine pack or one of their swollen leather bags.

"The lantern's smoking," I whispered. "Can you see?"

"You know I can."

Once more I swung my arm solemnly and it all leapt to

view—the dog, the scattered shoes, a tall medieval chest that smelled of iron spikes, the broad and sagging wooden bed whose tight percale sheets and a little hasty bouquet of hyacinths again revealed my wife's impulsiveness. At the foot of the bed and on his scrap of dark blue carpet, the dog was sleeping on his back with his paws in the air. Carefully I lowered the lantern, the smoke rose between us, side by side we were standing in the midst of their transient lives.

"You're thinking of your children."

"Yes. My children."

"Tomorrow," I whispered, "we'll teach you and Hugh to play the grape-tasting game."

"All right."

She did not move, together we waited. And I knew again that it was time to act and slowly, distinctly, and gesturing about the room with my upraised chin: "In all this confusion," I whispered, "can you find your pajamas?"

"Yes."

"Put them on. I'll be back in about twenty minutes."

"All right."

Elation? Tenderness? Guilt? Had I, who did not believe in trivial, tedious seduction, maneuvered her after all into a kind of uneasy submission? It was possible that hers was a troubled or low-pitched acquiescence or even worse a defensive gesture motivated more by the lyrical sex-play in the lemon grove than by her internal needs and the attention I was interested in giving her. By dawn would she feel nothing but distaste? Or would I return to find her deep in sleep? But no, I told myself (walking with careful step and heavy purpose past the grape arbor and on toward our own dark villa) no, I could not have been so very wrong, could not have so underestimated the flesh of her womanhood or so mistaken the sound of her voice. Small fears, perhaps, but no disappointment. No unfortunate deception or painful aftermath. Could anything be more unquestionable than love undertaken in the presence of her sleeping children? She had passed the test of the children, I told myself, surely had forgotten the cries coming from the lemon grove even before we had strolled away from the grapes.

Yes, I told myself (abruptly detecting Fiona's absence from the now familiar darkness of this room we ordinarily shared together) and emptying my pockets, putting aside Fiona's helpful talisman, removing my large white tennis shoes, undressing once again though not for sleep—yes, of course I had read the cues and inferences correctly because now I recognized once more those first sensations of inevitability, certainty, slow emotional assent that had characterized the early hours of my most vivid relationships throughout the years. And my companion? Was my soft and unexplored companion now pacing me on the other side of the funeral cypresses, I wondered (climbing into my cerulean pajama bottoms and adjusting the ties, buttoning the top) or was she already waiting for my return and the approval guaranteed in the slowness of my embrace? Waiting already, I decided (thrusting first one arm and then the other into the cool loose sleeves of my maroon-colored dressing gown) but selflessly, patiently, since this was our first time and even now she must know that my lengthy preparations were all for her. Tying the sash, tugging at the silken lapels of my dressing gown, feeling about for handkerchief, black cigarettes, tortoise-shell brush and comb, and brushing my hair and then rinsing my mouth at the round mouth of a small earthenware vessel that tasted of Fiona's lipstick and timeless clay—in all this I found myself pleasurably confirming once again my own modest belief in the theory that, whenever possible, it was always best to make the gift of love intentional.

At the last moment I decided that it was easiest to wear the tennis shoes on my naked feet as protection against the thorns that were bound to lie embedded in the dark path between the villas, and so took a little extra time and put them on.

"Cyril? Is it you?"

The sleepy voice was coming not from the lemon grove but from the grape arbor, though I could see nothing and did not know if they were sitting on the stone bench so recently vacated or on the ground with their knees drawn up.

"I know it's you, baby. Stop hiding."

I paused, allowed the cigarette to hang between my lips, and smiled at the sleepy quality in Fiona's voice which meant more than that she was tired of running and that her feeling for the one-armed man was lapsing predictably but only momentarily into girlish grief. Fiona habitually imagined the death or departure of a potential lover within the first few hours of any unexpected passion. But generally such moodiness was short-lived.

"It's me," I called softly and laughed. "You know it is. How are the grapes?"

And then clear, sleepy, fading: "We're going to sit up and watch the sunrise, baby. OK?"

"Great idea, Fiona. Great."

I heard nothing more, no sighing, not even the solace of a deliberately noisy kiss, and I shook loose the skirts of the dressing gown, walked on. To me the sunset was always preferable to the sunrise, but there was no way I could help them back there in the arbor and of course Fiona was too good a woman, inside or outside of marriage, to brook any interference with her romantic views. It would have to be the sunrise then. But at least in a sense I had given her the secluded arbor, since apparently the lemon grove, like the night itself, was not enough.

"Is it you?"

"Of course it is."

"I'm over here."

The lantern was out but I had followed the sounds of the dog and in my absence she, my waiting partner, had forced open the rotten shutters so that now the same faint light that Fiona no doubt was noticing in the grapes was also turning my partner's orderly white pajamas into a beckoning yet somehow modest concentration of mute phosphorescence. The old dog lay as before, still dreaming his way toward death, and still the villa was filled with the pleasing chaos of scattered children, scattered signs of temporary life. Carefully I nudged aside what appeared to be one of her husband's shoes and half facing the head on the pillow, sat down slowly on the edge of the bed. Her eyes were turned toward mine, her legs were heavy, her arms were at her sides. With gentle fingers I discovered that in her nearest hand she was holding the stems of Fiona's impulsive little gift of flowers.

"Was I long?"

lidn't mind waiting."

ting my hand, leaning in her direction, knowing that
she was as conscious as I was of my soft lips pressing together, parting and then pressing together again, slowly I
slid up the bottom of her pajama jacket and exposed a few
inches of her wide stomach and then withdrew my hand,
leaving the soft broad belt of skin exposed. Her hardly
audible vocal throb subsided, she did not move. I swung
away and for a moment devoted precise fingers to the carefully tied laces of my tennis shoes.

"I wonder if they're lying in bed together right now," she
whispered. "Like us."

"Would it change anything?"

"It might explain what I'm doing here with you."

"Do you think so?"

"No."

I was standing barefooted beside the bed and untied the
large bow I had made in the sash. "As a matter of fact," I
whispered, "they're just sitting up to watch the sunrise. Is
that better?"

"That makes it worse."

"Why?"

"I don't know."

Seated once more on the edge of the bed and laughing:
"I can give you clarity," I whispered, "but not understanding."

Only then did I remove my spectacles and for safekeeping put them inside my left tennis shoe beneath the edge
of the bed.

"Don't be prudish."

"I'm not."

116

"Don't worry," I whispered, "just relax."

Eyes shut, mouth dissolving, oblivious to snoring dog and absent husband and little nearby unconscious witnesses but not to me, slowly she moved at last, waited, moved again. Her head had fallen to one side but she was listening to me, to all my voices, and watching me in the depths of her smothered eyes.

"Your shoulder's cold," I said, and covered it with a soothing hand. Murmuring, waiting, stroking her hair, smiling at the thought that her soft arms were hardly able to reach around my back and that her hands had not been able to preserve their desperate grip on my enormous tough rump—beyond all this I the white bull finally carried my now clamorous companion into a distant corner of the vast tapestry where only a little silvery spring lay waiting to restore virginity and quench thirst.

Later, and into my ear and softer, much softer than before: "I guess I wanted you all the time," she whispered. "But I never thought we'd be in bed together."

"Glad you were wrong?"

"Yes. I'm glad."

The sunrise, as later I happened to see for myself, was brilliant.

Steady wind, hard clear light, the four of us holding hands on the rocks that faced the squat ominous remains of the fortress across the narrow crescent of dark water now harboring only four or five half-sunken wooden boats with high prows, broken oars, red chains. Moody, we were bound together by wind and light and hands. All eyes were on the ruined penitential structure just across the water that was apparently unchanged, unnourished by the sea crashing on three sides of us. All eyes were on the gutted shape of history, as if the clearly visible iron base and broken stones and streaks of lichen were portentous, related in some way to our own presently idyllic lives. But I for one was conscious of bodies, hands, squinting eyes, positions in line, was well aware that Fiona stood on my left and Catherine on my right and that Hugh was doomed forever to the extreme left and could never share my privilege of standing, so to speak, between two opposite and yet equally desirable women. Even on our promontory of sharp wet rocks it amused me to think that, thanks to Hugh, our sacred circle would remain forever metaphysical. Nothing more.

But what was he saying?

"That fort, boy . . . soon . . ."

"Good idea," I shouted and, nodding my head up and down, again I was struck with the perception that he was black while I was gold. But a ruined fortress was not a safe place for a man like Hugh, and though I did not yet understand the basis for so much oblivious intensity, still I admired his courage and was beginning to share his eagerness to undertake the expedition to that unwholesome place of bone, charred wood, seaweed.

Suddenly I felt the pre-emptory childish tugging on my left hand and the cold lips against my ear. Fiona's words seemed to lodge immediately and permanently in the still room of my brain.

"Do you know where we are, baby? Tell me quick."

Surprised at her sudden and atypical desperation, but laughing and aiming my mouth toward the hint of white cartilage buried like an arrow in the now violent cream- and sable-colored hair: "Sure," I shouted, "we're in Illyria. Like it?"

"I like you, baby. You."

WAKING, WRINKLING MY NOSE, ROLLING OVER, I HEARD my hand slap accidently against my own thick mottled thigh and realized that despite our early agreement intended to safeguard children and husband alike, I had dozed off, so that now we were only a few hours from dawn. I was faced with precisely the situation we had thought it best to avoid. Slowly I climbed out of the bed and found the polka-dotted pajama bottoms and put them on, lit the lantern, yawned, made my way toward the cry that I had recognized as coming from the little tight-lipped mouth of Meredith. And then there was the battle of whispers, one side tormented, bitter, the other dismayed, calm as usual.

"What's the matter?"

"Nothing."

"Your nose is bleeding."

"It's not."

"Stop being a child."

"I'm going to tell my father."

"Let's do something about this nosebleed."

"He'll probably kill you for coming here."

"Hold still."

Despite the eyes of the injured eaglet and her obvious efforts to escape the touch of my hand (cowering, hunching the thin white naked shoulders), she could no longer defend herself from my kindness because the blood was running into her mouth and down her little pointed chin. Her nostrils became dilated, the head drew back. But with the tip of Fiona's pink sheet, which was already bloody between my fingers, slowly and carefully I wiped her face and pinched her nose until finally the gushing stopped and coagulation started. I cradled her damp head against my chest, waited, then by the light of the lantern satisfied myself that only a few dried streaks and stains now betrayed the lonely extravagance of Meredith's nightmare bleeding.

"You can wash it all off in the morning," I whispered. "Now go to sleep."

In the immediate afterglow of the extinguished flame her face hung below me a moment like the small white mask of some sacrificial animal. But though the eyes were still fearful and unforgiving, the mouth, after all, was growing soft.

WE TURNED, STARTING UP THE HILL TOGETHER, CLIMBING one of the high narrow twisting streets of the village without purpose, without destination, drawn upward together by the air, the light, the dusty steep grade of the little street, by the abrupt seasonal invasion of the wild flowers that had taken root, matured, bloomed all in a single night. The flowers lay in bright masses of wet color on walls, tiles, flat stones, or packed like some kind of floral mortar in cracks and fissures around slanting doorways and beneath crude window ledges. So the two of us were climbing together and admiring the flowers when suddenly the village street looped again and there above us, amidst priest and children and a crowd of barefoot men, stood the white boat.

Yesterday? Only yesterday.

I was taking slow uphill strides and smelling the flowers, asking myself why I had had such unhappy luck with Catherine, wondering how I was ever to win her to all the sensual possibilities of the intimacy I had in mind, persuade her to give me her complete attention, to look at me, to live on with Cyril.

Yes, I thought, there in all this suffusion of flowers is the familiar *Physanthyllis tetraphylla*. The ripe and fruity vinelike plant with its wet green leaves, yellow buds and faint traces of silver hair, lay spread across the entire surface of the dusty village street, and I could hardly fail to note its tendrils drifting off into silence, its nodules cup-shaped, as usual, in pulpy succulence. And wasn't that the *Pisum elatius?* Yes, I thought, Fiona's favorite.

But Catherine, I asked myself, why doesn't Catherine know by now that I am enough, that she is enough, that we are all interchangeable, so to speak, and that our present relationship is already as unlimited and undeniable as our past affair? After all, there is something glorious about standing together in time as two large white graceful beasts might stand permanently together in an empty field. And yet how could I convey the truth of all this to Catherine?

At least she was wearing her pea-green slacks (glancing over my shoulder, waiting for her to close the gap between us, frowning at her obvious reluctance to catch up with me), exactly as if her children had yet to smear their little hands in the folds of my dissolving tapestry and we, the four of us, had yet to follow the angular black-haired shepherd into the still grove and then beyond to sun, sea, joyous ruins, long nights, distant piping. At least the pea-green slacks, a white sweater, an old pair of heavy dried-out leather sandals on bare feet. At least there was the clear sound of her matter-of-fact exertion—the sounds of her breath, the grating comfortable sound of the sandals. But nothing more. No corresponding glance at my own black suit and white shirt open at the collar and golden hair beginning to curl at last into tight sprightly barbs over the ears and down the back of my neck. No smile. No music in the way she moved. Nothing for Cyril.

And then? Then it burst upon us, so to speak, the spectacle, the processional, the very message of our actuality. Suddenly the narrow street was looping again, rising more steeply than ever, and in one single instant priest and children and barefoot men and white boat were poised above us. Suddenly Catherine and I were thrust against high stone walls on opposite sides of the narrow street. The two of us stood upright and facing each other with our flesh and even our bones flush to the rock, precisely as the village priest tried to wave us back down the street and out of the way of the white boat whose lunging destructive descent was prevented only by the crowd of men.

"Don't move," I said across the space between us, "there's plenty of room."

"What are they doing?"

"Just trying to launch their boat. Don't worry."

The entire procession was upon us in clamorous motion. Gesticulating priest and darting boys and barefoot men strained backward against the full weight of wood and brass and shouted to each other, calling out in violent square-mouthed appeal to some archaic and obviously indifferent deity. But only the wide, high-prowed boat itself appeared to move as it groaned, listed to one side and then dragged its ragged half-naked attendants another few feet down the steep grade toward Catherine and me. I saw the golden fish on the white prow above my head, watched the broad gunwales swelling from stone wall to wall and filling the street. And if they let go? Or if one of them stumbled or too many turned away to drink from the several black wine bottles passing from man to man? And if the enormous white sun-struck prow then veered toward Catherine, veered toward me?

"We'll let them pass," I called, "and then we'll join the procession. OK?"

But already the great curve of the towering white prow was slipping between us, stopping, inching on again. Now Catherine and stone wall and little street were gone, obliterated by the white enamel sweep of the boat and the sudden presence of the men who were clutching her gunwales, clutching her sides, and struggling, sweating, laughing, warning each other of collision and disaster. High on the prow they had fastened a handful of *Lobularia mari-*

123

tima, and I found myself nodding because the flowers were white and implied fleeting tenderness on the part of even these boatbuilding villagers.

How like them, I thought, to lay the keel in some tin-roofed shed up here on the high edge of the village, laboring with crude tools and rusty old circular saw until their boat finally stood finished not within reach of the dark tide but gleaming and massive beside the boatbuilder's cottage. Of course they were a dark-eyed people, I reminded myself, and not entirely ignorant, because if they had built this enormous empty vessel up here amidst their tethered goats, and had employed typical perversity and illogicality in its construction, nonetheless they had managed to lift it, transport it, move it down these steep and treacherous streets with a display of what I could only call true primitive ingenuity. Despite their sweat, their shuffling, their grunts of *fagag, crespi fagag* and their shouts of *croak peonie,* the desperate movements of their naked feet, the anger and sudden lapses to childish carelessness, wasn't all this anomalous effort nonetheless an unmistakable example of their practicality?

Yes, I told myself, of course it was. Because these very men who were adept at mending nets and whose feet were bare and cracked and whose voices were tuned to nothing more than shouting to each other throughout their long hours of night fishing, even these same men had apparently held council. Suddenly and together they had leapt from emotionalism to cogency, from baffled dream to rationality, and in one moment of lucid silence had overcome the problem of a graceful and necessary white boat constructed witlessly in the wrong part of the village.

Simple, I thought, and pure, mysterious, crudely logical (seeing Catherine's head and then her shoulders reappearing gradually on the other side of the enormous white canted hull), because it all depended on a few oblong blocks of cream-colored wood and on the agility and stamina of two small boys who were sweating even more than the shouting and laughing men. Yes, I thought, how like them to rely on children and to see in a few pieces of scarce wood a somehow religious solution to a mechanical problem. They had cut the blocks, shaped them, in the center of each had chiseled a half-moon indentation broad enough and deep enough to hold the boat's keel. In that tin-roofed shed above us, out of sight, they had raised the prow and forced the front block beneath the keel and shoved, pushed, pulled, and had driven the second block beneath the keel. They had continued this process until the greased wooden blocks were spaced out evenly in the form of a movable and slippery track across which their enormous empty white boat was sliding painfully but safely down through the entire steep length of the village toward the beach and sea.

Religious insight. Primitive ingenuity. And the two small boys? Even now they were moving in their assigned positions, one of them staggering forward with a great block in his arms and reaching the prow, daring to stoop and drop the heavy block directly in the path of the advancing keel. The second small crouching boy fell to his knees and tugged, dragged, lifted into his arms the full weight of another cream-colored block that had emerged from beneath the stern and, grimacing and wobbling, ran forward to dispose of his load as had the first small boy.

But did it matter to Catherine, I wondered, that they had greased their dozen or so oblong blocks of wood with a dark thick shiny substance that was obviously blood? Amidst flowers, noise, dust, the tilting of the black wine bottles, the sudden lurching of the boat and shouts of fear, had Catherine begun to discern the religious insight implicit in their use of partially coagulated blood as a rich and appropriate lubricant? Perhaps, I told myself, deciding that in all likelihood Catherine had in fact observed the thickening stains of blood just as she must have seen the few loose sprays of *Lobularia maritima* affixed to the high prow of the boat. Priest, blood, *Lobularia maritima*, procession —how could it have been more plain?

"You're strong," she was saying then, "why don't you help them?"

Together, side by side, slowly we retraced our steps downhill at the rear of the crowd as if I had never been the headless god nor she my mistress, but as if she and I were simply the two halves of the ancient fruit together but unjoined. The dust was rising, Catherine was pushing up the sleeves of her sweater, her very profile made me think that she was responding at last to me as well as to the white hull. Why not assume that she was beginning to value my mental landscape? Why not assume that a now invulnerable Catherine and reflective Cyril were starting over? Why not?

"Let's get closer," she was saying, "I want to see."

All the sounds in the air were suddenly co-ordinated to Catherine's voice. There below us the priest was chanting prayers across the bright water, someone was striking authoritarian chords on one of their old stringed instruments, dogs were barking.

"It's a big affair," I heard myself saying above the noise. "Like it?"

"Yes. I like it."

"Remind you of anything?"

She was looking at me, shrugging, beginning to smile, preparing to express some kind of recognition. But suddenly we were pushing downhill with the rest of them, past open doors and hanging nets, pursuing the white hull that was rocking and grinding down the last incline of the village street. For one instant the entire crowd flung hands and shoulders against the sides and stern and ran, shoved, not attempting to restrain the descent of the boat but rather leaning into it and contributing to the possibility of that very crash which all this time they had been attempting to avoid.

And then the shuddering cessation, the shock of stopping, the thick and absolute immobility of the boat's dead weight on the beach. The hour had fled, the light had changed, the stones and doorways of the dark village had given way to a thin strip of gray sand and the smell of the sea. Behind us the rising village, to our left the distant fortress, somewhere off to the right but hidden from view the cypresses and the twin villas, in front of us the brilliant sea. And men and boys were laughing and standing still while the priest stood shouting brutal, imperative instructions to an agile old man with a deformity between his shoulders and the face of a goat. The high white prow was pointed directly toward the horizon, unmoving and yet soaring, an aesthetic actuality that belied the work required to convey all this curving weight across the sand to the life of the foam. Surely the grace of the boat itself went far beyond the necessity to feed a few dark mouths from the depths of the sea.

So our feet were deep in the sand, I lit a cigarette, the boat was balancing between the loosely divided halves of the launching party. Beneath the plane tree, a young man was seated alone beside a bare wooden table, and it was he who played the archaic heart-shaped stringed instrument. I took it all in—the assembled villagers, the enormous white crescent of the waiting boat, and the dogs, the children, the black shawls, the impoverished young man whose metallic Eastern music was now reaching out toward the rolling sea. And here we were, Catherine and I together at last in the festive air. The sun was overhead but close to us, close and orange. Once more the invisible nets were spread.

"It's all right," I murmured, "take the glass. The old fellow just wants you to toast his boat."

At that moment the old goat-faced man himself was suddenly before us and smiling, holding out to Catherine a little battered tin tray bearing not one of their black bottles but a small dirty glass half filled with a colorless drink more powerful, I knew, than the dusty wine. He extended the tray, raised one shoulder, looked into Catherine's eyes and into mine. Little more than a commonplace event, an instant in time, only a small disreputable old man with a gray shirt ripped open to the waist and partially unbuttoned trousers loose at the large hips. But thanks to his agility and bright blue eyes and stubby fingers, I realized

128

immediately that he was a friendly guide who at a glance had read Catherine's past and mine in the very shape of our middle-aged bodies that were so much larger than his.

"Take a sip," I said. "I'll drink the rest."

Catherine held the glass to her lips, I nodded my approval of the clear fierce taste that suggested both the salt of the sea and the juice of the heavy lemon. I left him a few drops which he licked with his fingers, laughing and tilting the little dirty glass above his burnished head. For another moment the glass hung high in the air while the old man patted Catherine's arm, shook my hand, pointed with expansive admiration toward the boat still propped upright and waiting for the first touch of the uncontrollable sea.

The glass fell to the beach, the grip of the vanished hand lingered in my empty hand, Catherine smiled exactly as if the old man had not yet disappeared. But he was already gone and even now was rousing the villagers to the final effort of pushing the majestic slow boat across the sand to the sea.

"Well," I heard myself saying, "recovered yet?"

I glanced at Catherine, the heart-shaped instrument leapt between two or three high notes and one smashing chord, Catherine held her bared elbow still tingling, no doubt, from the touch of that unfamiliar hand.

"I don't know why I feel this way."

"Excited?"

"It's lucky he found us."

"Look," I murmured, "here come the oars."

Two youthful figures ran down the beach with a pair of long virginal oars suspended between them. The distant fortress was cupped in the shriveled palm of desolation. The orange sun descended, the open sea undulated in slow fleshy waves. The old man and the angry priest were arguing about a few half-submerged brown rocks which apparently lay directly in the path of the boat. Catherine smiled. Heavy-headed Cyril smiled. The boat was in motion.

Yes, in motion, and Catherine had already removed her sandals, already I anticipated the sight of Catherine's green slacks wet to the knees and the sensation of my own black trousers weighted at least to my bulky calves with dark sea water.

The upheld oars protruded above the sweat-dampened heads of those men straining at the stern of the boat, to one side and at the edge of the beach the priest stood with his skirts awash and the large and radiant silver cross held aloft in both extended fists. Again the two small boys were filled with self-importance and were hard at work. The forward motion of the boat was slow, painful, continuous, unmistakable, and bore no relation to priest, struggling men, old women. No, I thought, that white boat was moving only for the sake of Catherine, me, and for one agile and ageless village elder obviously deformed at birth. Quietly I smiled at the symmetry of orange sky, chunks of bloodied wood, oars that projected into nothing more than air, boat that still lay several yards from the vast tide that would float it into life and yet would one day reduce it to nothing more than a few cracked wooden ribs half buried in sand.

"Remind you of anything?"

My smile was embedded in those slow words, and as soon

130

as I spoke I knew that my voice was exactly as audible to Catherine as it was to me, as if all those other sounds (water, music, laborious breathing, grinding of wood on wood) were only a silence for me to fill or existed only that Catherine and I might listen more attentively to what each of us had to say. Catherine glanced over her shoulder and her eyes were larger than I remembered.

"I'm not sure. Tell me."

"How about the day we met?"

Had I gone too far? Summoned too abruptly our missing shadows? Merely ripped open old graves, old secret bowers? Exposed myself to more conventional grief and unjustified accusation? Was she less perfectly healed than I had begun to assume? But no, her hands were on her womanly green hips, her head was turned in my direction, the immediacy of her amber-colored eyes was still undimmed. Yes, I thought, she was looking directly at my golden spectacles and into my warm eyes and the white boat was exerting more than ever its pull on the fringes of Catherine's consciousness.

She spoke without insistence, without emphasis, clearly: "I never expected to talk to you again."

"I know," I murmured, lending her strength.

"But I've changed my mind."

"Catherine. Doesn't it remind you of a wedding?"

"Not ours."

"Positive?"

As if my voice and the very depths of my broad chest were not enough, suddenly our heads were together. We stooped, splashing ankle-deep in the first slow reddish swell, stooped just in time to see the rounded bottom of the bow slide within inches of the red tile and the first clear drops of spray already trickling in a bright pattern of transparent bubbles down the steep curve of that thickly enameled white wood. Was Catherine gasping? Was I gasping too? But even as Catherine and I perceived the clear bubbles splattered like an ever-changing necklace on the lower portion of the gleaming and steeply pitched white bow, the bow itself moved forward and sank, obliterating the first signs of spray and foam at the very moment they leapt up and settled expressly, I thought, for Catherine's pleasure and mine.

"Careful," I said, "not too close."

The men fell back. The boat was free. Catherine laughed. We were wading in soft water up to our thighs, and all around us the men were floundering, the villagers were wading in behind us, the golden fish on the bow of the boat was flashing. A figure leapt high (hair wet, face contorted in both grief and joy) and snatched away the white flowers and flung them off to float bereft and abandoned on the surface of the deep sea tinted with blood.

"Look, Catherine. There he is."

"I see him."

Yes, he was there. Yes, we saw him. Impish, angular, energetic, indomitable, immersed to his armpits but ready to spring, ready to take possession of what was his, dark head and narrow shoulders distinctly visible as the white stern twisted and rose above him and the orange sun came down, coagulated, turned time itself into a diffusion of thick erotic color.

"Help him," Catherine said.

"Don't have to."

We waited. Our shoulders touched. The water that was saturating Catherine's pea-green slacks was filling my pockets. Somebody shouted, the oars clattered, the white stern came down. And then the old man jumped and seized some fragment of glossy wood and in full view of ancient women, small boys, shouting friends, two strangers whose spiritual relationship he somehow shared, propelled himself upward so that in the next instant, as the now orange-white stern towered above us all once more, the old man also towered above us, balancing up there on his spread knees that were wiry, insensitive to pain, and naked. Yes, naked, because he had had the forethought to rip off his ragged trousers before committing himself to frenzy and determination, had kicked them off at the edge of the beach before the white boat had rolled, pitched, begun to float. The stern was at the top of its arc, Catherine and I were staring up into the orange brilliance of the old man's aged nakedness, and his shanks were dripping, his buttocks were dripping, his obviously unspent passion was hanging down and rotating loosely like a tongue of flame.

We looked, we waved, Catherine's eyes met mine.

"Starting over," I murmured and laughed, straightened my spectacles, wiped the spray from my face. Catherine smiled. At last, I thought, we had come under the aegis of the little crouching goat-faced man half naked at the end of the day. What more could we ask?

W̲E BROKE, WE RAN, WE SCATTERED UPWARD ON THE FACE
of our favorite hill like birds or like children, and because
I was last in line, lowest figure in that bright pattern, and
was holding back as usual (tail of the kite, conscience and
consciousness of our little group), I found myself general-
izing the visceral experience of the moment itself, found
myself thinking that our days were idyls, our nights dreams,
our mornings slow-starting songs of love. On my extreme
right Fiona was already halfway up the hill (hands waving,
large woolen bag slung over her shoulder army-style and
bouncing on a lean hip), Hugh was angling in sly pursuit,
off to my left Catherine was stumbling loosely and happily
toward the bare crest of that familiar hill, while behind
them all and on a clear tangent between Hugh and Catherine I brought up the rear heavily, gracefully, varying my
speed, saving my breath, and wondering what effect this
kind of dawn exertion might have on the ruthless fist
lodged in the blackness of Hugh's chest. The early morning
trip to the hill was Fiona's idea, of course, and I suspected
that even had she known of Hugh's secret ailment, which
apparently she did not, there would have been no change
in Fiona's plans, no slacking of Fiona's pace.

"Come on, boy," Hugh shouted over his shoulder, "quit
lagging."

I waved him on. In the chilly air and on the tawny slope
between two darkly nesting growths of small olive trees, the

four of us constituted the four major points of the compass oddly compressed, distorted, oddly disarrayed, and Fiona sprinted girlishly toward the top where the silence had no direction and the sun in another moment or two would be rising.

Like birds, I thought, like children. In a glance I recorded Catherine's dark brown slacks, Hugh's black bell-bottoms, Fiona's white shorts cut low on the waist and high on the thighs (tight elasticized garment winking above me in the dawn light), my own soft cord trousers hastily donned in semidarkness and stuffed into the tops of large and only partially laced chamois boots now slow and rhythmical on the stubbled surface that smelled of dead grass, sharp spice, sweet dust. My faded denim shirt still unbuttoned and flowing away from massive breast with its bronze luster and sleep-matted hair, Hugh's black turtleneck, Catherine's plain mustard-colored blouse, Fiona's pink shirt unbuttoned and merely tied at the waist—even these simple details of careless dress reminded me of Fiona's whimsical leadership and unaccountable energy. Thanks to a nudge from Fiona's elbow and the sound of her voice, we were all four of us only minutes away from the twin villas and still sleeping children. A few details of clothing revealed at least to me our haste, our dawn dishevelment, our desire to please each other, our sense of well-being against that panorama of steepening hillside and wiry dark green trees.

"Don't say anything, Cyril. Don't spoil it."

The top. The silence filled with the smell of thyme. And I who might well have been first came last, climbed over the crest and smiled at Fiona's eager words and squeezed into my place on the fragment of stone wall between Catherine, who was out of breath, and Fiona, who was always breathless yet never out of breath. I drew up my heavy knees and wiped my mouth on the back of my arm and sighed. Hugh's heart was pounding, Catherine's dark hair was loose. From Fiona's bare stomach came a faint brief purling sound of some internal agitation, Hugh cleared his throat, Catherine shifted audibly on the cold stones. And clasping my knees and leaning to the rear so that I was able to glance at Hugh behind Fiona's firm curving back, for a moment I caught Hugh's eye and smiled. Was he attempting to convey some kind of masculine detachment in the grip of Fiona's enforced silence and rather theatrical poetic expectancy? I could not be sure. At least I could afford to nod and smile at the narrow sweat-drenched stony face and did so.

"What's all this about the sunrise, boy?"

But before I could answer: "Shut up, Hugh. For God's sake."

I respected Fiona's need for silence, always respected the stillness that contained her sudden electrical sense of purpose, and so refrained from remarking that dawn was Fiona's hour and that everything about my wife suggested the flights of dawn and excitement of the first light, despite her admitted shivers of theatricality and the interference of Hugh's crude temperament. Behind Fiona's tight back I shrugged, glanced away from Hugh, and allowed this first clear chilly breath of morning to fill my chest. Fiona said nothing more, Catherine leaned forward and crossed her legs. Like Fiona, I tilted my head back into the rising light and contented myself with the paradox that while Fiona was concentrating on the sunrise Catherine was no doubt thinking of nothing more than the possibility of turning and placing a gentle hand on my bare chest. Again Hugh cleared his throat.

So we sat together, waited together, on a fragment of stone wall in this sacred spot. At our feet lay the abrupt and nearly vertical and rock-strewn descent, and down there the windy darkness of the miniature valley contained one field of waist-high grass (remembered now from previous occasions rather than seen) as well as a single line of small pungent olive trees marching, so to speak, across the soft floor of that sheltered contour of darkness, gloom, silence. But beyond it all, beyond perfect valley and rock wall and Fiona, Hugh, Catherine and me (four witnesses seated flank to flank in the uninterrupted tension of Fiona's rare feminine interest in natural phenomena), three low purple hills and a sweep of bare silvery horizon belied witnesses, lyricism, grape-bespattered joys of love, sleeping children, sleeping invisible village, belied the sunrise itself. Once more it occurred to me that the splendor of ominous distance reflected a side of Fiona and even an aspect of my own personality which Hugh, for instance, would never appreciate. After all, Fiona enjoyed the sight of moody colors and somber landscape—why not? Only Hugh's compulsive interest in Fiona's more obviously active life blinded him, I decided then, to the understandable necessity of Fiona's silences. Fiona was sexual but hardly simple.

"Look, baby," she whispered clearly, "an eagle."

"Big one," I murmured, "a real beauty."

"Where, boy? I don't see any eagle."

"Take another look," I said after a moment. "He's there."

It was a small matter, of course, and yet the sky, it

seemed to me, was empty except for rolling darkness and cold bands of silver. I looked, I squinted (seeing dark hills, inhuman sky, nothing more) and assumed that this was merely another instance of Fiona's occasional inaccuracy for the sake of a deeper vividness, for the sake of an important mood. Between Fiona's voice and Hugh's sometimes brusque insistence on reality there was, for me, no choice.

"I see him," Catherine said, and pointed. "Up there."

"She's right, boy. He's unmistakable."

Nodding, suddenly identifying the crooked speck at the end of Catherine's finger: "A sign," I murmured deeply, agreeably, "it's a doubly significant sign, Hugh, don't you think?"

"Keep quiet, baby. Please."

Correct and incorrect, I thought, right and wrong. And yet at bottom my sense of the situation was essentially true, and I felt only pleasure at the sight of this new justification of Fiona's vision and my own supportive role. Unmistakably, as Hugh had said, the eagle was now hooked almost directly above us on bent but stationary wings in the black and silver medium of the empty sky. Stark, unruffled, quite alone, a featureless image of ancient strength and unappeased appetite, certainly the distant bird was both incongruous and appropriate, at once alive and hence distracting but also sinister, a kind of totemic particle dislodged from the uninhabited hills and toneless light. Here, I thought, was a bird of prey that would utter no cry, make no kill. And for some reason his presence brought to mind the handfuls of dark cherries which Fiona was carrying in the off-white woolen bag still slung from her firm shoulder.

But was the bird descending, drawing closer to us, a deliberate herald of the rich desolation that lay before us, fierce bird of prey somehow attracted to large lovers and the cherries in Fiona's bag? Was he singling us out as further confirmation of Fiona's essential soberness and lack of fear, or even as a reminder of the terror that once engulfed the barbarians and from which Hugh, for instance, was still not free? At any rate the bird was descending and the hills, like distant burial mounds, were dark. Slowly I put pressure with my upper arms first on Catherine's shoulder and then on Fiona's.

All eyes on the approaching eagle. Fiona began to shiver, Catherine returned the pressure of my affection. But Hugh, I thought, was growing impatient, was much too preoccupied with his own doubts and desires to realize that sometimes the faceless eagle heralds not only the breath of dead kings but the sunrise.

Yes, the sunrise. And now, quite suddenly, the sunrise was so immense, so hot and brilliant that Fiona found it necessary to respond in kind and leaped to her feet, all at once was standing upright between Hugh and me and taking swift athletic breaths of the golden air, apparently unconscious of my own hand steadying her right calf and Hugh's her left. The black and silver sky turned orange and foamed for miles behind the stationary air-borne eagle, and the purple hills dissolved, reappeared, revealed on thick green slopes a clear pattern of thistle, clay, warped trees, a few abandoned stone huts. Mist filled the valley at our feet and then lifted. The cold air grew warm, the eagle suddenly glided downward to the east and was gone, simply gone. The day was ours.

"What's that, baby? Listen."

I listened, we all listened, Catherine's ring hand was on my thigh. Across from us the large round sun had already outlived its bright circumference, its glorious round orange shape had already given up its enormous singular shape to time, had become only the light of our day, the undefined brilliance of our morning song. But that clear random tinkling sound from the valley? That metallic musical sound too unstructured for music and yet harmonizing, so to speak, with the sweet smell of our still unexplored valley?

"Sheep bells," Catherine murmured. "That's what it is."

"By God, boy, do you see what I see?"

"Couldn't be better," I said, and drew Fiona's upright leg more tightly to my rib cage and with my other hand signaled Catherine through the brown cloth on her hip.

Because cold dawn had given way to hot morning, the sun had yielded to light, the eagle had flown off only to return to us as a flock of long-haired semidomesticated animals.

"Goats," I said pleasantly, "not sheep."

"But the girl, baby. Look at the girl."

It was the new day's gift to Fiona, nature's final gift to my wife. Yes, the random tinkling sound we had heard was produced by bells fastened around the necks of goats, small rusty pear-shaped iron bells hand-forged by peasants oblivious to the sad melodies that unknown cultivated strangers might hear in their noise. And goats, an entire flock of them, wearing long brown shaggy robes the color of Catherine's slacks but more shiny, and bearing bone-colored curling horns on the tops of their nodding heads, now suddenly filled our valley with motion, color and the sound of their bells. From where Hugh and Catherine and I sat

140

and Fiona stood, we could see that these stately animals were attended by a young girl wearing a large white hat and running, slowly running, through the tall grass.

"I want to talk with her. Right now."

"How can you talk with her?"

"I'll find a way."

"Don't you worry about Fiona. She'll do what she wants."

"Of course she will," I said and laughed. "But there's the problem of language. And the hill's too steep for Fiona, Hugh. Believe me."

"Cyril," Fiona said, and the calf of her leg was hard and trembling, the skin was cold, "she's just a child."

"A young woman," I heard myself saying. "About seventeen. But sit down, Fiona. You'll fall."

"I'm holding her, boy. Don't worry."

The moment passed. I made a low humming sound of affirmation in my nose and throat and said nothing. And who was to say which was the more remarkable, I asked myself, the girl or the goats? The goats were overly large, their coats long, here and there were the obvious bell-carriers, the jangling sunlit leaders, and it was quite apparent that the entire flock had come in slow hungry pursuit of the tough little black leaves of the olive trees, was following some purely aesthetic instinct to feed at dawn on the resilient branches laden with dawn's oldest and most meager fruit. We could hear the hooves, the bells, the grass, the rubbing of long hair which was either dry and regal or still damp from the recent discharging of white milk. And the girl? This girl who carried no crook and appeared to feel no responsibility for lost kids or straggling elders? How could her slight vaulting presence down there be anything if not more remarkable than the indifference of her ancient goats?

"Baby. She sees us!"

The girl was waving. Standing still and waving. And in this instant, the very moment of correspondence between the girl's world and ours, Catherine returned her wave, Fiona suddenly tightened her fingers in my hair. Hugh laughed because the largest goat had discovered the largest olive tree and like some tall but malformed adventurer was standing on his hind legs and nibbling in tenuous balance at the dusty leaves. It was like Hugh, I thought, to care more about the rising, unnaturally distended old goat than about the girl.

The goat chewed while the girl ran to us. Full of trust and candor she skirted a creamy boulder, she sped through the grass. On bare feet she raced toward the rocky, precipitous slope that separated the hilltop where we watched from the secluded green valley where her unsuspecting goats were feeding. But where had she gotten her clothes, the castoff garden hat and tattered dress so clearly unintended for rusticity? How could she be so unaware of girlhood, so unaware of the fact that the goatherd, in this lonely world, was usually a sullen boy or unshaven, unfriendly man?

"Here she comes," Fiona cried. "Help her."

How many times had we sat on this same fragment of rocky wall composed of stones that certainly were the teeth of time, sat together on this hill of ours and watched the transformation of hills and air, hemlocks and clouds, roots and rocks into a clear and sunlit but always lifeless panorama that we never ceased to admire? And now eagle, goats, unlikely girl. Perhaps Fiona had appealed to the sylvan sources in a voice more winsome and undeniable than ever before. At any rate I could not begrudge Fiona the exhilaration that was now removing her, distracting her, from Hugh and me.

"Don't frighten her, Cyril. Please."

I stood. We all stood. My very posture acknowledged the voices behind my back and welcomed the girl. Like one of her charges she scrambled up to us, raising dust, clutching at loose stones and tufts of grass, discovering crevices with her bare toes, laughing at the ease with which she emulated the climbing ability of her silken goats. Her face was round, her eyes were dark, the enormous flimsy hat remained somehow on the back of her head, there was a faded pink bow fastened to the bodice of the threadbare gown that fell below the knees and yet swirled and mingled with the bright air and dust she raised. She clung to the hillside, laughed again, glanced up and took her bearings and then lowered her eyes and without hesitation scrambled the last few feet into our waiting arms.

"Made it," I said aloud, and placed the flat of my open hand on the small of her back, helped her over the wall, stepped aside for Hugh. We crowded around her shamelessly, Catherine took hold of a bare elbow, Hugh vied with Fiona for a closer look.

"She's mine, baby, all mine!"

"Fiona saw her first," Catherine said. "Let Fiona try to talk to her."

"That's right," I murmured, "Fiona's more bucolic than the rest of us."

"Never mind. I'll give each of you a little taste!"

We laughed. In unison we lapsed suddenly into silence.

143

With unnecessary delicacy and concern for her feelings we stood around her—and stared. Not so the girl, who wanted to talk and did, and who was young but by no means a child and large though not as large as Hugh, Fiona, Catherine and me. Yes, it was the girl rather than ourselves who was outspoken in curiosity and who began and sustained our conversation, wanting to know us, wanting to tell us about her life. She spoke in a constant uninterrupted rush of sound and gesture, assuming our comprehension of the barbaric syllables and girlish pantomime. Up went the soft arm shaded with faint hair. She shrugged in the direction of the valley. She sighed, she extended both empty hands. She smiled, held up six fingers. She smiled, shook her head, touched both breasts, clapped a small hand to her unprotected loins. But all this was unimportant, she seemed to say, because she was only a goat-girl. Whereas we, she knew, were men of mystery, women of beauty. And she recognized us, she seemed to say, though she had never expected the goats to lead her to the good luck of this encounter, which she did not intend to spend on mere self-preoccupation. Hardly.

"Make her stop talking, baby. It's time to eat."

But she would not stop, was unquenchable, even while I raised my eyebrows and smiled and demurred and Fiona, lovely tense barelegged Fiona, opened the widemouthed sack and passed around the cherries. No, hands laden with that suggestive fruit and mouth stuffed with cherries, lips pursed to spit out the stones, on she talked—singling out each one of us for analysis, glancing to the rest of us for confirmation of her judgment, her appreciation, her right to associate herself with our mystery, our beauty. She overlooked Hugh's missing arm, was simply not interested in his missing arm, but concentrated instead on Hugh's little black pointed beard, reached up and stroked it with fingers juice-stained and knowing. She had tousled with the horns of the largest goat, she knew that the affinities between certain men and certain animals were to be respected. She touched her bare foot to Fiona's bare foot, giggled when Fiona giggled, then swung about and exclaimed over Catherine's breasts and filled her wet hands with Catherine's hair. And then? And then she turned to me.

Or rather she glanced at Fiona, glanced at Catherine, and then once more gave me the sight of her perfectly round eyes which for the moment were certainly a match for the cherries. But no gesture of awe, no smile, no uncomfortable burst of shyness, no quickness of breath. Nothing. She did not care that by now half her flock was beginning to climb the further wall of the valley. She counted on Fiona and Catherine for tolerance.

"Kiss her, baby. She probably thinks you're some kind of god."

"Of course she does," I said, and bent down and obliged Fiona as always. My face was half again as large as the girl's, my lips were full while hers were thin and remarkably pink in color. The kiss was a mere stitch in the tapestry of my sensual experience. The distance between the goat-girl and singer of sex could not be bridged by a single kiss, prolonged or not, agreeable or not. But I who had kissed how many girls at Fiona's bidding now kissed this one, and beneath my hand I felt a sprig of clover, a spray of green growth snagged from the field. At least there was a pleasing moisture on my cheek and mouth, at least the goat-girl

145

considered herself loved by the unattainable man whose name she would always try to remember and say aloud to her goats.

"Hugh," I said, turning away and glancing first at Fiona and then at Catherine: "How about it?"

"Pass, boy. For me, one woman's plenty."

"Oh, Hugh, kiss her just once, like Cyril. Catherine doesn't mind."

"I don't care if he kisses her or not."

"Doesn't care, boy. You hear that?"

"I mean it, Hugh. Kiss her, if that's what you want."

"Cyril, baby, save us!"

"No," I said, laughing and taking hold of Catherine's arm, "fun's over."

"Oh, you're just trying to spoil my morning. All of you." And turning, laughing, staring at Hugh, pulling at the elastic of her tight shorts: "If you won't kiss our little goat-girl, baby, kiss me instead!"

"Anyway," I said softly, "she's gone."

Were they listening? Were they interested? I would never know because I had already waved at the tiny white figure once again watching us down there in the midst of her girlish vigil beneath the largest olive tree, had already begun to guide Catherine down the other and more gentle slope of our sunlit hill. We walked slowly and heavily, listening to the tread of my chamois boots and Catherine's worn-out green tennis shoes, moved slowly down the hot pastoral grade with arms about each other's waists and faces raised to the sun that was dissipated, invisible, yet uniformly present wherever we looked. Our bodies were free, our temperaments were in accord. And near the bottom of the hill we paused, and Catherine rested her head on my shoulder. Her voice, when I heard it, was low and sensible.

"What was the trouble last night?" she asked. "Meredith again?"

I nodded.

"More nosebleeds?"

I nodded.

"She's had them for years."

"Don't apologize," I said. "I'm fond of Meredith."

"Are you?"

"Of course I am."

We kissed each other. The goat-girl and I had kissed each other. Surely on the hilltop we had just abandoned, Hugh and Fiona were kissing too. So my theory of sexual extension, I thought, was taking root, already new trees were growing from the seeds we had spit so carelessly onto that barren ground.

"FIONA IS PERPLEXED, BABY. LISTEN A MINUTE."

"I'm listening."

"We were standing together in the dark, like this. We were nude, like this. The whole thing was a duplication of us right now, but different."

"Well, I hope it was different."

"Please, baby. Be serious."

"I had an idea we might talk tonight. Tell more."

147

"I was giggling. Just a little."

"Sure you were."

"What's the matter with you? Stop fencing. And you could control your delicious hands. I want to talk."

"Control your own."

"If I can't talk to you, I'm lost."

"The difference, Fiona, the difference."

"It's not just that he's thin and bony and was trembling. I love all that. It was something else."

"Don't stop now."

"God, you're irritating."

"Sure I am. Why not?"

"Baby, please."

"Start over, Fiona. My love can wait."

"I want you, baby."

"Keep talking."

"We were standing here in the nude, like now. About three o'clock in the morning, and I thought you were on his mind because he seemed taller than ever, bonier, and he was cold, baby, cold. I had my arms around his neck and crossed, like this. Loosely. I didn't care about his hand on my behind. I hardly knew it was there. I guess I tugged on his beard a little bit with my teeth. But that's all. I was just hoping that he'd know how good he made me feel and begin to relax."

"Sounds all right to me. What's the problem?"

"I wish you'd stop caressing me. God!"

"Caressing stops."

"Kiss me."

"Let's finish the seminar. What happened."

"You smell good, baby."

148

"You, too."

"That's enough, now. Please."

"What's wrong?"

"Just stop being Cyril a minute, can't you?"

"You're the one who's puzzled, Fiona, not me."

"It's just that he was doing something funny with that hand of his. I began to feel it. He was making me uncomfortable, and I didn't know why. I was conscious of something a little different and I couldn't get it out of my mind. I was beginning to lose what you call my crispness, baby, I was beginning to smile the way I do when I'm not sure what's happening. He was making me think, he was making me fish around inside for a little clue about what he was doing and how I was supposed to respond. It was such a small thing, and yet suddenly I couldn't think about him or me but just about what he was doing back there with that hand of his. Not him, but his hand. Not me, but my behind. It wasn't exactly a tickling, but it wasn't sweet. I was uncertain, baby, uncertain. I whispered something to him, but he didn't care. I tried to move, but it didn't matter. I wasn't unhappy, just uncertain. Uncomfortable but interested. And then I got the idea, because he was pulling on me. Just pulling on me. He wasn't rough, he wasn't tender. Just holding half my little melon as hard as he could and pulling. He forgot me, baby. He forgot himself. And I did too. Because suddenly I got the idea that he must be working in collusion with some great big lovely satyr with hair all over his shanks and a lot of experience with little girls' behinds. But he wasn't. There was no satyr. Nothing."

"Nothing?"

"No, baby. Nothing at all."

"Poor Fiona."

"Now I can't think of anything else. Who'll be my satyr —you?"

"Shaggy shoulders, horns, a lot of experience. OK?"

"You're fun, baby, you really are."

A︎FTER ALL, I TOLD MYSELF, IT HAD BEEN A LONG HOT dawn, and emerging now from the dragon's mouth of the dark green cypresses, I found myself once more in this mild extremity of a familiar mood. There was no longer any point in being dressed for the night, everything about me revealed the pointlessness of a garb that had already served its purpose. The dressing gown untied and hanging open like a pair of splendid maroon-colored silken sails bereft of wind, the carefully tended hair uncombed and rumpled, the clear eyes cloudy, the fresh mouth numbed with fading taste, the cord of the pajama bottoms no longer tied in a perfect bow but sleepily knotted, the feet unaccountably bare, and brows furrowed, hands in pockets, no message on lips that were nonetheless working together in sensual emptiness, not even a cigarette to prolong the vaporous moment —all this told me that the negative account was full and that my usual and fastidious preparations of only a few hours past were now used up.

Catherine was no doubt sleeping. And Hugh? Fiona? The villa concealed on the other side of the wall of cypress trees behind me was dark, the villa lying directly ahead was also dark, concealing what contented faces or whispering mouths I could not predict. Would I hear them? Glimpse them? Join them? Or merely feel my way into a trysting place that would prove white and shadowy and empty after all? Was I, a lover, seeking the companionship of two more lovers or near lovers who might be thickly awake and just as interested as I was in a few moments of drowsy speech? I could not be sure.

I felt the dew on the soles of my feet, I saw myself sitting on the edge of Catherine's bed and fumbling, as I had, with spectacles but not with tennis shoes. I smiled to think that the spectacles were crooked on the bridge of my nose, smiled to think that for once I had deviated from my usual habits and had walked among the pines and beside the dark sea, had returned without special purpose to Catherine's villa. I had pushed my way through the cypress trees, had strolled in the lemon grove that fanned out soft and silent at the edge of our lives. Why, I asked myself. Why? And replied with another smile, a keener appreciation of the weight of the silk now dragging down my shoulders and brushing my calves.

Voices. One of the children demanding comfort from Catherine? But no, I told myself, walking squarely through the scented darkness that separated trees and villa, and feeling the irises growing large in eyes no longer as lackluster and heavy lidded as they had felt in the first portion of this wasted dawn—no, the voices were not high enough or querulous enough for the children's. Thoughtfully I approached the rotten shutter locked open on the night and darkness within, avoiding stealth I approached so close to the irregular oblong of Catherine's window that I might have peered inside, had I so desired. I stopped. I listened. I was close enough to see the morning-glories twining in the broken slats of the shutter, and yet even now the voices inside the familiar room were muffled, unclear, loud with intimacy but indistinct. I recognized the burden of the dialogue if not the words, and suddenly recognized the voices themselves because one was tired, insistent, reluctant, and belonged to Catherine, while the other was ingratiating, importuning, and obviously issued from a dry throat that could only be Hugh's.

But Hugh? Bare-chested? Fresh from his own trampled garden and wide-awake? Was that really Hugh in there, in this late hour sprawled across a sagging bed more mine than his? Hugh propped up on his one good eager arm and filled with clumsy confidence, talking to Catherine as he had never talked to Fiona, Hugh now singing his happy but constricted version of my sweet song? No doubt of it, I told myself, our paths were crossing, and I moved closer.

I listened. I asked myself what was unusual about this pattern of sounds. I followed the rhythms of Catherine's voice, the rhythms of Hugh's, and then I understood. Even before I heard any actual words I understood that Catherine was employing a variety of defensive responses, whereas Hugh was saying the same words again and again as if the ease with which he had apparently shifted from Fiona's stimulation to Catherine's struggle justified his use of repetition. But why had Fiona let him go? Why must Catherine struggle?

I could not make out any of Catherine's negative phrases, and decided that she was hiding her face, speaking into the pillow. But no matter, I told myself, since Catherine's declamations came readily to mind (those words and phrases of conventional denial), and since what most concerned me now, as a matter of fact, was the precise content of what Hugh was saying, the exact nature of those particular words which had borne the freight of his sexual needs for all the years of his marriage.

For a mere instant he raised his voice. For an instant I heard him as clearly as if Hugh had popped his head out of the window and spoken not for Catherine's benefit but mine.

"Don't be afraid of Daddy Bear," he was saying, "don't be afraid of Daddy Bear . . ."

So this was what we had bargained for, Fiona and Catherine and I—this sad and presumptuous appeal from a man who had spent all the nights of his marriage fishing for the love of his wife with the hook of a nursery persona. The dew was a cold bath on the soles of my feet. My shoulders were heavy, my hands were more than ever resigned to the large pockets of the indifferent silk dressing gown. Instantly Hugh's voice sank, subsided, once more rumbled along its subterranean road. The translation went hand in hand with the sounds of his voice, simple text and desperate message were one in my ear, and it took no great effort to identify the source of his words. Of course, I told myself, the honeymoon. What else if not a few words stolen in desperation from the vocabulary of the cheapest myth of childhood and spoken aloud unwittingly but successfully into Catherine's ear in the first surge of crisis? Yes, I told myself, those words had worked, had carried Hugh with surprise and relief across that first rough spot of Catherine's ignorance and thereafter had become the only lyrics to his monogamous song.

But why deny the humor, I asked myself, why give way to pity for Catherine and contempt for Hugh? Was there any conventional privacy that might not yield up its unique embarrassment? While the morning-glories were straining to unfurl, while Hugh lay floundering in constricted speech, while Catherine struggled to interrupt his persistency and I stood listening—why not concentrate, I asked myself, on the consolations? At least Hugh still wanted to assume his sentimental bestial shape. At least the mode of his approach was nothing new for Catherine. At least their rituals and formulas of marriage were still in force. And whatever else might happen, I told myself, my insight of the moment and Fiona's elegance would consort together to safeguard her from all the means of self-betrayal Hugh might devise.

But Hugh was winding down at last, Catherine was beginning to give in to habit, or perhaps more than habit. I noted the first light in the sky, I moved one step closer to the window and assured myself that they would have a few minutes yet before all three children arose and came leaping into that shocked and harried bed. Yes, I thought, Hugh had slipped off one schedule but gained another. Their house was in order, so to speak, the roles had changed.

I turned away, calmly I tied the ends of my forgotten sash. And straightening shoulders and spectacles alike, I returned along the empty path that stretched endlessly from villa to villa. It amused me to discover that I was walking slowly but with a step reflecting nonetheless the rhythms of the central phrase in Hugh's proposal, as if an old drummer were beating a brief and muffled paradiddle in my head, my inner ear, my heart. Would he find my tennis shoes? Would he begin to understand that there could be no limits on our exchange and that in the circum- scribed country of Illyria a grassy wind was bound to blow away the last shreds of possessiveness? I hoped he would.

In all this darkness and silence I smelled the dead roses, saw the open door and warm rows of tiles, heard the clear but sleepy voice of Fiona calling to me from deep within our thick white walls and timeless collection of vases, earthen pots, artistic tokens of harmonious life. Her soft clear voice was coming as close at it ever did to peevishness, she might have been lying in the dew at my feet. I yawned, I approached the door, I noticed that our morning-glories were doing better than Hugh's.

"Cyril? Is that you?"

"Expecting someone else?" I murmured, and entered the darkness, listened for another brief volley from her hard sweet sleep-ridden mind.

"Just you, baby. You."

"WHERE'S MY MOTHER?"

"I told you, Meredith. They're bringing the wine. You can't have an idyl without wine."

"I'm sick of your old idyls."

"You're lucky to be here. If it weren't for me, you and your little sisters would be back at the villa where Hugh, for one, thinks you belong."

155

"It's not my father who doesn't want us around. It's you."

"Look, Meredith. We need flowers, lots of flowers. You can't have crowns without lots of flowers."

"I don't want any old flower crowns."

"Your sisters do."

"How do you know? They can't say anything."

"Of course they can. They speak the language of children. But take my word for it, Meredith. All little girls like flower crowns in their hair."

"I know what you're doing. You're just trying to impress my parents. That's all. You're just trying to fool them again."

"I'm simply going to bedeck their daughters with flowers, Meredith. It's a nice idea."

"It's dumb."

"That's enough. I want you to gather all the flowers you can. Understand?"

"God, you're mean."

"To work, Meredith, to work."

She turned, she hiked up her baggy shorts, she tried to shake some kind of curl into the chopped-off hair now wet and dark and stuck midway to her ears, she attempted to appear undaunted. But she knew I was watching her, had once more felt the weight of my interested wisdom bearing down on the brittle sticks of her suspicion, and as if my gentle insistence on obedience were not enough, had already begun to respond reluctantly to my idea of the crowns. Even Meredith was not above the idea of a little self-beautification, not exempt from the hope of one day becoming glamorized, idealized, in the eyes of preoccupied parents. Already the green shoots were popping up in that small dark brain of hers, she was trapped in my smile.

"Come on," I said. "Dolores and Eveline and I are waiting."

She glanced at me over her shoulder and then muttered something, stopped, and yanked up a fistful of *Cyclamen persicum* without regard for the pink petals scattering, bleeding, or the soft heads clutched in her hand.

"Not so hard," I murmured. "And leave longer stems."

"I want my mother. I don't like your silly games."

"Put the flowers over here. We'll make a lot of piles and then we'll start weaving."

Without turning she flung her poor crushed offering toward my feet. But she had heard my voice, she was drenched in my patience, she could not deny the laughter of Dolores (or was it Eveline?), and her fingers were stained with the juice of the torn *Cyclamen persicum.* She could hardly help but see that our glen, our golden glen, was filled with clumps of pink flowers, and red and yellow and white flowers, and already she must have envisioned all those helpless buds entwined in little Eveline's hair and in her own. She could not resist. She squatted. She began to pick.

But Cyril among the children? Alone, absolutely alone, with Catherine's two identical female twins and one hostile girl? And only the old black sleeping dog to share my guardianship? It was not a typical situation for me. To serve as liaison between the adults and children, now and again to break off from the four-pointed constellation of our adulthood and sail away, as it were, in order to intercept the small three-pointed heavenly figure of the children and

157

stall its approach, contributing to the freedom of the adults I left behind and creating unenthusiastic coherence among the children I took in hand—all this was one thing and understandable. But to propose separation at the outset and before it was necessary, to make the suggestion casually yet willingly that it might be fun for the children were I to lead them on ahead to the glen—this was quite another thing, and had prompted surprise from Fiona and Catherine, scorn from Hugh, sullenness from Meredith, and mere acquiescence from the little twins. Then why the halfhearted magnanimity, the atypical gesture? Why this minor sacrifice, this exposure to boredom? Meredith was partially right, of course, but I was a better judge of motives than Meredith, and perhaps there was something more to my plan than deception, selfishness, showmanship. Perhaps I wanted to spare Catherine a moment or two, perhaps I wanted to ensure Hugh some time alone with my wife and his, perhaps I was simply inclined to amuse the twins for once and to appease Meredith in the process, show her my other side, give her a half-hour of my attention. Perhaps I wanted to share my capacity for different games, for love on another plane. Who knows?

"I thought you were going to help."

"I am, I am."

"Then why are you just standing there like that?"

"You need more of the *Echium diffusum*."

"Huh?"

"Those little red flowers, Meredith. Over there."

The boredom was not exactly boredom, the distance between myself and the children was not intolerable. I was enjoying myself. The soft green dusty tumors were hanging from the branches of the fig trees just above my head and within easy reach, the infinitely soft and idle grass pillowed the sitting twins and the sleeping dog, a denser species of brushy pine ringed our glen, the fragile flowers were embedded in remarkable variety in the tissue of the ash-blond grass, the sunlight was descending through the green leaves and speckling all four of us. I heard Meredith crawling about this gentle place intent on my work, I saw the polka dots dancing, so to speak, on the ruffled jumpers of the two smaller girls seated side by side in the warm grass and holding hands, blowing chubby laughter in my direction as if they had never seen me before. And the peace, the warmth, the stasis, the smell of it—in such circumstances how could I help but enjoy my own immensity of size or the range of my interests, how help but appreciate the adaptibility of certain natural scenes which, like this one, allow for the play of children one minute and the seclusion of adults the next? I felt a coolness between my porous thin white shirt and the skin of my chest. In linen slacks and alligator belt and hard low-cut shoes the color of amber, I sensed the consciousness of someone carefully dressed for taking care of children. The children themselves were decked out for the occasion in ruffled jumpers, and in baggy but laundered shorts and sleeveless top.

"It's hard to tell your little sisters apart, Meredith. Very hard."

"It's easy."

"At least your mother could dress them differently. Blue polka dots for one, say, and red for the other."

"She likes them the same."

"I see."

"Eveline has bigger teeth."

"I don't think they understand our game. Let's teach them."

No answer. No effort to show me anything except her back. Was she engaged at last? Lost in the scent of the flowers and distracted in the dream I had offered her? Or was she eluding kindness, going through motions, feigning preoccupation, reminding herself that she disliked the sound of my voice and disdained my game? Was I dealing with Meredith the spy, who was filled with duplicity and fear of what she took to be my own duplicity, or was I now in charge of Meredith the harmless child, as I had first assumed? Engaged, I decided, and only the harmless child, because now her small white haunches were frozen where she had just been crawling in the still grass, her head was turned, one hand was raised, in poignant shyness and feminine delicacy she was holding up to her small pointed nose a single bud of *Tolpis barbata* and sniffing in pleasure unmistakably her own. The thin hand quivered. I was sure that her eyes were closed.

"Well," I murmured, "if you won't help your sisters, I guess I'll have to."

"Go ahead."

"I'd prefer that we work together, Meredith."

And pausing, thinking, and then deciding to relent: "Dolores," she said, "Eveline, pick the flowers."

I rubbed the patina of soft dust from one green pendant fig, I watched as Meredith broke a few more stems and abruptly propelled herself toward a clump of *Cistus ladaniferus* worthy, I thought, of any young girl's breathlessness. But obviously Meredith was more attentive to the situation than to the flowers, was listening for some remark from me or some sound from the twins. She waited, she shrugged, until conscience and impatience overcame the lure to beauty and elicited a brief example of the pre-emptory maternal tone she always adopted when addressing the twins. "Come on, come on," she muttered, "just pick them. Pick a lot of them."

"That's fine, Meredith. But Dolores and Eveline don't understand. Let's help them."

"They won't be able to make crowns anyway."

"Of course they will. But if we're going to surprise Fiona and Hugh and Catherine, we'll have to hurry. There isn't much time."

"Who cares?"

"Listen, Meredith. Let's make yours out of those pink and lavender flowers and the white ones. They're best for your eyes."

"I'm not a child."

"Maybe I'll wear one too, who knows."

"What are you doing now?"

"Just sitting down, Meredith. Do you mind?"

Cyril descending among the children. Cyril reclining on the floor of the fig tree bower. Fiona's husband reposing within arm's length of Catherine's two smaller girls who appeared to have been dropped like heavy seeds into our dark-eyed glen. Amuse them, I told myself, control them, don't frighten them, don't awe them with effusion or excessive magnificence. And how easy it was to avoid boredom, repugnance, or exceptional condescension. Of course Meredith was watching me, ready to pounce on my first slip, and of course the twins were watching me, waiting for what chance to erupt into private persecution or unpredictable rebellion I could not be sure. If they fled, if they pummeled each other, if they began to shriek—what then? Above all I expected serenity from all three of them, was determined to see for myself that even these three were capable of charm and of conforming to my own concepts of playful sport that would entertain not only them but me. And yet it turned out that I had only to incline my back, extend one leg, seize the upraised knee of the other and smile, first at Dolores and then at Eveline, to cause both children to blink, to roll apart, to come to me.

"Look what you're doing. You're kicking my pile of blues to pieces."

"Sorry. Just gather them up again."

Supine, I was lying partially supine and wondering whether it was Dolores or Eveline who had flopped belly down on my heavy thigh, Eveline or Dolores who was attempting to perch herself on my upraised knee. But of course one name was as good as the other, I told myself, and for a moment longer tolerated the inertness of the little stomach flat on my thigh and the slow persistent movements of the short legs against my massive calf. But at least there was no tugging on Cyril's hair, no poking at spectacles, no bouncing. Only the polka dots, the two fat bodies, the two sets of large brown eyes brooding impossibly on mine. The little stomach was sighing, the fat legs were searching for a grip. All this I tolerated for the sake of the apparent depth of feeling with which they were clambering upon the bemused figure of the man who kissed their mother and knew the way to the glen.

"Now we're going to help Meredith pick the flowers. I'll show you how."

They understood, they disengaged legs and stomach from my knee and thigh, they stepped aside and waited (plump, somber, square-faced, bright of eye), and without hesitation they followed my example as I descended to all fours and moved through the speckled sunlight and between the dusty trunks of the fig trees appraising, selecting, admiring, but picking (endlessly picking) the flowers that most caught my attention or most appealed to little Eveline or little Eveline's twin.

"You like this one. Take it to Meredith."

"Don't bother. We've got plenty of those."

"Never mind, Meredith. Eveline likes this kind."

"God . . ."

Like my small white purely artificial sheep with its stifled cry and faint accusing expression on the small face that was neither human nor animal but something of each, they drifted about in the fig tree bower together, all three of them, clumsy industrious children engrossed in gathering armfuls of goatsbeard, ghostly asphodel, and the heavy lidded *Anemone coronaria*. I led the way. My industry, though of a different sort, matched theirs. Eveline, I noted, remained at my side while her twin preferred more independence and was given to nibbling certain prime specimens of the *Cistus salviaefolius*.

"She's eating them. Make her stop."

"Dolores is enjoying herself, Meredith. Let's leave her alone."

"She's ruining everything. You want her to."

"Not at all, Meredith. Not at all. But look, it's easy to make the crowns. You simply take a few flowers from each pile and a few green leaves and bind them together with these slender stems until you get a chain long enough to fit around your head. Then you fasten the ends, of course, into a beautiful circlet of all kinds of flowers. These little milky stems are like string. Think you can do it?"

"God, what a question."

"You and I will have to help your sisters. But I'm sure that you can make a beautiful crown without any help from Cyril."

"Why don't you just stop talking?"

"I don't suppose your mother ever told you that Theophrastus was the father of botany. Well, Meredith, he was."

She scowled. I cajoled the two smaller girls until they were finally seated in a row with Meredith facing what I thought of immediately as the feast of the flowers. Bent heads, sounds of dismay, hands tangling, tears of innocence stuck between chubby fingers or falling onto their little immobile legs. Their silence made mine the more melodious as I watched all of them struggling with tissued gems, their peaceful though unsuccessful employment heightened the serenity of my own involvement in what was, for me, an easy and, as it were, poetic task. I worked swiftly and my progress kept pace with their frustrations. Meredith was not as clever or dexterous as I had at first assumed, her sisters could do no more than mangle my prized flowers in helpless palms. Yes, I thought, their ineptitude was certainly my skill, their strain my relaxation, their dubious fun my pleasure.

164

"Having trouble?"

"No."

"Some of those stems are a little short for weaving. But that looks pretty nice, Meredith. Good choice of colors."

"It's falling apart."

The occasion was mine, and I was determined that each child should have her luxurious and perfectly executed crown. It was up to me, and so I wove all three of them, though not before I created a great thick yellow wreath of *Laurus nobilis* and *Genista cinerea* that was heavy, majestic, sweetly scented and much too large for the head of a child.

"Like it?"

"God, you're selfish."

"I simply knew it would take longer, Meredith, so I made it first. Now we'll fix up yours and your little sisters'."

"I thought we were making them just for us."

"Who's being selfish now?"

"You don't need one. Why do you have to have one too? They're only for children."

"If you want me to make you a flower crown as nice as mine, how about a little politeness? Shall we finish the game or stop right here?"

"It has to be as good as yours. Promise?"

"Promise."

Yes, all three children wanted wreaths like mine, and so I wove them—tossing aside my splendid yellow concoction, adjusting the spectacles, smiling into those three little expectant faces. Meredith put an arm around Eveline's shoulder, through their eyes I saw the familiar and freshly turned-out man become the flower god at play. Why not?

165

Sentimentality was hardly a problem, my estimation of the circumference of each of those three small heads was more accurate, say, than Hugh's. And if despite this good judgment of mine I erred somewhat in the size of Meredith's little queenly crown so that it sat low on her slender brow and obscured her eyes? And if the other two were hastily made and were identically composed of nothing more than leftovers from the bed of *Odontospermum maritimum?* Could such trivialities detract from the eagerness of those cross-legged children or from my own composure? Not at all. The satisfaction of adjusting each delicate crown on each little bowed waiting head was mine. The satisfaction of seeing their self-consciousness was mine. The transference was actual, the flowers of the glen leapt from their hair, drooped over their ears, with a few good natural strokes I paid my debt to Iris and to all the other imaginary nudes of a more distant time.

"On your feet," I murmured, "they're coming."

The three girls in a silent row, I leaning back against the bare trunk of the tallest fig tree—thus they found us, Fiona and Hugh and Catherine, when I called out, directing them to the passage through the pines. They veered our way, laughing, Hugh pursuing his dark unrhythmical shadow, our two wives carrying between them the wicker-bound demijohn of white wine, and found the passage and entered our fig tree bower.

"Hugh, look what he's done!"

"Catherine, what do you think of what Cyril's done to our little girls?"

"They're sweet, baby. They really are. But what about

yourself? I want to see you wearing a great big floppy crown of flowers."

"I've got one."

"Well, put it on, baby. Let's see."

I shrugged, reached down and slowly retrieved the wreath at my feet. The children watched, Hugh laughed. Cathernie's eyes met mine. With both hands I settled that outspoken yellow mass into the heavy texture of my blond hair. I felt the tree at my back and slowly glanced up through the speckled light toward the clear sky that accompanied all our days of idyling.

"God, boy, what a sight."

"Don't ever take it off, baby. Ever."

I HAVE MADE IT PLAIN TO CATHERINE THAT IT IS A GOOD idea for the two of us to poke around, as I put it, in the remains of my tapestry. She agrees. She now understands my reasoning. My moody psychic organization is becoming hers, together we have been touring this landscape of old deaths and fresh possibilities. The lovers have become companions. We are equally inclined, at last, to share the pleasure of turning up the occasional familiar relic or of visiting one of the crevices or hollow enclosures once known to our foursome or perhaps threesome, or even to Catherine alone or to me alone. What else is my tapestry if not the map of Love? I know well its contours, its monuments, its abandoned gardens, its narrow streets, and Catherine is beginning to know them too. In an atmosphere of peaceful investigation we are traveling together from sign to sign, from empty stage to empty stage. We turn a blind corner, we hear a distant bell, we discuss a handprint on a fragment of stone wall, suddenly we recognize the featureless head of a small child sculpted in white stone. What we both know, we share. What Catherine does not know, I tell her. The monuments, the places to visit, are inexhaustible.

For instance, not far from the squat church (within sight of its little mordant cemetery, as a matter of fact) stands a small aboveground granite cistern built by the barbarians in the same era as the construction of the squat church itself. Its mouth is open, a few crude steps lead down to pestilent green water, the vaulted ceiling reflects the greasy surface of the irregular clay tiles, the small and crumbling protrusions carved on the columns suggest a spiraling array of curling leaves, as the original artisan must have intended. Yet more important, a pear tree grows in this unlikely place, has taken root in the mud that lies beneath the polluted water and has flourished, has burst the masonry of the vaulted ceiling so that now it flowers high above the large ragged hole its green head once forced through the blanket of hard tile. It is a curious spectacle, this fusion of pear tree and ancient cistern. And sitting side by side on one of the low steps, hips touching and shoulders touching, elbows on knees and chins on clasped hands, smelling the stench and staring into the darkness of the cistern and the light let down by the heroic tree—what better spot, I told her, for concealing the wooden arm which had been stolen by Fiona and Hugh and retrieved just in time, I thought, by me.

168

After all, the arm could not have been returned to the church, and our villa was not the place for displaying a religious theft. And so it was into this very water that late one night I flung the heavy arm, risking Fiona's petulance but satisfying the dictates of my own good sense. At the time of our visit, Catherine and I speculated on the possibility that it must still be there, sunk in the deep fetid water toward the rear of the cistern, and waterlogged, still gaudy, still unattached to human form. Perhaps it is, though no hand rose to the surface when, that day, I tossed a few smooth stones into the echoing darkness and, in a sentence or two, evoked the past. But at least the tree stands, the cistern stands, while the shadows of love, as I told Catherine, are still flickering.

Or, to take another example, not far from the church and the cistern and cemetery stands a perfectly simple and unadorned statue of a small nude figure which, at first glance, appears to be that of a young girl. The stone is disintegrating, the lower legs and feet have long since been destroyed, the slender arms are cracked, the head is gone. The figure is little more than a small torso standing somewhat higher than my waist and covered with a leprous pink skin of dust that is the residue of its own deteriorating stone. Unprepossessing? The very antithesis of voluptuous intention? A mere weed beside the fiery bloom of the conventional greater-than-life-size female nudes sculpted out of muscular marble or cast in bronze? Yes, at first glance the breasts are small and soft, nothing more than suggestions of latent womanhood, the hips are undistinguished, the belly seems to have been molded by the hand of a sexless creator. And at first passing glance the eye resists and then dismisses the one blemish, a disproportionately large and perfectly round black hole drilled upward between those small helpless thighs.

Why then this decided sensation of erotic power? Why the implication of some secret design? What brilliant and, so to speak, ravaging guile could possibly be concealed inside that slender and merely partial form? Why did I smile immediately and Fiona cry out in happy recognition at the black hole driven so unaccountably into that small portion of the stone which, realistically, should have revealed no more than sexual silence?

Of course I knew the answers then as I know them now, knew them with as much warm pleasure as I knew them only weeks ago (or days?) when Catherine and I were standing alone in that same sun-filled abandoned place and talking together, contemplating the very same stone figure that had once so mystified my eager friend and aroused my wife. Observing Catherine's hand on the little sloping stone shoulder and seeing Hugh's bafflement in Catherine's eyes and hearing Hugh's questions in Catherine's mouth, I could do no more than point out to Catherine that these two situations of discovery were dissimilar and yet similar, while no matter how many times the small pinkish torso gave up its little secret, the actual grace and power of this small figure remained undiminished. Because in the first situation, as I reconstructed it for Catherine, Fiona had verbalized the secret whereas I had relied on demonstration, Fiona putting her arm around Hugh's waist and explaining in a lighthearted speech that the beautiful stone figure was really a little boy as well as a little girl, I searching about in the grass until I found the missing piece which, when inserted into that large and perfectly round black hole, demonstrated the statue's double nature already defined in Fiona's words. And searching in the grass again, at first with no success and then with good luck, once more finding the handy length of polished stone where I had apparently dropped it so long ago, and repeating the demonstration for Catherine, softly I filled in a few more details, recalled a few more instances of forgotten speech, forgotten sensation, describing how Fiona had enjoyed this human toy, had swiftly taken over the demonstration from methodical Cyril and had exclaimed repeatedly that the figure was a girl for Hugh and me but was always a boy, a beautiful little boy, for her. Fiona had been right, as Catherine agreed, and Catherine admitted that she too preferred the missing piece in place and yet understood my sympathy for Hugh who had repeatedly attempted to seize it from Fiona's hand and yank it out so long ago, so far in the past.

And so it stands in that gentle half-demolished enclosure where three of us once frolicked and later, much later, two of us talked, and where Catherine and I may further contemplate it whenever we wish to view ourselves again in light of the handmaiden and youth combined.

Of course the cistern, with its resemblance to the squat church, and the little pink hermaphrodite, with its obvious resemblance to the yellow and vaguely female figure whose history is still fading high on the interior walls of the squat church, are merely two landmarks perused at random from our inexhaustible supply. There are other examples (the Byzantine grave marker on the beach beyond the pines, the table that still lies overturned in the lemon grove, the bend in a rocky path where I sponged the oil of roses onto Catherine's soft back, a bed of crab grass) and some are more important, some less. And yet how can we choose, Catherine and I, what difference does it make which kiss we recover, or which single laugh or which faint cry we hear again in silence? The tapestry hangs down, the map is spread, one road is as good as the next.

Love beckons.

I DID NOT KNOW HOW LONG I HAD BEEN STANDING THERE with hands in pockets, legs crossed at the ankles, left shoulder slowly and heavily inclining against the flimsy and yet tightly fastened shutters, but I was quite aware of Hugh's persistent silence and of the obvious fact that if I wished to open the shutters, as indeed I did, I had only to flip the hasp and give them an easy push with a finger or two. Still I waited, keeping my back to Hugh and preferring not to unfasten the shutters but only to lean against them with increasing pressure. I smelled the canal that lay outside at the back of the wall, I heard Hugh rattling his photographic equipment, I heard a solitary pigeon strutting above our heads on the roof. And I dismissed the sound of a liquid chemical slopping into one of his developing pans, I ignored Hugh's silence, I asked myself what I was doing here with Hugh when I might just as well be embracing Catherine behind our favorite oleander tree. But then shoulder and shutters crossed some kind of threshold so that thanks to no apparent volition of mine they burst open, those ancient tightly secured shutters, and swung back on the light, the gray water, the stone embankment, the rusted body of the old motorbus now the color of red lead.

But I knew full well why I was here with Hugh, knew what Fiona wanted and what was coming, and perhaps should have been more ready than I was to enlist Hugh's agony in dialogue. And yet I waited, allowing myself to wonder what had become of the woman I had once seen waving from this window where now I leaned, allowing myself to wonder again why the pitted and rusted vehicle down there in the water was more real, so to speak, than the one I remembered. But the lonely pigeon fell into view for a moment, Hugh moaned.

"What's the matter," I heard myself saying. "Something wrong?"

"I'm sweating, boy, can't you see?"

"Chest again?"

"No, boy, it's not my chest."

"Well then," I said, and paused. "How about Fiona?"

"Fiona?"

"Sure," I said mildly. "Why not?"

"God, boy. Do you know what's happening?"

"Let's talk about it."

But would I be able to bear down on Hugh's problem? Could Hugh be comforted? He had not selected this room for nothing, it seemed to me, and I could not have been more aware of sagging floor, wet plaster, the crude and heavy bench covered with tin pans, blind cameras. Even the photographs scattered here and there on the white walls were stuck to the rancid plaster with thick and rusted nails that were more appropriate to beams, coffins, heavy planks, than to the glossy and curling enlargements of nude girls. And everything about Hugh himself bore out the nature of his purpose, the extent of his self-created pain, his determination to infect this hour, this day, our two lives and more with his despair. How could I miss the acid stains on the long and skimpy cotton shirt that clung to his chest? How miss the gray discolorations on his long cheeks, the beads of sweat in curling beard and knifelike mustache? How miss the black sailor pants on one side left unbuttoned from loin to waist? Or the fact that he had not even bothered to fasten the left sleeve with the usual safety pin, so that below what should have been the elbow there was merely the empty sleeve, the ghost unheeded but nonetheless in his way? How miss his eyes, his height, his agitation? And against all this I had only patience, tolerance, my systematic personality, Fiona's silent prompting, the sun at my back. Was it enough?

"You just don't know what's going on. That's all."

"Do you?"

"I'm appealing to you, boy. Don't let it happen."

"Well," I said slowly, "you've had your eye on Fiona since the beginning. Let's reason from there."

"She's got a husband."

"You've got a wife."

"I'm talking about you, boy, not me."

"And the torment," I said and paused, "yours or mine?"

"You don't know what's going on in the shadows, boy. That's all."

"Tell me."

"If we don't work together, if we don't stop this thing, you'll lose her."

174

"To you?"

"To me—to me. Don't you see?"

I smiled, I shook my head, I waited. I leaned back in the frame of sunlight and glanced toward Hugh. And as I expected he began to pace, to stride from thick wall to wall, towering, lanky, disheveled, determined to keep us both captive in this little second-story dungeon of his and, in the bargain, to keep Fiona waiting. I watched him, wary and yet at the same time patient, and in that silvery monastic gloom his black bell-bottoms were flapping, his small black eyes were the eyes of a familiar saint. And he paced, he stopped, he tore down one of the photographs and stared at it with aching eyes. I took a long slow breath and tried again.

"Of course I care."

"A dirty nest, boy. Is that what you want?"

"I suppose you're trying to blame Fiona?"

"How about a little virtue, boy?"

"Fiona's the most virtuous woman I've ever known."

"She wants me, for God's sake."

"Yes," I murmured, "I think she does."

"She laughs. She looks at me. She's always talking about Catherine and me . . ."

The pigeon, I could hear, had returned to the roof and alone up there was pecking, scratching, fanning its tail. Now Hugh stood upright, and taller than ever in the right-hand empty corner of this oppressive room, reminded me in pointed ears, hard eyes, bitter mouth, that the face of Saint Peter was very like the narrow large-eyed face of Saint Paul. And were the ligaments beginning to part, the flesh to tear? Was his breathing under control at last? Was he beginning to appreciate the tone of my argument? For a moment I closed my eyes and when I opened them there he was, directly in front of me, legs spread, expressionless, with his good arm raised and all his long bony fingers rigidly extended and cupped to the little black pointed beard on his chin.

"It seems to me," I said gently, "that what you're really after is my permission."

I sighed a low leonine sigh and waited, watched the black eyes turning red, listening for the next gagging sounds of his confusion. Would the stony fingers tighten on the pathetic beard? Would he extend his arm and place the full weight of his murderous stone hand against the fern-green field of my expansive breast? But he merely took a step closer and slowly, unconsciously, began to rake his long curving ribs with the spread and rigid fingers of his single hand.

"You don't mean it," he whispered. "You can't."

"Put it this way," I murmured, "you want to play footsy with Fiona . . ."

"No, boy, you're wrong . . ."

"And you want me to sanction the bare feet under the table."

"For God's sake, I don't."

"But why should I? Why won't you play footsy with Fiona and leave me out of it?"

"Don't hurt me, boy. Don't make it worse than it is."

"Look," I said gently, "do we really have to have all this male camaraderie in matters of love?"

But my confidence was exactly what he was fishing for, of course, and even as I spoke I realized that my last remark

could do no more than goad him on to exactly the sentimentality I had hoped to avoid. Fiona was waiting, Catherine was waiting, the wine was chilled, the thick-lipped bell
was tolling in its bird's nest of iron on top of the squat
church. Yet here I stood, drinking from the sack of Hugh's
bad conscience and knowing full well that there was no
stopping him and that I could not deny his confusion, his
deflating misery, his annoying dependence on Fiona's bored
but sympathetic husband. At least I was ready for him and
did not flinch when the long arm rose, as it did then, and
the hand fell and clamped itself to my shoulder.

"I thought you'd listen, boy. I thought you'd get me out
of this mess."

"What more can I say?"

"How much has she really told you?"

"If you want to know what Fiona calls her little trade
secrets—ask her."

"I don't believe she's told you a damn thing. There it is."

"Well," I murmured, "the only problem is that Fiona's
afraid you don't like her enough."

"Don't like her enough."

"That's right."

"You mean she's unsure of herself? Fiona? And worried
about me?"

"Looks that way."

"I just don't understand, boy. I can't believe it. She
couldn't just confide in you like that. Manhood rebels at
infidelity, it's only natural."

"If you must know," I said and laughed, "she calls you
Malvolio. She says she loves her Malvolio best. Will you
believe me now?"

"That's crazy."

"Ask her yourself."

"She doesn't love me best. She couldn't."

"Oh well," I murmured, "you know what she means."

I shrugged. Slowly and gently I dislodged his blind hand, and turned and carefully drew in the shutters, hooked them tightly closed. And above the sound of Hugh's stony breath and the distant bell, was that of the voice of a young girl sitting somewhere in a doorway beyond the canal and pining in loud crude song for a lost love she was not yet old enough to know? I hoped that Hugh was not too preoccupied to catch a bar or two of that high song and plainly sexual refrain.

"Feeling better?"

"Do me a favor, boy. Don't tell her about this . . . talk of ours."

"Fiona? I won't tell her a thing." I crossed the room, dragged open the warped door and waited for Hugh to follow. "And by the way," I said, "I won't tell Catherine either. OK?"

It was not the last I would hear of Hugh's medievalism, I knew, but at least for a moment the lid was once again in place on his poor troubled pot.

"ARE THEY COMING?"

"Not yet, I guess."

"Cyril? Are they staying away from us on purpose?"

"It's only been a few hours, more or less."

"It's been a day, a whole day."

"Perhaps they just don't want to intrude."

"Cyril? Give me a kiss."

"You're not the least bit interested in kissing old Cyril. Why pretend?"

"You're right, baby. How did you know?"

Waiting? Letting the day die? Bridging our islands, as Fiona always said, with a few friendly sex allusions and silences that suddenly drifted away in passion? But was it possible that I had spent these six hours, eight hours, whatever they were, slumped in a wicker chair and arranging a half dozen common violets in the high narrow neck of a small clay vase the color of dark earth? Was it possible that the cigarette I had begun to puff somewhere around midmorning was still burning now, still turning to hot ash in the little white saucer not inches from my ring finger hand? Apparently so. And in her own way had Fiona passed this first day, which was already gone, merely changing her clothes, appearing now and again for my silent approval in gray slacks, rosy shorts, ankle-length gown of flaming silk, virginal white frock which must have won my approval and hers and which she was now wearing? Yes, I told myself, she had.

"Nice flowers, baby."

"Glad you like them."

"Maybe they're not going to come to our little party."

"Maybe not."

And avoiding the arbor? Avoiding the lemon grove? Doing little, saying little, going our separate ways, keeping a safe distance from the dark and scented wall of funeral cypresses? But listening? Had I too been listening for a voice, two voices, for whatever sound of life might reach us from beyond the trees? Yes, I realized that throughout the day even I had become aware of moments of passing disappointment that Fiona's eavesdropping had not met with more success.

"How do they keep so quiet over there?"

"God knows."

Fiona disappearing inside again, the cigarette burning, Fiona scratching her right thigh in a flurry of thoughtless exasperation, the recollection of a small half-eaten yellow crab on a large white plate near the crook of my elbow, the watery violets defying the aesthetic pattern I had in mind —yes, everything confirmed my impression of the typical first day as a slow and sluggish reflection of the first night. It was always the same, Fiona's briefly pantomimed reassurances, my slumping revery, her thoughts, my thoughts, the curious sensation that the adventure begun in the dark was somehow obscured, discolored, drowned in the bright sun.

"Cheer up, Cyril. Please."

Had I glanced at her book? Had she dipped her fork into the broken shell of my cold crab? Had she stared into her tall goblet while I drank from mine? Had I missed her in the midafternoon and then glanced up to see the hand on her hip, the slow consoling smile on her distant face? And had this dying sun waked the two of us and driven Fiona to an endless toilet and me to a hot cup of coffee ground from a handful of dead and blackened beans? Yes, this was how the day had passed, true to form.

Once again I found myself observing that while the

first night of adventure was always sober, despite darkness and excitement and fresh uncertainties, the first day was inevitably somnolent and oddly drunken, despite the sun overhead and the return of what I thought of as private consciousness. And once again I found myself observing how different we were, Fiona and I, and yet how similar. Because if it had taken her all day to arrive at the white frock, whereas I had climbed into the old white linen jacket without thinking and as soon as I had drunk my coffee, still my slightly rumpled white jacket and beige shirt unbuttoned at the throat revealed precisely the same taste and motivation as Fiona's frock. Unspoken traditional decorum was always the handmaiden of unconfessed anticipation. At least our new-found friends on the other side of the funeral cypresses would appreciate if not understand the significance of the way we looked. Unless this was to be another one of those rare first days that sometimes ended, as they began, in silence.

"Oh look at them. They're all dressed up."

"Pretty formal, don't you think?"

"But sweet, baby, sweet."

So time was leaping out of the shadows after all and I was standing, Fiona was hiding one hand behind her back and hitching at a fresh pair of panties beneath the frock. The diffusion of the sunlight was already jumping into the clarity of approaching night. And simply because of a powdery blue jacket, a necktie obviously tied by a woman's hand and a gray dress with a bright red sash at the waist? That's all it took, I thought, a few twists of clothing and a few shared memories of a night that was not dead and only lengthening, starting over.

"Found this in the luggage," Hugh said. "I thought you'd like it."

"Oh, Cyril. Cognac."

"Let's try it."

"No, thanks, boy. Not me."

"Hugh's been sick."

"But Hugh, what's wrong?"

"Cramps. Diarrhea. Weakness."

"Feeling better?"

"Ask Catherine, boy. She'll tell you."

"Hugh's all right, baby. You can see he is."

"Yes," I said and laughed, "great Pan is not dead."

Meeting. Mingling. Greeting each other. And I shook Hugh's hand, Hugh shook Fiona's hand, I put my arm around Catherine's waist, Fiona took a sudden firm grip on my white linen sleeve. And the day? Gone. The night? Deep. The sunlight? Green. We admired the bottle of cognac, we glanced from face to face, Hugh assured us of his recovery. We told Hugh that the weakness would pass, Catherine admired Fiona's frock. Fiona suggested that I open the bottle of cognac covered with black mold, but I suggested we wait.

"But, baby, what shall we do?"

"Well," I said, "before it gets too dark, let's look at the grapes."

"Oh, Cyril, the grape-tasting game . . ."

"Want to play?"

I turned, led the way. I stepped inside the arbor and waited for Fiona to join me at a run and for Catherine to notice the empty stone bench and empty glasses, waited for some sign of Hugh's obvious disappointment. The trellises of thick green leaves, the sandy floor, and overhead the dry and silent clusters of purple grapes—for me this was clearly the place for the bedding down of lovers. Whereas Hugh's initial reaction, I expected, would be distaste for the grapes and impatience at what now amounted to his sudden confinement not only with Fiona but with wife and presiding host as well. But he would wait, I thought, we could all wait. Never had the grapes been this heavy on the vine, never had the fat clumps been this brown, this blue, this purple. Here even Hugh might awaken to the smaller joys of my harvest.

"All right," I said quietly, cheerfully, "come close."

"What's on your mind?"

"You'll see."

"Cyril is a pastoral person. Aren't you, baby?"

"Sure I am."

"I don't know about the rest of you," Catherine said in the shadows, "but I could stay right here forever."

"But it's a little silly, boy, isn't it?"

"Oh," I said from somewhere in the center of my chest, "it's not so silly."

I looked from face to face and noted with satisfaction that Hugh was somber and was buttoning his ill-fitting jacket while Catherine, despite her soft words, was glancing about the darkened arbor in a large vague gesture of shyness, uncertainty, apprehension. But for once Fiona was standing still, perfectly still, and was studying my collected features with bemused and yet unfeigned admiration.

"Come on, come on," I said again. "Closer."

I had been careful to position myself where the weight of the grapes was greatest. And to this spot I now drew my wife and Hugh's wife and Hugh, so that in the green light and in oddly appealing discomfort we were all four of us standing shoulder to shoulder with the lowest grapes nesting in our four heads of hair. I felt myself warming to mock seriousness, I knew that each one of us was witness to the other three, I knew that individual and group self-consciousness was mounting as Hugh attempted to dislodge a flat green leaf from the side of his head and Fiona gave me her bright level stare and Catherine shifted slowly from foot to foot. For a moment I allowed myself to concentrate on the distant scent of orange blossoms and the nearby complacent song of some little member of the thrush family.

"It's easy," I said then in low tones of solemn confidence, "we just keep our hands behind our backs and go after the grapes—with our mouths."

"No grapes for me, boy. No thanks."

"Oh," I said and laughed, "you don't need to eat them. Just try to catch them in your lips and pull them down."

"Why not pick a couple of bunches with our hands," Hugh said, "and go sit under a tree?"

"Let's do what Cyril says, Hugh. Please."

"Baby, I want to be first. OK?"

"No, Fiona," I said slowly, "I'm first."

For a moment longer I took all the time I wanted—adjusting spectacles, letting arms hang loose, cushioning the backs of both clasped hands against upper thighs and lower buttocks, unlimbering the torso inside the old white linen jacket. And then I rose on the balls of my feet and simply stuck my face up among the grapes. But strain? No. Exertion? No. Yet Hugh and Catherine and Fiona could hardly help but be aware of my lifted chin, the soft open planes of my tilted face, the heavy and tightened flesh of my bent neck. And was Fiona fidgeting? Hugh grunting? Catherine sighing in disbelief? I heard them, I too was amused at their vision of my bulky athletic figure sporting with playful aesthetic hunger among the grapes. Yes, I told myself, my large head poking for no apparent reason into the symmetrical fat clumps of purple grapes was no doubt an amusing sight, as I intended it to be. But more, much more. And now the grapes were sitting on my round lenses, rolling down my nose, bobbing against my hard closely shaven cheeks, lolling and falling across the tops of my ears. I set one in motion with my tongue, I reached out for another with ready lips, it popped away. But I persevered, methodically I sucked in that single plump dangling grape and gave a tug, closed my mouth, split the skin, began to chew.

"God, boy, I see what you mean . . ."

"Come on, Catherine," I said and laughed, "your turn."

"But what about Fiona?"

"That's all right, baby. Catherine's next."

Hugh grinned, Fiona clapped her lean hands silently, I nodded encouragement. So up went Catherine on tiptoe and with her eyes open, her mouth open, her jaw thrust forward. But as soon as she encountered the first grape, felt the first grape bouncing with a will of its own against her upraised chin, Catherine shuddered, stumbled, looked at me with a long soft look of unmistakable recognition. Was this what I was thinking? Was the sensation she had just experienced the same as mine?

"You missed," Hugh said. "Try again."

185

"I lost my balance."

"They're only grapes," I said under my breath. "Have some."

"Nipples, boy, that's what you mean."

"Suit yourself," I said, and laughed. "But they're just grapes."

Again I nodded, stuffing large hands into jacket pockets, and again Catherine stood on tiptoe and to my surprise began nuzzling and nudging the very cluster which, only moments before, I myself had abandoned to the green night. And there—her throat was exposed, her hair was loose, her lips were pursed, the crushed grape was going down. Only the mother of three children being a little silly in a fairly commonplace arbor in which, nonetheless, the fruit of the field grew ripe in the air? Yes, I thought, that was all. But I enjoyed the sight.

"Baby," Fiona whispered, "did you see?"

"But what's this, boy—arm around my wife's shoulders?"

Yet even as I replied in kind to their rhetorical questions and pantomimed my congenial and self-evident assent, already Hugh was stretching like a man attempting to chin himself without the use of his hands, while Fiona's cool white brow was rising to the touch of the grapes. Eyes disappearing among the leaves, lips in shadow. Catherine and I were watching them, of course, and Catherine was so turned that somewhere below my armpit I could feel the undeniable pressure of her right breast settled against my waiting side.

And Hugh? Fiona? Their heads were together temple to temple, one of his darkly trousered legs was canted across one of her bare legs, the grapes (the entire sagging arbor of pulpy grapes) were swaying and rippling to the sound of their laughter, the movements of their open mouths.

"Oh, baby, I want to nibble each one of them!"

So much, I thought, for the viscera of the cornucopia.

Barefooted but otherwise fully clothed, Hugh leaps about waist-deep in the rough and sunny water with the short length of rotted rope tight in his hand and the small tar-covered boat lunging and rearing in slow circles. Fiona and the children tumble from bow to stern, four wet energetic figures bailing and attempting to transform a broken oar into an imaginary mast. Catherine and I sit watching from the brief pebbly incline of the hot beach. Hugh shouts in the spray, and for answer Fiona leans over the gunwale and thrusts down her faunlike and naked face. We wave.

Or I round the point and discover Fiona squatting in a rocky crevice with her face toward the sea, the tide at her feet, her back to the vertical ledges of pink stone. And on top of the little cliff that hides Fiona and safeguards her modesty sits Hugh—rigid, one leg drawn up and the other dangling in the clear air, his silent face peering down at us in raucous and privileged enjoyment.

Remember?

"WHAT'S THE MATTER," I CALLED, "GETTING OLD?"

Though we had started out together and with every intention of remaining together throughout a day this timeless and bright and clear, nonetheless we had once again drifted into pairs and begun to separate, to pull apart long before reaching the commencement of the breakwater. By the time Catherine and I first set foot on the breakwater and moved out from the shore, Hugh had already swept himself and Fiona far ahead, the two of them long-legged and impetuous and receding, growing smaller, flaunting their eagerness and similarity of temperament until, flanked on either side by sun and sea, they had all but disappeared. Yet midway on the breakwater between shore, village, beached fishing boats and at the other extreme, the ruined fortress, suddenly the two of them, Hugh and Fiona, had seated themselves on a couple of flat white rocks where now they waited for Catherine and me, the slow strollers, to close the long clear empty space between us.

"Not as old as you are," Hugh shouted back through the silence, and planted his single elbow, I saw, in Fiona's lap.

"There's no hurry," I said to Catherine, and squeezed her hand. "Let's take our time."

"Why does he want to explore that ugly place?"

"God knows."

But now that the village lay at our backs, there was nowhere to walk except forward across the high narrow breakwater into the open sea and toward the squat and ominous pile of dark stones that revealed in the midst of its wreckage the shape of the former fortress. How strong, I asked myself, was my empathy with Hugh's present eagerness? What could account for the rather special quality of desolation that appeared to characterize the abandoned structure now awaiting the sound of our four voices, the cautious tread of our feet? When did an ordinary stroll become a compulsive quest? And why did I now identify that unspectacular and essentially uninteresting ruin with the dark caves of the heart? Self-imprisonment, which was what we appeared to be heading for, was hardly my own idea of pleasure. And yet I was beginning to feel something of Hugh's elation. Today of all days my empathy with Hugh, I decided, was fairly strong.

"Does Fiona really want to climb around in there?"

"I suppose she does."

"Well, I don't."

"We could have stayed with the children."

"I'd never let him take Fiona in there alone."

"Jealous?"

"If she goes, I have to go. That's all."

"Fiona might fool us both. You never know."

"How?"

"But then," I said more to myself than to Catherine, "it's Hugh's expedition. We'll just have to wait and see where it leads."

One glance backward, and I knew what I would see: dark hills, brief and distant panorama of tiled roofs and whitewashed walls, black little boats ranged on the gray beach and, far to the south, the fragile landmarks of the funeral cypresses. And yet all this was gone and for us there was only severance, isolation, the sensation of proceeding outward from the familiar shore and into the uninhibited world of blue sky, black sea, penitential fortress. We might have been walking down a country road, Catherine and I, except that the rutted track we followed across the high surface of the breakwater was white, not brown, and was composed of rock and crushed shells, rather than of dusty earth, and carried us not safely among the olive trees but precariously across deep salty water and into the light that had no source. We shaded our eyes, looked out to sea. No wonder Hugh had insisted that the four of us wear rubber-soled shoes. No wonder he had packed his enormous khaki-colored rucksack with rope, torch, knife, rolls of bandage and bottles of disinfectant. But was this clear vista of peace and treachery, space and confinement, reason enough for Hugh's excitement? I suspected not.

"Hey there," Hugh called, "what do you think of it?"

"Interesting," I called back, "but let's stay together."

"Graffiti, you two. Come look!"

"Can you read them, boy?"

"Sure can."

"Oh, baby, what do they say?"

No doubt the large and indecipherable signs were the work of passing fishermen who in their crafty loneliness had used pieces of soft and chalky masonry to inscribe their private sex legends on these dead walls. Appeals to big-boned virginal women said to inhabit small green islands lying somewhere beyond the horizon? Songs to a young girl of our own village? Ribald declarations of one grizzled fisherman's love for another and much younger fisherman?

190

Whatever the content and whoever the lovers, for us these public testimonials remained no more than secret and unreal scrawls, since no sooner had I begun to gather Fiona and Catherine close to my sides, no sooner begun to scan the massive walls for clues to the specific sense of the abandoned messages, then Hugh was already shouting from the interior of this impressively dismal place and urging us to forget the graffiti and to follow him inside.

"Are they all about the singing phallus, baby?"

"I guess they are."

"Don't you know, for God's sake?"

"I'll read them to you another time, Fiona. OK?"

"Hurry," Catherine said then, "Hugh's alone in there."

"Well," I said, gripping Fiona's hand and Catherine's elbow, "it's too bad we can't all share Hugh's rather boyish interest in old fortresses and so forth. But on we go."

"I love these old masculine places," Fiona said. "You know I do."

Still I hung back, surveying the light that shone only at sea, the incongruous mustard-colored stone walls which on three sides descended at a steep angle into the dark random tide, the entrance that was low and rounded and deep. And I noted what I suspected Hugh had failed to note in his characteristic haste and determination to see it all at a glance and to find his own lean shadow wherever he looked: the briars clotting the entrance way, the ringbolts and fallen rock, the iron bars driven into the rounded arch and now bent aside. Yes, I thought, herding Fiona and Catherine into the dark mouth of the fortress, yes, the gates were gone and the marble monsters no longer stood on their sunken pedestals. But nonetheless the mouth of the fortress remained guarded, oddly protected, within its own matter-of-fact condition of disuse, and only a man like Hugh could rush through this brief tunnel unaware of ancient armaments and present obstacles to passage. Catherine stumbled, I gripped her arm, Fiona's uncertain voice echoed down the wet walls.

"Look," Hugh shouted then, "burned!"

Chin high, legs far apart, rucksack lying brown and lumpy in the weeds at his feet, there stood Hugh waving us into the hot and empty courtyard and at the same time indicating with his long good arm the high walls, the blackened doorways, the cracked tower, the vacant blue sky overhead. I saw immediately that he was right, because all four walls had been deeply and viciously scorched by some devastating blaze so that they were streaked and seared with enormous swatches of unnatural color—intestinal pink, lurid orange, great blistering sheets of lifeless purple. And everywhere the weeds and fallen pediments were encrusted with the droppings of long departed gulls.

"Burned clean, boy. There's nothing left."

"No juice of the growing fruit, "I murmured, "that's for sure."

"Don't be cryptic, baby. Please."

"You can't even smell it, boy. No ashes. No smoke. Nothing. It's just a reflection—a reflection of some fiery nightmare. Don't you see?"

"Sure," I said and laughed, "if that's what you want. But I prefer a little more than weeds and discoloration. How about it, Catherine?"

"Oh, Cyril, stop arguing."

Everywhere I turned I could see that these burned walls

were punctured with small charred doorless entrances leading no doubt into a labyrinth of pits and tunnels, cells and niches for birdlike archers. Never had the four of us been so starkly confined, starkly exposed. Hugh and Catherine and I were dressed appropriately for whatever ordeals might come our way (Hugh in his castoff Navy denims, Catherine wearing her gray slacks with the patches, I dressed in sweatshirt and chocolate-colored corduroys), whereas Fiona had disregarded Hugh's instructions and was wearing only her eggshell sandals and mid-thigh tennis dress of shocking white. Stark, alone together, exposed, self-conscious. But despite my predisposition in favor of the lyrical landscape or any of those places conducive to my own warmer inclinations, and despite my conversational reluctance of only a few moments past, nonetheless I too was beginning to understand Hugh's feeling for the condemned courtyard and gutted fortress, was already partially willing to forego my kind of pleasure for his.

"Well," I said, and picked up Hugh's rucksack, "what now? The tower?"

"No, boy, the dungeons."

"Treasure," Fiona said. "What fun."

"OK," I heard myself saying pleasantly, "I guess you know what you're doing. Let's go."

So I slung Hugh's clumsy burden from an easy shoulder, commiserated with Catherine in a long good-humored meeting of eyes, grinned at Fiona, trudged off across the courtyard toward the most distant and least inviting doorway in the northeast wall. Hugh leapt gaunt and spiderlike into that charred darkness, Fiona ducked after Hugh, Catherine entered head down and heavily, I whistled softly to myself and then pushed my way out of the sunlight and through the cold, tight, irregular doorless opening. There followed the typical moment of disorganization, confusion, pretended panic, while the four of us stood in single file and bumped together, enjoyed the last noisy sounds of indecision before starting down. I attempted to rummage inside the rucksack and dig out the torch, and discovered without surprise that Hugh's torch was a nickel-plated, long-handled affair that was obviously filled with greenish and partially corroded batteries. I flicked on the weak beam and passed the torch from hand to hand to Hugh. Catherine had turned her back to me and appeared ready, now, to undergo Hugh's childish adventure to the end.

"Cyril? Are you there?"

"Sure I am."

"Steps, boy. They're pretty steep. Careful now."

The darkness was like the water in a cold well, the roof of the narrow corridor became the sounding board for Hugh's loud voice. With slow shoulders and spread hands we felt our way along the slick invisible walls and occasional gritty patches of leprous masonry. In single file and breathing audibly, on we crept toward the diffused beam of Hugh's torch which he was flashing in all directions now to indicate, as he said, the beginning of the steps. Above Fiona's strong jasmine scent and the smell of the throbbing seaweed there drifted the unmistakable smell of human excrement—an undeniable fresh smell that could hardly help the tone of our quest, could not help but make Catherine uncomfortable and Fiona displeased. For a moment I allowed myself to muse on the odor of human offal, thinking that men inevitably relieved their bowels in all the ruined crypts of the world and that the smell struck some kind of chord in other men but to women was merely distasteful. What then of Fiona's earlier asssertion of her love for the places of masculinity? Was that particular love of hers unqualified? The smell of the offal and Fiona's sudden silences were the first indications that it was not.

"Well," I heard myself saying, "we're like a bunch of kids."

"Speak for yourself, boy."

"At least you could shine the light this way once in a while. Might help, don't you think?"

"I'm cold, Cyril. What'll I do?"

"There are a couple of sweaters in the rucksack, boy. Why don't you pull one out?"

"No," I said. "We'll wait until we reach the bottom."

I heard our three pairs of spongy rubber-soled shoes making soft contact with the first half dozen steps, distinguished the hard leathery sound of Fiona's tissue-thin sandals on the stone. I saw Hugh's haste registered in the jerky disappearance and reappearance of the light of the torch. I hoped that Hugh would find something to make this expedition of his worthwhile, I hoped that whatever he found would please Fiona and prove to be of interest, at least, to Catherine and me. I hoped that the last hours of the day would find Catherine and me alone together in one of those dense harmonious places of my choosing rather than Hugh's, and would find Fiona once again running free and nestling with a more appreciative and agreeable Hugh.

"If there's nothing down there," I called, "what then?"

"It's there, all right. I dreamed about it."

195

"Stop him," Catherine whispered in a flat voice. "Can't you do something?"

"Too late," I whispered back. "Besides, he's enjoying himself."

"Why can't we all hold hands?"

"Wouldn't do much good. It'll be over soon."

"Hugh," Fiona said. "Tell us the dream."

But even the timbre of Fiona's voice was oddly diminished, and the restraint and poignancy of this second brief appeal made it only too clear that even Fiona was beginning to have reservations about the intensity of Hugh's descent. And treading the dark air, sinking, fumbling, following each other down, once again it occurred to me that Hugh was somehow more than oblivious to Catherine's fear and resignation, more than insensitive to Fiona's now obvious misgivings and disappointment, more than indifferent to my quiet presence behind him at the end of the line. Perhaps our very compatibility was at last at stake. In all the thoughtlessness of his clearly secret self, perhaps his true interest was simply to bury our love in the bottom of this dismal place and in some cul-de-sac, so to speak, of his own regressive nature. Perhaps he was as indifferent to the male principle as he was to me, and was not searching for some sexual totem that would excite a little admiration in his wife and mine, but was instead determined to subject all four of us to the dead breath of denial. Who could tell?

"Oh, baby, look at the view."

Suddenly we paused, leaning against each other, and crowded together at a high narrow aperture cut with beveled edge through the dark thick mass of what we now understood to be the outside wall, so that in the sudden funnel of clear light and with our heads close and hands on shoulders, arms about familiar waists, the rucksack pressing against Catherine's hip as well as mine, suddenly we found ourselves sharing relief from the darkness and uncertainty of our now interrupted downward progress into this stone shaft. Silent, subdued and yet attentive, relieved and yet immobile, unemotional, touching each other and yet unmotivated by our usual feelings of mutual affection—for one brief somber moment we stared out toward the vacancy, the sheer distance, the brilliant timeless expanse of sea and air. Hugh had hiked himself as best he could into one corner of the empty aperture and was a grainy and rigid silhouette leering seaward. The scantness of Fiona's tennis dress was pressing against the stiffness of Hugh's denims, the breadth of my chest was partially straddling Fiona's left shoulder blade and Catherine's right arm, Catherine's waist was soft and comfortable beneath the casual pressure of my left hand. There were no boats on the horizon, no birds in the air. Only the four of us, the silence, the fortress heavier than ever above our heads, the stones larger and darker and more imprisoning, only the constricted view of the inaccessible water with its all-too-real surface of white transparencies and maroon-colored undulations.

"Hugh," Fiona said then, "why don't we just climb back up and go swimming? I feel like a little swim. Right now."

"I hate this place," Catherine said. "I want to leave."

"It's just not much fun. I want us to have fun, that's all."

"Hugh knows about my claustrophobia, don't you, Hugh?

But at least you could listen to Fiona if you won't listen to me."

"The view's attractive, but the rest of it just isn't turning out as I thought it would."

"Hugh's selfish, that's all."

"Don't you want to go swimming with me, baby?"

"Of course he does. But Hugh's not about to change his mind. He'll deny us the same way he denies the children."

"But Hugh, we can't even have a little hugging and kissing down there. Don't you see?"

"He doesn't care. He won't listen to either one of us."

"Help me, Cyril. Tell Hugh I always mean what I say."

Laughing, leaning into both Catherine and Fiona and squinting heavily for another look at the gently shifting dark sea: "Don't pay any attention to them," I heard myself saying, "our wives don't want to admit how much they like this little dangerous hunt of yours."

"You'll be sorry, baby."

"No threats, Fiona."

"I'm bored. I'm not going to say it again."

"How about it, Hugh? Ready?"

Yes, I thought, my empathy was real enough, the tone of the position I had decided to take could not be missed. But did Hugh care? Had he been listening? Or was he more than ever oblivious, as I had at first suspected? Did it matter to Hugh that I had chosen sides—I who could always absorb the little resistances of his wife and mine, after all, with nothing to lose? Or was my support merely one more irritant that somehow enhanced Hugh's feelings of remoteness in this our first small disagreement?

It was then that I recalled the morning's trivial domestic

incident described to me by Catherine in one long breath of privacy before we had assembled into our usual foursome —I leaving, Hugh returning, Hugh lunging into his rightful bed, Hugh appealing in hypnotic whispers for Catherine's nakedness, Dolores entering that room of circular love, Hugh bounding up and striking his head against the rotten shutter which I myself had opened only moments before. But had Hugh sensed my intervention in both Catherine's nakedness and the state of the shutter? Or had he simply viewed the unwitting appearance of the sleepy child along with the crack on his head as somehow deserved or as a deliberate manifestation of the dream he was still keeping to himself? Had the interruption accounted perversely for his morning's cheer? But if all this were true, as suddenly I thought it was, and if the day's expedition had in fact begun for Hugh with this misadventure, then of course the invisible lump on his head in some way accounted for his present leering confidence and refusal to talk. Surely the lump on his head fit in with his plans.

Still saying nothing, Hugh merely turned and once more started down. We followed, of course, and the light was gone, the vista of the bright sea was gone, a sudden vacuum in the dark air told me that Fiona was hurrying to catch up with Hugh in spite of herself. Catherine was doing her best, the walls were wet, the steps were steeper and the passage more narrow than before. From somewhere far below, the sound of Hugh's creaking denims drifted up to us. And suddenly from those depths below us came Fiona's faint cry along with an abrupt rush of pattering sounds that could only mean that one of them had fallen.

"What's that?"

"Accident."

"You better come on down here, boy. Your wife's in trouble."

"Keep going," I said to Catherine, "but don't try to hurry. Be careful."

Fiona was sure-footed. Fiona was not one of those women who convert minor injury into an instrument of will whenever the neutral universe fails to conform in some slight particular to the subtleties of the female vision. She was strong, she was agile, she could not have fallen merely to teach Hugh a lesson or merely to hasten the swimming party which, however, I knew full well she intended to enjoy before the last light of the day. But that faint cry, that soft cry tinged with the barest coloration of accusation, I had heard it and recognized it immediately as the clear cry Fiona never uttered unless she needed my help. So as unlikely as it seemed to me, perhaps she was hurt. Perhaps there would be no swimming after all.

Beyond the suddenly visible bulk of Catherine's shadow, I saw the white dress pulled up to the loins, the lifted knees, the slender face, the cavern floor, Hugh's crouching shape, the circle of dim light. We were below sea level and now we were crowding together in a small wet space hollowed out from stone and thick with echoes.

"What happened?" I asked. "Are you all right?"

"I slipped, baby. Me! I went down about twenty steps."

"Well," I said, laughing, fumbling with the rucksack, finding the sweater, "let's see if you can walk."

"I hope you're satisfied, Hugh," Catherine said. "Fiona might have broken her ankle."

"Climb into this sweater," I murmured quickly and calmly, "and then we'll check you out."

But was she indeed hurt? Catherine was kneeling beside Fiona, Hugh was crouching, in his one hand gripped the now dying torch. Fiona herself was still prostrate on the cold stone. For a moment I had the decided impression that Hugh had bolted into these ruins and dragged us into these wet depths of vaulted darkness for the sole purpose of discovering nothing more than Fiona herself lying flat on her back in the faint eye of the torch like the remains of some lady saint stretched head to toe on her tomb. The expression on Fiona's face seemed to bear me out, since her head was turned to the sound of my voice and since the slender construction of Fiona's face and the willful eyes and thin half-smiling lips were raised to me in something more than mere personal concern for the immediate situation of unlikely accident. What else could that expression mean if not that she understood what I was thinking and was momentarily aware of her own body and expressly erotic temperament as the very objects of Hugh's subterranean design? How else account for Fiona's expression of puzzlement and appeal if not by knowing suddenly that Hugh was quite capable of attempting to transform my faunlike wife into a lifeless and sainted fixture in his mental museum?

"Give me your hand, baby. Help me up."

But still no word from Hugh? No hint of his usually exaggerated concern for Fiona's interests, pleasure, well-being, safety? Not even taking advantage of the darkness to thrust himself against Fiona who was now holding my hand and scrambling to her feet and was nothing if not responsive to Hugh's slightest touch? But it was true, all too true. He must have known that today there would be no hugging and kissing, as Fiona had put it, long before Fiona had voiced that sad little conviction of hers, long before he had had his dream, long before he had banged his head on the rotted shutter.

There was nothing to do, I thought, except to hold wide the neck of the sweater and help Fiona, however clumsily, to pop her head through the opening and feel her way into the sleeves so absurdly long and tangling. And then, quite simply, I would demand the torch from Hugh and lead us calmly back up to the limitless pastel light of the burned court.

"As long as we're here," Fiona said then, "let's look around."

"OK," I said, once more changing my mind, shifting my stance. "There's nothing to see. But we'll take a quick look anyway."

I realized immediately that there was more to come, that Hugh had not yet shot his bolt of poison and that Fiona was not going to comply with my helpfulness and had already refused the possibility of wearing the sweater. But at least I managed to drape Hugh's sweater across her shoulders and loop the long sleeves around her throat. In due time Hugh, not I, would lead us back up to the court-yard. Agreed.

"There's no way out," Hugh said. "We're at the bottom."

"Buried, you mean. Buried alive."

To hear Catherine's determined voice, to hear Hugh's silence in response to it, to know that Fiona was once again looking for Hugh in the wet darkness, to be aware of this cold timeless space hollowed from the very roots of the sea —suddenly I wished again that Hugh's poor torch would discover a real effigy with a stone cowl, stone feet, stone hands pressed together and pointed in prayer. Or would discover a real row of iron-headed pikes along one of the vaulted walls. Or a steel glove, the blade of an ax, a gold cup, anything to justify all this shadowy suspension of our lives of love. Surely this empty place should offer up some little crusty memento to justify my separation from sun and sea and grass, to justify the unspeakable content of Hugh's dream. But then the memento, as it were, did in fact appear.

"Now, boy—how do you like it?"

"If I were you," I said softly, slowly, "I'd leave that thing here where you found it. That's my advice."

"Leave it," Catherine said quickly. "I don't want to know what it is. I don't want to see it."

"Old Cyril knows what it is. Don't you, boy?"

"Yes," I murmured, "of course I do."

"Tell us, baby. Tell us!"

"No, Fiona, it's up to Hugh."

"Damn right it is!"

And I who had never exposed Fiona to discomfort of any kind, I who had taken the exact same care of Catherine, I whose handsome and bespectacled face had always stood for sensuous rationality among the bright leaves, I the singer who spent my life quietly deciphering the crucial signs of sex, I who only moments before had decided that Hugh would discover nothing, nothing at all—now it was I, I alone, who shared with Hugh clear knowledge of the ise nature of what Hugh was dangling from the neck of the torch, as if I myself had sought it and found it and inflicted it on all four of us, silly and pathetic and yet monstrous memento of Hugh's true attitude toward all of our well-intended loves.

"It's a bad omen, Hugh," I said. "Leave it behind."

"My God, boy. Where's your sense of humor?"

The voices echoed in the waxen blackness. Three figures squatted around Hugh's pit, and Hugh himself stood waist-deep in this very pit which had emerged from beneath the beam of his torch only moments before. The cavern was empty, its wet walls and floor were empty, as I had thought. But the pit was not. Suddenly Hugh had found this small rectangular hole in the cavern floor and had leapt up to his knees in the refuse of coagulated fishing nets, broken clay pots and charred ribs of wood. In the midst of this pulpy refuse, he had poked with the torch itself until we heard the dull yet tinny sound of metal on metal, had thrust down the head of the torch and hooked what he was looking for and slowly, in rigid triumph, had raised the unmistakable object of his lonely search.

"I knew it was here. It had to be."

"OK," I murmured, "you found it. Now put it back."

"Not a chance, boy not a chance . . ."

Then we were climbing, and in unchanged order (from top to bottom, from first to last), Hugh was perspiring in the lead, Fiona had obviously forgotten the effects of her fall and was pacing Hugh with renewed agility and fresh anticipation, Catherine was treading on Fiona's heels, while I went chugging upward with my concentration divided between the gloom of the coming moment, as I envisioned it, and the pleasure of the daylight burning somewhere above our heads. Yes, I thought, Hugh's exhibition in the courtyard was unavoidable. But after, after the silence, the disbelief, the dismay, perhaps then we would move on to long naked strokes in the bright sea or to a rendezvous of sorts with the small earthen-colored nightingale whose secret song I had recently heard not far from the villas. Or would the strains of this day dog us into the future, disrupt our embraces, diminish the peaceful intensity of all those simple idyls I still had in mind?

We stopped, we slipped, we climbed on.

"Thank God, baby. We're safe!"

Fiona with the empty sweater clinging to her back like the cast-off skin of some long-forgotten lover, Catherine with her eyes tight shut and hair awry and broad cheeks brightly skimmed with tears, I shading my face and easing off the uncomfortable and partially opened rucksack, Hugh holding aloft his prize and leaping through the weeds to a fallen pediment, Hugh turning and facing us with the little copper rivets dancing on his penitential denims and his mouth torn open comically, painfully, as if by an invisible hand—suddenly the four of us were there, separated, disheveled, blinking, and yet reunited in this overgrown and empty quadrangle that now was filled with hard light and the sweet and salty scent of endless day. I dropped the rucksack, squinted, fished for a fat cigarette. Fiona caught hold of the sleeves of the sweater at the wrists and pulled the long empty sleeves wide and high in a gesture meant only for the far-off sun. Catherine sat on a small white chunk of stone and held her head in her hands, Hugh tipped his prize onto the altar of the fallen pediment and flung aside the torch, reared back, and waited.

"But is that all, baby? It doesn't look like much."

"Take a better look," I said quietly. "You'll change your mind."

I filled my mouth and lungs with the acrid smoke, I squinted at Hugh, at Fiona, at Catherine. We ached with darkness, our eyes were burning with the familiar yet unfamiliar return to light, as lovers we were exhausted but not exhilarated. Hugh lifted his right leg and cocked his foot on the fallen pediment and rested his right forearm on the upraised thigh.

Catherine sighed and climbed to her feet. Fiona approached the cracked and fluted pediment, slowly Catherine and I moved into position so that all four of us were grouped around Hugh's improvised altar upon which lay what appeared to be only a thin circlet of pitted iron—frail, ancient, oval in shape, menacing. I looked at Fiona, she looked at me, all four of us stared down at the pliant and yet indestructible thin loop of iron that was large enough to encircle a human waist and was dissected by a second and shorter loop or half circle of iron wrought into a deliberate and dimly functional design.

"No," Fiona whispered, "no . . ."

On the opposite side of the pediment from Hugh, I also raised one heavy leg, placed one mountain-climbing boot on the gray stone, rested my forearm across the breadth of my heavy thigh, allowed myself to lean down for a closer look. Our four heads were together, in our different ways we were scrutinizing the single tissue-thin contraption that had already revealed its purpose to Fiona and now, pected, was slowly suggesting itself to Catherine as something to wear.

"It looks like a belt," I heard her saying. "But what are all those little teeth . . ."

I felt Fiona's lips against my cheek, my upraised hand was wreathed in smoke, the delicate and time-pocked iron girdle was lying on the gray stone and, I saw in this hard light, was the brown and orange color of dried blood and the blue-green color of corrosion. I concentrated, we were all concentrating. Thinking of the blue sky and mustard-colored walls and brittle weeds and this bare stone, I studied Hugh's destructive exhibition, studied the small and rusted hinge, the thumb-sized rusted lock, the rather large tear-shaped pucker of metal and smaller and perfectly round pucker of metal that had been hammered, shaped, wrought into the second loop and that were rimmed, as Catherine had just noted, with miniature pin-sharp teeth of iron—kept my eyes on this artful relic of fear and jealousy and puffed my cigarette, listened to Catherine's heavy breathing, wondered which strapped and naked female body Hugh now had in mind.

"Anyway," Catherine said, "it's too small for me . . ."

"No," I murmured, "it's adjustable."

"Don't be afraid," Hugh said. "Pick it up. Show us how it works."

"Baby. Let's go, baby. Please."

"The only trouble is that we've only got one of these things instead of two."

"Shut up, Hugh," Catherine said, "for God's sake."

"But maybe one's enough. What do you think?"

And relenting, changing her mind, Fiona reached out one bare energetic arm and suddenly cupped Hugh's frozen jaw in her deliberate hand.

"Do you want me to try it on for you, baby," she said. "Is that what you want?"

Later that day, much later, I knew that Hugh was by no means appeased. The hot coal of desolation was still lodged in his eye. For the first time he stripped to the waist, discarding his denim jacket on the beach not a hundred paces from the villas where the three children shrieked, for the first time he exposed to us the pink and pointed nakedness of his partial arm. But nonetheless he refused to strip off his denim pants and accompany our nude trio into the black-and-white undulations of that deep sea. And every time I came up for air, curving thick arms like the horns of a bull and sucking in broad belly muscles and shaking spray, looking around now for Fiona, now for Catherine, inevitably I saw Hugh stretched out on the black pebbles with one knee raised and his good hand beneath his head, the little black iron trinket clearly visible on his white chest.

"You haven't seen the last of it," he called out once, "believe me."

But then Catherine came rolling toward me through the waves, over my shoulder I caught a glimpse of the dark and distant fortress, I felt a splash, and suddenly Fiona's wet face was next to mine.

"Baby, baby, baby, what can we do?"

NEED I INSIST THAT THE ONLY ENEMY OF THE MATURE
marriage is monogamy? That anything less than sexual multiplicity (body upon body, voice on voice) is naïve? That
our sexual selves are merely idlers in a vast wood?

What is marriage if not a vast and neutral forest in which
our own sexual selves and those of our first partners wander
until momentarily stopped in the clear actuality of encounter? Yes, the best of marriages are simply particular stands
of pale trees sensuously stitched into the yet larger tapestry,
which is not to say that our entire troup of sexual partners
(other than wives or husbands) need necessarily be composed of women or men who are themselves in turn already
committed to their own matrimonial partners. There are
exceptions. Not every finger is ringed. But why voice what
simply runs in the blood and fills the mind of any considerate man who has sat with another man's wife on his lap or
of any woman who has cast off prudery and tugged at cloth
and moved out among the trees? Only, I suppose, in peri-
odic answer to nagging detractors, only for the sake of those
who detest my convictions, scoff at my theories, denounce
my measured presence in the world of love. And only for
the sake of those other detractors, that handful of the soul-
less young whose lives of privileged sexuality have condi-
tioned them merely to deride my lyricism. But none of
them, none of the bitter aged and none of that arrogant
handful of the contemptuous young have tasted the love

lunch, for instance, or know anything at all about the sexual properties of my golden wheels of ripe cheese. Old and wheezing detractors should curb their judgment of a man who knows, after all, what he is talking about. To young detractors I will say only that if orgasm is the pit of the fruit then lyricism is its flesh. Marriage, or at least the mature marriage, is the fold that gathers in all lovers nude and alone.

WHEN CATHERINE COLLAPSED THAT DAY ON THE COLD stone floor of the squat church and in the midst of Hugh's meager yet highly emotional funeral service, it was Fiona who first thought of the three fatherless children, Fiona who made her immediate and selfless decision to take upon herself the responsibility of the children and carry them off.

To sum it up, as only last night I finally summed it up for Catherine, Hugh died and Catherine gave way to more than grief and Fiona departed with all three of those young and partially orphaned girls. Fiona and I knew exactly what was happening and what to do. Fiona knew her part and I knew mine. She went. I stayed. Fiona assumed management of the children as if they were hers, I undertook Catherine's recovery as if she were my wife instead of Hugh's. Fiona went off to impart womanhood to those three little growing girls, I stayed behind to explain Hugh's death to Catherine, to account for her missing children, to convince her that I was not, as she thought, responsible for all her losses, to renew our love.

Last night I talked and Catherine listened. My voice grew thick and confidential in the darkness, she put her hand on mine, she asked questions, every now and then she suddenly raised her wineglass and quickly drank. Exhilaration in the palm of peace? A further step in the dark?

Last night we sat beneath the grapes, Catherine and I, sat together side by side at the little rickety table in the arbor and ate the soft flakes of fish and the grapes on our plates and the bread, the wedges of cheese, sat together comfortably and tasted the dark red acidic tang of the wine and talked together, lapsed into silence. Arm over the back of my chair, glass in hand, I insisted on the accidental nature of Hugh's death, explained to Catherine that Hugh's death was an accident inspired, so to speak, by his cameras, his peasant nudes, his ingesting of the sex-song itself. It was not our shared love that had triggered Hugh's catastrophe. It was simply that his private interests, private moods, had run counter to the actualities of our foursome, so that his alien myth of privacy had established a psychic atmosphere conducive to an accident of that kind. Hugh's death hinged only on himself. And yet for that death even he was not to blame.

"Hugh was not a suicide," I murmured, "believe me."

Last night I covered that ground with all the simplicity and delicacy I could muster and shifted back to Fiona's motives in going off with the girls. My final low note of reassurance was that Fiona's departure was not, like Hugh's death, a finality. With or without the children, I said,

Fiona herself would one day be coming back to us. At any moment, or at some time in the distant future, Fiona would simply come looking for us through the funeral cypresses. It was not a certainty, of course, but that had been the tenor of our farewell. Nothing was fixed.

ROSELLA (OUR SMALL, DARK-EYED, SULLEN ROSELLA) HAS spurned them all. The brazen village lover no longer spends half the night calling to Rosella through the lacy darkness of the cypress trees, the married fishermen have abandoned hope of holding Rosella's hand. Even the old man who was the most vigorous and insistent of the lot, a short and barrel-chested old widower full of aggressive appreciation, no longer appears each dusk to tie his little female donkey in our lemon grove and to shake my hand, to glance covertly at Catherine, to tempt Rosella with his garrulous promises of lust and tenderness. Yes, I tell myself, they are gone, the lot of them, including the old man who left us one night forever with one hand thrust into his ragged pants and his great dark lecherous old face smiling in the grief of his last denial. Any one of them might have given Rosella a honeyed tongue, a life independent of the headless god. The old man would have put her back to work in the empty field, would have given her the donkey to lead along narrow thyme-scented paths of crushed shell, each night would have given her all the chuckling and naked magnificence of his uncountable years. But they are gone, all of them, and now the nights are filled with Rosella's would-be lovers brooding separately in their far-flung huts of stone. And reclining on the wicker settee next to Catherine, I smoke, I listen, I notice Rosella watching us. I think of the old widower rubbing his squat knees in the darkness. I miss him (simple-minded old man with an itch for love), Catherine misses him, Fiona would never have let him go. Only Rosella is indifferent to the still night and all her absent suitors spurned for me. She is here, she is a shadow, she is Hugh's last peasant nude.

How like Fiona to insist on helping Hugh, I thought. While Catherine walked with the children in the middle and I brought up the rear with the rusty shovel, my wife joined Hugh at the head of our burial party and, staggering slightly under her share of the weight of the coffin, helped lead the way. Fiona's mood was serious, her face was white, it was she and she alone who had to help Hugh carry the coffin. So from silver handles at either end, the small black top-heavy coffin swung between slender woman and slender man and journeyed slowly through the gloom of the noonday trees toward the hole which I, of course, would dig.

"Listen," I heard Hugh say under his breath, "am I going too fast for you?"

"No, baby. It's all right."

For a moment they looked at each other—two heads in significant profile, two lovers joined by their shiny burden.

213

I saw their glance, I valued it, I noted the tightened muscles of Fiona's bare arm, I balanced the rusted shovel on one shoulder and smelled the breeze. In my left hand I gripped the pitted iron shaft of the Byzantine cross. Widely separated, speckled in soft light, we were moving, softly moving, and underfoot the carpet of brown pine needles could not have been more appropriate to Meredith's misery or to the solemnity that Hugh and Fiona were casting over the occasion. For once Hugh was the father, Fiona had become a beautiful dry-eyed priestess for the dead dog and little girls. Catherine was doing her part, though Meredith refused to be consoled, and for the time being the two smaller children were behaving themselves. I too was enjoying the spirit of this unlikely hour.

No more old black dog, I told myself. No more wheezing in the darkness or paws on our bed at night. And how like Hugh to come to Fiona and me with the dead dog in his arms, how like him to leave the old animal's body for an entire day behind our villa while in one of the narrow streets of the town he managed to find an actual coffin that was small, black, thickly ornamented, and intended obviously for a child. Now only Meredith was sniffling, Meredith who would not hold Catherine's hand and who walked alone, while in our various ways the rest of us played out Hugh's game of burial.

"We can stop and rest if you like."

"It's OK, baby. It's OK."

Fiona believed in the grief of children. I, of course, did not. Fiona's short yellow shift and slender naked feet meant nothing, in no way contradicted the intensity of her mood as pallbearer. But that faint ring of impatience in Fiona's voice? Yes, that brief sound told me that Fiona herself suspected Hugh's motives, suddenly disliked his evident concern for her well-being at a time like this, doubted that the death of a fifteen-year-old decrepit dog justified all the elaborateness of Hugh's formal plan. No matter what I might think, Fiona was walking through this grove of death because of Meredith. Whereas Hugh was apparently moving to the rhythm of some dark death of his own.

Muted path, dark green light, rough music of Meredith's unhappiness. And Catherine, for whom all of this could only be one more domestic incident, was carrying little Eveline high on her hip and I was strolling after them and swinging the cross, shouldering my long-handled rusted shovel. Naturally it was Catherine, I mused, who had discovered the lifeless body of the dog, Catherine who had summoned Hugh, Catherine who had undertaken the job of telling Meredith. Yes, I thought, merely one more domestic incident for Catherine. But as a matter of fact, perhaps she was just as susceptible to her oldest daughter's grief and her husband's game as was Fiona. Why not assume that she was moved somehow, and like me was quite satisfied with her more pedestrian role in this makeshift ceremonial affair?

"Meredith, baby, stop crying. Please."

But crab grass? Familiar crab grass? Full circle at last? And was it really possible that Hugh had brought us full circle through the gloom of the trees and across the carpet of pine needles to this thin strip of gray sand and frieze of sharp-toothed brittle grass which had once concealed his outstretched body from Fiona's eyes but not from mine? Did he now intend the pitted cross in my left hand to mark not only the grave of the dog but also the very location where he himself had once sprawled dreaming his naked dream? Had he deliberately selected this spot of his lonely passion as the site for the pathetic grave? But was I reading the signs correctly? Was this in fact the same gray sand, the same black and fibrous crab grass? Yes, I told myself, none other, because now my field boots were sinking ankle-deep into familiar sand and Hugh's shadow was already stretched out and sleeping in that low and narrow plot behind the crab grass where I would drive the shovel.

"Don't say anything to spoil it, baby," Fiona whispered at my elbow. "I'm warning you."

So now the sonorous gloom of the trees had given way to the clear light of the empty beach. We were standing motionless together between trees and sea with the soft blue sky above us and, at our feet, the small and heavy casket stark on the sand. Bare-chested and thinking idly of incense, white-walled cemetery, family of anonymous mourners, white chapel housing a faceless priest, slowly I struck the shovel upright in the sand and glanced at Fiona, acknowledged her unnecessary admonition, gave her to understand that, as always, she had nothing to fear from her strong and acquiescent Cyril. But Fiona did not return my smile and my imaginary peasant mourners of a moment before were gone.

"Look what they're doing," Meredith said then. "Make them stop!"

Catherine glanced at Hugh, Hugh scowled, Fiona began to fidget though her eyes were gentle. For the first time that day I studied Meredith's little pinched pragmatic face and saw that she had been rubbing her eyes and nostrils with the back of her hand. Something was always wrong for Meredith, obviously something was already wrong with the funeral. Even the sight of Cyril leaning ready and sober on the handle of the upright shovel was not enough for Meredith. Not now at least.

"Dolores," Hugh said, "Eveline. Get away from the coffin."

"They're just playing," Catherine said. "Leave them alone."

"They're not playing," said Meredith, "they're trying to open it. Make them stop."

"Listen, Catherine. I'm telling you to get those children away from that coffin. Now do it."

More tears? Fresh cause for adolescent accusation? Or sudden shrieks of pain from the two small girls? Meredith in flight from the collapsing funeral and Hugh stalking off with Fiona? And all because the two fat little girls were flopping and climbing on the coffin at last and, in happy silence, were in fact tugging at the heavy lid which Hugh himself had feverishly screwed in place? Even while we four adults looked on (tall, quiet, silhouetted in the salty breeze, immobile, reluctant to move), now those two small children were setting upon the coffin with all the animation they had held in check from the moment our slow procession had first started off from the villas. Dolores was sitting astride the truncated high-topped brightly lacquered black coffin and riding it, beating upon its thick hollow-sounding sides with both fat hands. Little Eveline was pulling in fierce and speechless delight on the right-hand silver handle and laughing, kicking the sand, suddenly looking up at me. But now they were reversing themselves, scrambling to change places, so that Eveline was riding the fat black dolphin of the casket while Dolores was struggling on hands and knees to push the whole thing over. Eveline shouted, Dolores suddenly rested one plump cheek coquettishly against the slick hard surface of what she would never know was the old dog's lead-lined resting place. The casket moved, Hugh glowered. The casket tilted and sank a little deeper into the gray sand. I saw the cry of anger leaping to Meredith's thin lips.

"Don't just stand there, baby. Do something."

But then Catherine stooped down in matter-of-fact slow motion and pulled them off, drew them away, removed their offensive presence from the austere object of Meredith's despair, led them safely and with a few obvious maternal words to a low hummock of spongy grass and sat down holding them close against her upraised knees and warm and comforting torso. Hugh took two strides and put his long arm around Meredith's narrow and bony shoulders. Fiona sighed. Catherine squeezed her little culprits. I rubbed my chest. Once more funereal peace was ours.

"Meredith says she wants to dig the grave herself, boy, if it's all right with you."

"Sure," I said, turning away from the shovel. "It's hard work, but let her try."

So Hugh relinquished Meredith, whose eyes were more pink-rimmed than ever, I saw, and positioned himself close but not too close to Fiona, while in silence I aligned myself, so to speak, with Catherine. In our semicircle around the would-be grave we allowed ourselves no talking, no more secret signals, as if at last to convince poor Meredith of our complete attention.

"Whenever you want me to take over, Meredith," I said, "just let me know."

But she recoiled from my offer as I knew she must, and thin, disheveled, with her outgrown childish light green frock only partially buttoned up the back (having refused Catherine's early morning commiseration, having allowed no one to button the dress or comb her short-cropped hair), she bent herself to the task which she could not possibly accomplish. The handle of the shovel was much too long for Meredith, the flat rusted blade much too heavy. Never had she been so insistent, never had she been so cruelly indulged, while the four of us silently waited and looked on.

The shovel scraped in the sand, she held her breath, she twisted and swung her arms, a little shower of moist sand fell through the breeze. On she went, concentrating, wearing down, glancing at Hugh between each stroke. And then Meredith simply threw down the shovel. She broke her awkward rhythm and admitted defeat, not by making some kind of agreeable teary appeal to the waiting and bare-chested friend of her father, but simply by turning full in my direction, hefting high above her head the shovel, holding it aloft in both stiff and frail arms, and then flinging it down. It was a gesture far more vehement than I had expected, and yet no doubt Meredith's sudden display of unmistakable temper was preferable to any soft-voiced appeal for my assistance. And at least this little wasted interlude was at an end.

"Listen, Meredith," I said, passing her, deciding suddenly

that fury might be a symptom of true grief after all, "whatever wakes up has to go back to sleep. Think about it, Meredith. OK?"

My fully rounded words, my wrinkled forehead, my athletic size, the faint smell of lemon juice on my sun-tanned skin and the hazy smell of white wine on my breath—none of it meant anything to Meredith, of course, who walked deliberately within striking distance of my seductive speech and refused to answer. I saw the fresh tears, the angry eyes, even the pale strawberry-like impression of the vaccination on one bare upper arm, and I was as close as I would ever come to feeling what Meredith must have been feeling at the loss of her dog. But it was hopeless, and I could only shrug and lean down, removing heavy hands from tight hip pockets, and seize the abandoned shovel and prepare to dig.

"Take your time, boy," Hugh called gruffly. "Make it deep."

With the first full thrust of the rusted shovel into the coarse sand, I both destroyed the original dark drifting mood of our death party and restored it. On the one hand I was breaking ground, making irreparable crunching sounds with the shovel, merely digging a hole in the wet substance of a narrow strip of gray beach. And yet on the other hand the grave was opening. Yes, I thought, poor Hugh's funeral fantasy had given way suddenly to one large half-naked man working slowly and steadily on an empty beach. Grief had given way to industry. And yet my thoughtful exertion pointed toward the moment when the pitted cross would stand in place and the contemplation of mystery (if that's what Hugh thought it was) could be resumed.

220

My physical labor, my concentration, my upper body beginning to shine mildly with sweat, the unmistakable flashing movements of my golden spectacles and large and low-slung belt buckle of dull pewter, the serenity of my dripping face, and the deepening trench, the flowering grave—all this was exactly what Hugh wanted in spite of himself, I knew, and so I prolonged the brutal practicalities and continued to dig, to shave the walls of my wet pit in the sand. I recalled Hugh's tactless confession of a few hours before ("She asked me if you and Fiona had to come along, boy. I said you did.") and realized that if Meredith had had her way, had in fact been able to disrupt the firm community of our two families, there would have been only Catherine to dig the grave or to share that task with her mournful and disabled husband. But better me, I thought, better old Cyril with his good wind, two good hands, steady arms, brown and hair-tinged abdomen hard as a board. Yes, this work was to my liking, I told myself, and noted that both Hugh and Fiona were staring out over my bent or rising figure as if they could see some distant apparition of the black dog yelping and floundering on the horizon. Alone as I was for once, alone with my cream-colored calfskin field boots sopping up water and my tight denims gritty and streaked with sand, still I could not help but admire Hugh's fierce expression and Fiona's refusal to hold Hugh's hand or touch her hip to his.

"Done," I called, and tossed out the shovel and climbed from the grave in one slow unobtrusive motion appropriate to the man who had dug to the center of Hugh's fantasy and laid bare the wet and sandy pit of death. Slowly I brushed at the wet sand on my denims, took a fresh breath

221

and surveyed the deep empty trench and the remarkably high pile of inert yet trickling sand. Deeper than necessary, higher than necessary, stark. Already my chest and arms were drying and I did not regret the magnitude of those expressive scars on the beach.

"Look," I heard myself saying then, "a visitor . . ."

"But, baby," Fiona whispered, "he's got a dog!"

I nodded, though Fiona had already turned to stare again toward the dark trees and tall approaching man and leaping dog, as had Hugh, whose fist was clenched, and Catherine who had climbed to her feet and was holding close her small and obviously frightened girls.

"He's a shepherd," I murmured. "And he may not be quite right in the head. You can tell by that odd angular gait of his."

"We've got to get rid of him, boy. Send him off."

"When he sees the coffin, he'll want to help us mourn."

"Oh, baby, how awful."

"Be friendly, Fiona. That's all we can do."

"But that damn dog, boy. It's just like ours."

"Yes," I said, "too bad for Meredith."

"Tell him the party is private, baby. Please."

"Can't offend him, Fiona. Bad luck."

He raised one long black-sleeved bony arm in innocent greeting. Carelessly he swung a long white slender crook in time to his steady but unrhythmical gait. He was fast approaching, and all the incongruous details were clear enough—the shapeless and once formal black coat and trousers, the absence of shirt or socks or shoes, the short black hair suggesting the artless conscientious work of the village barber, the stately and yet ungainly size, the slender crook. Yes, I told myself, hearing his sharp whistle and noting that the whistle had no effect on the fat and mangy black dog bearing down on us, in every way our approaching stranger exemplified the typical shepherd who was bound to keep an illiterate family in the village and yet spend his days and nights roaming from thorny field to secret watering spot with his nomadic sheep.

"Hugh, baby," Fiona whispered then, apparently forgetting Catherine, Meredith, me, the funeral itself, "he looks like you."

But before I could comment on this latest of Fiona's aesthetic judgments, suddenly the appealing and yet repellent figure of the shepherd was standing a shadow's length from the casket and frowning and crossing himself, while now his dog lay groveling and whimpering in the sand at Meredith's feet.

"It's a different dog, Meredith," I said. "He's a lot younger than yours. Besides, he's got that white star on his chest. Listen, if you pat his head a few times he'll leave you alone."

"Never mind, baby, it's all right. We'll pat him together."

With obvious disregard for everyone but Meredith, quickly Fiona stepped to the child's side, knelt down, put a thin strong arm around her waist and firmly began to stroke the head of the dog. It was a small but totally absorbing example of Fiona's swift feminine purpose, another one of Fiona's golden pebbles dropped into her bottomless well of rose water. We heard that sound, we saw her move, we watched.

"Look at the way your shepherd is staring at Fiona, boy. I don't like it."

Had the circumstances been other than what they were, had there been no children, no coffin, no open grave on the beach, and had we four met the tall intruder while swimming or among the pines in some dense secluded grove where we might have sat with our spread white cloth and Fiona's array of wicker baskets, then surely Fiona would have been her usual self and would have touched the man's arm, paired him up with Hugh, would have softened to his fixed smile, his indifference to loneliness, his broad and crooked shoulders. But not now. She had made her decision. She was concentrating on Meredith and the shepherd's dog. And did he know all this? Had he understood this much of my kneeling wife in that single frank sweep of his dark unfocused eyes? Had he caught the pretentious tone of Hugh's remark and decided to heed that hostile sound? Was he more concerned with our funeral than with Fiona?

Slowly he stepped forward and offered his bony right hand first to Hugh and then to me, and in the grip of those cold and calloused fingers even Hugh must have begun to comprehend what our unwanted intruder meant to say: that he had slept in dark caves, that he had buried countless dead ewes, that he also knew what it was like to bury children, that only men could work together in the service of death, that death was for men, that now his only interest was in the one-armed man and bare-chested man and the coffin. The rest of it (our wives, our children) meant nothing to him. Only death mattered. He had joined us only because of the coffin.

224

"Meredith," Hugh was saying then, abruptly, gruffly, "the shepherd is going to help Cyril and me. You better watch."

Together Hugh and I lifted the coffin, moved in unison through the crab grass, and approached the wet hole where the mute and barefooted figure already stood waiting, shovel in hand. The flatness of the sea before us reflected the gloom and silence of the wall of trees at our backs. The hole, soon to be filled, was ringed, I saw, with the deep fresh impressions of the shepherd's feet. No birdcall, no tolling bell. Only the sound of Hugh's breath and the rising of the salty breeze and across the open grave the white face of the shepherd.

"You better gather around," Hugh said. "All of you."

"Meredith, baby. This is the way it is in real life. Don't be sad."

"Ready, boy?"

"Ready."

At either end of the grave we knelt and took hold of the silver grips and swung the coffin over the open grave. Together we eased the small black heavy coffin down until it rested finally in the sea-smelling dark water that lay in the bottom of the hole. I was sure that behind us Fiona was restraining Meredith. And was Fiona thinking what I was thinking? Was she too recalling the old half-drowned animal in my wet arms? No, I thought, Fiona did not share my interest in coherence and full circles. For better or worse, Fiona lived free of the shades of memory.

But it was not at all a question of restraining Meredith. She was not struggling to plunge toward the grave, as I had expected, but instead was kneeling with her hands clasped gently and her thin white face raised happily toward the black-and-white figure of the shepherd who was now filling the grave. Sitting back on her heels, Meredith appeared to be quite unconscious of Fiona's long fingers stroking her hair or of the dog's head resting in her lap. Only the shepherd mattered for Meredith, and despite his concentration and violent labor, the tall man was obviously aware of the admiring child.

"I'm afraid of him," Catherine whispered.

"No need to be," I murmured, and brushed the sand from the hair on my chest, felt little Dolores encircling my tight and heavy thigh with a stealthy arm.

Bare foot raised to the edge of the black and pitted blade, coat open, chest and belly now and again exposed in both a poverty and pride of nakedness, broad and crooked shoulders twisting suddenly to the thrust of the long arm and invulnerable bare foot—all this was observed in silence as slowly the pile of sand went down and the shadows lengthened and the light of the afternoon grew still more pale. In this physical act of covering up forever what he assumed to be the small body of an infant dressed for death, the shepherd was providing Meredith with a performance which I, had it been me, would surely not have attempted. But even now I suspected that Meredith, so seldom treated to anything she herself desired, had probably forgotten the reason we were waiting at the edge of this grave. And yet if Meredith was having a little excitement, I thought, what did it matter if momentarily she had forgotten her old dog? After all, I thought, the afternoon really belonged to Hugh.

"Oh, baby, a flute . . ."

226

From a pocket in his open coat the shepherd had produced a short wooden pipe on which he now played his reedy tune for Meredith. The light faded, the rising wind blew through the open coat, his unfocused eyes were fixed on Meredith, the bony fingers rose and fell on the holes of the crude pipe. Had he known all along that he would stand here playing his shepherd's pipe? Was this why he had joined us and taken up the shovel? Only to pipe his endless frail tune into the approaching night? At least Meredith would never forget those sounds, I told myself. Nor, for that matter, would Hugh.

He was still playing when I retrieved the shovel, still playing when once again we straggled back into the wall of trees. And still playing when from the darkness ahead, where Hugh and Fiona were quite invisible, I heard against the wind and that faint piping the clear tones of Fiona's voice.

"He was attractive, baby. But not as attractive as you."

IT IS ANOTHER ONE OF OUR MURMUROUS NONSEQUENTIAL midafternoons in Illyria. Together we lounge around the small white female donkey which only this morning Hugh discovered stock-still in the lemon grove. Hugh holds the donkey's rope. Catherine ties back her hair, Fiona smiles, all four of us have taken turns at the makeshift shower.

"Listen," Hugh says, "we can either pack the baskets on the donkey and walk. Or Cyril can carry the baskets and

Fiona can ride the donkey. What do you say, boy, shall Fiona ride?"

"Sure," I say, admiring the little trim white body and pearl-colored hoofs, "let Fiona ride."

"Help me up, baby. OK?"

We face each other, we kiss, we look into each other's eyes. I put my heavy hands on Fiona's waist and lift and seat Fiona sidesaddle (though there is no saddle) on the donkey's rump. I step away, Hugh gives the end of the rope to Fiona and puts his quick hand against the small of her back.

"I'll hold her on, boy. Don't worry."

Fiona waves. Off they go at a fast walk through the lemon trees which soon give way to orange trees white with blossoms.

"Wait," Catherine whispers, "they'll see."

"Can't wait," I say, and pull her into another full-length embrace, mouth to mouth with Catherine's hands in my hair and my own two weathered hands pressing the warm flesh beneath the blouse and beneath the wide waistband of Catherine's skirt. We hold each other, we erupt into a few choppy kisses, again we hold each other—Catherine and I who are too heavy to ride on donkeys, too large in each other's arms to move.

And yet I lift my head, Catherine lifts her head, for a moment we see that all this while Fiona has been riding back and forth between the trees, Fiona with her bare legs thrust out for balance and steadied at the same time by her smiling Hugh. They wave, the air is sweet, the small white distant donkey carries its laughing and weightless burden through the orange trees.

"Baby," Fiona calls, "we can do whatever we want to do. We really can."

Remember?

O<small>R IN THE SEA AND SWIMMING, ALL FOUR OF US SIDE BY</small> side in an undulating line of naked bathers peaceful, untiring, synchronized, stroking our slow way out from the pebbly shore behind us and forward toward the little island rising ahead. And today Hugh is as naked as the rest of us. Today he lies in the low waves beside Fiona and his body rolls, his tufts and patches of black hair shine in the foam, his thin legs are cutting imaginary paper, his stump is pink, his good arm is doing double duty.

"Think we'll make it, boy?"

"Sure we will. Only a few hundred yards or so to go. Nothing to it."

Porpoises. Four large human porpoises similarly disposed and holding formation, laughing, stroking the waves, and Fiona is swimming on her side, like Hugh, while Catherine and I are riding heads down and on our bellies, though now and again we swing together and bump and touch. With every breath we see each other through pink spray and across green foam.

"Baby, it's so beautiful. I could swim forever."

It is Fiona's idea, of course, these naked watery idyls to the little island that slopes up from the sea and gently turns like the bare brown sinuous shoulder of a young girl.

And the idea corresponds somehow to Fiona herself and to the experience—in the idea as in the sea itself we snort, kick, float, swim on as if the less familiar shore will never rise to our feet or as if the freshening depths will never give way to the warm shallows.

But it ends. We drift against the island, and Fiona is out and running, and silvery wet-ribbed Hugh is gasping for the breath of paradise but giving chase. Sea to sand, obviously it is another moment of metamorphosis which Catherine and I, still dripping, still knee-deep in the pale tide, share at a glance. Her hair is plastered to cheek, neck, upper chest, and down her left arm. Her small amber-colored eyes are fixed on mine. She is large but I am larger, and side by side we climb from the pooling sea and walk together across the few remaining feet of dry sand to the privacy of the nearest convenient rocks behind which I draw Catherine into another full-length embrace. And suddenly Catherine is all mouth, all stomach, all thighs and hands, all salt and skin and hair, Catherine sliding between my heavy legs and I between hers until later, much later, our knees can spread no wider and the brass voice resounding in the oracle of Catherine's sex and mine can sing no more. We extricate ourselves. We kiss. We smile. I strip the wet and partially graying hair from Catherine's cheek. Hand in hand we walk back to the clear green shallows for a rinse and then strike off across the sand for our usual cool rendezvous with thin Hugh and slender Fiona in the little abandoned seaside chapel at the eastern edge of this small timeless island.

Hugh and Fiona are already inside when we arrive, their sandy footprints already shine on the stone floor when we join them within the whitewashed wall of the little chapel. There is a cross of sorts on the roof but no windows, no altar, no iron bell, no icons, no religious furniture, as if the chapel itself had once been drowned in the depths of our green sea and then hauled to the surface and left to dry out forever. We enter, Catherine and I, knowing that Hugh and Fiona are already there. In silence we greet each other with eyes and fingers, we who are now four naked figures instead of two. There is light in the narrow doorway, the white and shadowed eruptions of this room reflect the nudity of our four tall bodies congregating, so to speak, in reunion. And if we are all comparing notes, as it were, Fiona smiling at Catherine and squeezing my arm, Hugh glancing slowly in my direction, Catherine watching the movement of Fiona's legs and thinking of me, I catching a glimpse of Hugh in Fiona's steady eyes—still we are all unpaired self-less lovers agreeably reunited in the island chapel.

"Baby," Fiona whispers, "I like us all bare together, don't you?"

I smile, Hugh tucks the tip of his injured arm against Fiona's ribs. We linger on.

Remember?

"YOU'RE WEARING YOUR NICE OLD DRESSING GOWN," Fiona was saying. "Have fun, baby."

"I could stick around here tonight just as well, Fiona. What do you think?"

"You're feeling amorous, baby, and she's expecting you. I can tell."

"This blue mood's not like you, Fiona. I'll stay."

"No baby. Go ahead. Please."

Yes, I was feeling amorous, as Fiona said. All day long I had sat outside our villa and watched Fiona's mounting silence, had sat with elbows propped on heavy thighs and blown halfhearted, stillborn, unappreciated smoke rings and watched Fiona walking back and forth with her head down and her two strong hands on her buttocks. We had stared at each other over the flashing rims of our wineglasses, we had had one of our love lunches, as Fiona called them, but had made no love. She had smiled, she had looked wan, she had made no move to walk beyond the villa. And all day long there had been no sign of Hugh. So now in the darkness there was no mistaking the message of Fiona's hand on my silken sleeve, no use arguing against Fiona's mood. She was determined that I go, that she stay behind, that she wait alone either for my return or Hugh's unlikely arrival. But Fiona was wearing her white and tightly belted terry-cloth robe instead of her lisle negligee, which suggested that she would spend the night with neither one of us.

"I won't be long."

"No hurry, baby. I'm going to read."

"Listen," I murmured, "if he shows up . . ."

But before I could allude to the innumerable incidents that might have justified Fiona's hopes, suddenly I felt her cold hand on my mouth and her thin fingers against my lips and could say no more. Was all Hugh's excitement to come to nothing? Was Fiona to be denied?

"I told you, baby. I'm going to read."

My hands were in the loose pockets of my maroon-colored silken dressing gown, Fiona's long insistent fingers were still pressed to my lips. The day that was like no other day in our lives was ended, the night that was like no other night would soon be gone. And nodding, aware of the narrow featureless white face in the darkness and the white tufted robe which I could not bring myself to touch, for the first time I contemplated the possibility that Hugh might have managed to keep himself in ignorance of Catherine and me, as a matter of fact, might simply waste all his obvious devotion to Fiona and hence hers to him. Was it over? Was it never to begin?

"It's just not going to happen, baby. I was wrong."

I thought of all she refused to let me say, I thought of Hugh and Fiona listening to the nightingale, I heard them laugh. I saw Hugh catching her close among the silent trees. And now only the two of us with our perplexity, our depression, our separate thoughts? We had had our disappointments in the past, our reversals, but nothing like this. Nothing quite as simple and stark and final as this.

"You better go, baby. Come back when you want to."

So the day had already struck the toneless note of the night's silence before darkness fell, and already the mood of the woman I was leaving had telegraphed itself, it seemed to me, to the woman I was about to meet. If Fiona was beyond my reach, I decided, Catherine was perhaps no better off. If my wife was pensive, Hugh's wife would be pensive too. Solitude did not bode well for amorous feeling. So even before I pushed my way through the funeral cypresses, moving slowly and more ruminative than ever, already I was anticipating the pauses that would precede companionship, the reluctance that would greet my tenderness. I too was moody. The night was a black heart. I misjudged the whereabouts of the rift in the funeral cypresses and was forced to retrace my steps and feel my way through the no longer familiar passage between the trees. Perhaps Catherine was sleeping. Perhaps she was not lying awake for me at all as Fiona had thought. And still there was no sign of Hugh and I did nothing to disguise the sounds of my slow approach, thinking that we lovers in fact were bound to suffer at the hands of the lovers in fancy.

But mistaken. Totally mistaken. Because as soon as I invaded Hugh's dark villa and entered that cold room, I knew immediately that it was worse than I thought, that it was no mere question of blue moods or vague romantic numbness, but that something was wrong, something specifically and painfully wrong.

"Catherine? What's the matter?"

The shutters were open, the low bed was empty. I waited. I listened for the sleeping children and sleeping dog, heard nothing. But there at the foot of the empty bed stood Catherine with her dark hair loose and arms at her sides and wearing the white translucent pajama top and pants. There she stood, immobile, opalescent, poignant, and suddenly I knew that she had been standing there for hours.

"Catherine. What's wrong?"

I saw the turned-down bed, from somewhere in the darkness of this thick-walled room I detected the scent of the three large cream-colored roses which I had picked and brought with me the night before. Nothing and yet everything had changed. But why, I asked myself, what had happened? Why was Catherine breathing with such deep regularity and watching me with such willful silence, as if Hugh himself were hidden bolt upright in one of the other darkened corners of the room? Or had he instead departed? Simply packed up his cameras and disappeared? But Catherine and I were alone, safely though uncomfortably alone, and no matter how Hugh chose to treat his wife, surely nothing could induce him to abandon the garden in which Fiona flowered.

"Catherine, what's happened? What's wrong?"

Mere empty bed, mere silent woman, mere smell of the night, mere fading scent of the roses, mere smell of useless cologne on my naked chest. But this could not be all, I told myself, and again I was convinced that Catherine was now more than ever in need of my patience, my tenderness.

"Listen. There's something you want me to know but don't want to say. What is it?"

I moved close to Catherine and placed my firm hands on her sloping shoulders.

"Fiona's not herself tonight," I said gently. "Neither are you."

"I wish you hadn't come."

"But you've been expecting me."

"Yes. But you'd better go."

"Is it Hugh?"

"It's not Hugh."

"Tell me. What's he done?"

"Nothing."

"Catherine, put your arms on my shoulders and your hands in my hair. Kiss me."

"I can't. I just can't."

"Well, I'm not going to leave you like this. You know I'm not."

"But that's what I want."

And if I did what she asked? If suddenly I assumed that Catherine meant what she said and that this new temperamental turn of hers was an ordinary, insignificant, familiar condition of only a single night's duration and nothing more? If I nodded, kissed her cheek, left quietly, retraced my steps? If I simply went back and shared the smoky glow of Fiona's lamp and spent the rest of these dark hours listening to Fiona read aloud? Was this the answer? But what then of Fiona's unhappy hunch? If I left this room, might not the import of Fiona's hunch prove as true for Catherine and me as for Fiona and Hugh? And what of Hugh? Where was he? Even now Hugh's absence was a sinuous presence in this cold room.

I withdrew my hands from Catherine's shoulders, dropped my arms, turned, tightened my silken sash, and sat down on the edge of the bed. I thought of Hugh yearning for Fiona and punishing all four of us with the fervor of his deprivation. And I thought of Fiona robed in white and consoling herself with her book of poems and sipping wine. Nothing and yet everything had changed.

"Join me, Catherine," I said. "You might as well."

Slumped on the edge of Catherine's bed, skirts of the dressing gown drawn prudently across my pajamaed knees, chin in hand, low-keyed invitation still unanswered—slowly I realized that Catherine was going to settle for docility. Without speaking, without argument, without emotion, as if all our former procedures preliminary to affection had never existed, Catherine accepted my invitation not by seating herself beside me in any kind of readiness to talk, but simply by stretching herself out behind me on that low bed. In another woman docility would have said only that sex was going to get us nowhere. But not in Catherine. In Catherine docility meant something else, something more. But what?

Carefully I moved, thinking of our mimosa tree bereft in the darkness, carefully I swung up my legs and crossed my ankles, lay back carefully and quietly beside the full length of Catherine's body. What else could I do? How else could I be except placid, undemonstrative, leisurely, totally considerate of Catherine's docile body next to mine? But if I could have been wrong, if I myself could have been mistaken about Fiona and Catherine and even Hugh? If Fiona had decided just for once on the necessity of deception, and had actually spent this day not inuring herself to loss but anticipating a secret assignation with Hugh? If terry-cloth robe and poems were a harmless ruse? If Fiona were now lying at last with her arms around Hugh on the rough and sloping floor of his darkened studio, and if what was wrong with Catherine depended only on her so interpreting Hugh's absence—if all this could have been true, then Fiona's pleasure would have been my pleasure while Catherine's jealousy would have been no match for the heat of my love. But the night was long and dark and silent. And it was not true. None of it was true. Fiona had never felt the need to deceive me in the past, so why now? Catherine had felt no jealousy since Hugh first made plain his self-thwarted attraction for Fiona. Why now?

"Confide in me, Catherine. What else can you do?"

She said nothing. She did not move. She remained flat

on her back in her own way determined to acquiesce, if that's what I demanded, but equally determined to offer me no encouragement, no help. So I shifted, rolled onto my left side, raised myself, stared down at what I could see of Catherine's shadowed face. Slowly but firmly I placed my free hand on Catherine's body. All this I did, not with any interest in arousing Catherine against her will but only as a matter of course, a tactile act of comfort. The movement of my hand was personal but not exploratory. I meant to convey the sensation of the palm of my large hand, not the fingers. But apparently even this, to Catherine, was more than she wanted. Apparently she was not as determined to acquiesce as I had thought.

"Stop," she said quietly and yet not so quietly. "I wish you'd stop."

But too late, I thought, too late. Because suddenly I felt beneath my hand the unmistakable presence of something hard, something foreign, something distinctly different from the soft malleable flesh of Catherine's waist. It was too late to stop.

"What," I whispered, with hand arrested, mind leaping forward, voice giving way atypically to surprise, "what . . . ?"

No light in Catherine's open eyes, no sounds of confession on Catherine's lips, no effort on Catherine's part to dissuade me, to disengage my heavy hand from where it lay on her waist. I paused, she waited. And suspended there in the darkness between my whispered exclamation and what I now knew with reasonable certainty to be its cause, slowly I felt a single cold drop of sweat trickling its telltale passage down my naked side. But was it possible? Was my hand touching what I thought it touched? One minute I was sweating for Catherine and the next I was sliding my hand beneath the edge of Catherine's pajama top and with my bare hand touching the band of metal which now I knew beyond a doubt was girdling her waist. And just as methodically I thrust my fingers between Catherine's unmoving thighs until beneath the mere breath of white cotton cloth I felt the little sharp pointed teeth of that elongated narrow tear of iron wedged tightly and unmistakably between her thighs.

"Catherine, it can't be true . . ."

"Yes," she said quietly. "I didn't want you to know."

"How could he do it? How could you let him . . . ?"

"He made me. That's all."

"All night long you've been wearing this wretched thing. . ."

Bruise? Blemish? Specific source of Catherine's pain? Her only answer was to disengage my hand at last. She did not speak, did not move, except to take hold of my hand and remove it slowly and gently from where it no longer belonged between her legs. I felt her hand, I smelled her hair, Hugh's message could hardly have been more clear. And I understood that it was meant for me, that message, and suddenly I understood that Hugh was not at all idling away those dark hours on the empty beach or brooding alone at the unshuttered window of his bare room above the black canal. I knew where he was. I knew exactly where to find him.

"What are you doing?"

"Nothing. I'll be back."

She made no objection. She asked for no explanation. And when I returned she would still be there, waiting in the darkness and making no effort to free herself from that iron web which Hugh had somehow brought himself to adjust to Catherine's size and lock in place.

"I won't be long. Trust me."

Of course, I told myself, the wicker settee. Where else would he be if not stretched out even now in the darkness of the grape arbor? How like him to wait for me on the very piece of furniture from which I had watched Fiona resolving herself to so much unnecessary solitude. How like him to wait for darkness and then steal onto our side of the funeral cypresses and into my arbor, which was what he must have done, to usurp my place beneath the grapes he scorned, only to lie inactive, silent, within easy earshot of the plaintive voice of the very woman whose calm unhappiness was the result of what she took to be his absence, his unknown whereabouts. But all that time he had been there and must have listened to Fiona's quiet declaration and heard all we said, quickened at the sound of Catherine's name and writhed, as it were, at my own words that sealed the purpose of my departure. And to him it must have seemed too late to undo the damage he had done to Catherine, to all of us, no matter what he might have felt upon hearing the sad ring of Fiona's voice. But perhaps our blue moods had meant nothing to Hugh. Perhaps they had only heightened his agonized elation over what he knew I was setting off to encounter in that dark villa of his. Love never had so fierce an antagonist, I thought, never had Fiona and I been so unfortunate.

"That you, boy?"

"You know it is."

"Well, I've been waiting for you."

"Yes," I murmured, "I guess you have."

From where I stood the glow of Fiona's lamp was invisible. High overhead the night sky was packed and streaked with colonies and continents of stars that gave no light. And yet I knew where I was, had already heard and answered the voice that had spoken up suddenly inside the arbor. It was obviously the voice of a man reclining, a voice that had accosted me from behind a thick invisible wall of flat and matted leaves, a voice so close and soft-spoken and yet at the same time so screened and deeply buried that in the very instant of sound it transformed my gentle arbor into a cavern of black leaves. Hugh was lying inside that cavern and filling it with his distasteful eagerness and, I guessed, the pain of all the dark time he had spent rehearsing himself for my arrival.

"Come on in, boy. I want to talk to you."

I felt the leaves in my hair, the leaves against the sides of my head, the leaves thick and black and suddenly meaningless against one silken shoulder. And now without answering Hugh's pathetic effort to gain the upper hand I simply entered the arbor, noted in silence the darker elongated mass of shadow that was only Hugh deceptively at rest, and seated myself, as I had known I would, on our now cold and otherwise empty bench of stone. I crossed my heavy and loosely pajamaed legs, leaned forward, clasped together my two weathered hands, found myself regretting that this my trysting place had now become the scene of tribunal. We were alone. We would eat no grapes, drink no wine. Again I became aware of the smell of my cologne. Despite the darkness, I was sure that Hugh was dressed for the night chill in his old pea jacket. And was Hugh as conscious as I was of the scent of my cologne? And equally conscious that I, unlike himself, was dressed for love and sleep and was perfectly at home, so to speak, in the night temperature? No doubt he was. But while I felt only indifference for all my advantages, nonetheless I made no effort to subdue the formidable seriousness of my presence on this stone bench in my ruined arbor.

"Why don't you smoke, boy? It'll be easier for you."

But I was resolute. I was sensible. I was silent. I let it pass. From where Hugh half lay, half sat in the darkness I heard the faint orchestrated sounds of the squeaking wicker, the dry fibrous sounds of Hugh's suddenly uncontrollable agitation. He could not contain himself. He knew he was wrong. Even while waiting to laugh in my face he was already trying to eliminate the traces of black scum from the sound of his voice.

"How's Catherine?"

"Feeling the way you do," I said then, speaking more promptly and impersonally than I had intended, "you have no right to ask."

"How is she, boy?"

"Let's just hope Fiona doesn't find out what you've done."

"Your little visit was pretty short. What's wrong?"

"You know what's wrong."

"She say anything? Or did she just throw you out as I told her to?"

"I got your message, Hugh, if that's what you mean."

"You got my message. Well, it must have been quite a shock."

"Don't you know what you've done?"

"I know you've been sucking two eggs at once, that's what I know. But it's over. It's finished."

"You haven't felt this way before. Why now?"

"Slow, boy, slow. But I found out. You understand?"

"So tonight's your night."

"Planned the whole thing beforehand, boy. And you fell right into it. I guess you just walked right in there and told my wife to strip on down as usual and then found out there's one easy way to stop that sort of thing. I made it pretty plain. The lid's on the jar. It's all over. You've been trying to get into my wife ever since that damn bus went off the road. And now you can't."

"Are you through?"

"For some men one woman's not enough. Some men would suck all the eggs in sight, if they could. But you're finished. From now on you're going to stick to just one woman, understand?"

"Listen," I said quietly, and stood up in the darkness of our trembling arbor, "Catherine and I have been having perfectly normal relations since the first night we sat right here together on this very bench. Normal, ordinary, uninterrupted relations," I said, hands in pockets, head in the leaves, "from that first night until a few moments ago. Why should they end?"

"I've been waiting for this. Keep talking."

"And now you decide to come on the scene. You make up your mind. You imagine the whole thing as if it began last night or the night before. You decide you're jealous. You decide to interfere. But you can't interfere and everything you say is wrong."

"There's nothing you can do about it. Not a damn thing."

243

"When I'm through with you I'm going back to Catherine. I'm going to take that thing off her as gently as I can. I'll try to undo the harm you've done."

"So you won't stop. You won't leave her alone."

"If Catherine doesn't want me to stop, as you put it, why should I?"

"All right, sit down. Let's have it out."

"I don't feel like sitting down."

"Vomit, boy. Think I'm going to vomit . . ."

"After what you've done to Catherine, you might as well."

"I can't bear this business. Catherine can't bear it either."

"Wrong again."

"She hates it, boy."

"You've hurt Catherine. You've hurt me. You've hurt Fiona. Catherine just hates your jealousy. All of us do."

"My villa . . my bed . . . my wife . . . with the children in the next room . . . and you in the nude and crawling all over my marriage . . ."

"Listen," I said then, tasting the night, feeling the dead sand beneath the soles of my tennis shoes, "there's nothing wrong with your marriage, such as it is."

Would he retch as he promised? Would invisible Hugh lean over the side of Fiona's settee and retch on the sand? Hugh tightly buttoned into his pea jacket and filling our cold cavern with the smell of his vomit? Hugh gagging and appealing to me for help? Yes, I thought, I would have welcomed even this most disagreeable act of Hugh's discomfort. But it was not to be, as I might have known, and even the passing threat of Hugh's nausea was already gone. And yet his next whispered words were so constricted, so sour, that he might well have coughed up the acidic spume of his agony in one silent heave while I waited, listened, heard nothing at all.

"She took off her clothes. She lay on her back. She tongued you, boy. With Meredith lying there in the next room."

"Meredith's mind is like her father's. It's time she grew up."

"Let me tell you something. You deserve that damn belt. Both of you . . ."

"All right," I said, quietly, slowly, "on your feet."

"At least it's ingenious. You have to admit it's pretty ingenious . . ."

"Hugh," I said again, "stand up."

"You think I'm afraid of last resorts? I thought the damn thing was going to come apart in my hands. But it didn't. It fit, it worked. I found my own way to take care of the problem. And you can't fight it . . ."

"For the last time, Hugh, on your feet."

"I'm crafty, boy, crafty. And that damn belt's a work of art . . ."

But behind Hugh's desperate whispering I heard the squeal of wicker, the expelled breath of exertion, all the slow begrudging sounds of Hugh pulling himself out of the settee and uncoiling, rising, standing half erect and wary in the darkness of dead grapes and forgotten leaves. Feet apart, single hand held before his face and ready, head averted, and waiting, licking his lips, listening—there he stood, invisible and yet to me defined by all I knew about him and by every furtive sound he tried to conceal. But did Hugh know that I was blocking the entrance to the arbor? And

was he even now expecting to join Fiona's always reasonable husband in some unthinkable scuffle here on the sandy
floor of this same arbor where all four of us had burned our
candles and drunk our wine? Yes, I thought, even now he
was perhaps attempting to feel out the direction of the first
blow, his or mine. How like him to so mistake my tone.
How like him to assume that I, for one moment, would
ever allow him to fall back on his lanky aggression. How
like him to assume that my wedding ring could ever split
the chin of Catherine's husband and the man Fiona loved.

"Where are you, boy?"

"Right here, Hugh. Don't worry."

"Jockeying for position, is that it?"

"I haven't moved."

"Well, here I am. What next?"

"If Catherine and Fiona could see us now," I murmured,
taking a step, pausing at the sudden eruption of defensive
shuffling sounds in the sand, "what would they think? How
would they feel?"

"Maybe I ought to go off. I'll leave. I'll let you have her.
Is that what you want? Maybe I'll just go off with the dawn
and be done with it. You don't mind if I take the dog and
just disappear—do you, boy?"

"Fiona would mind."

"Fiona?"

"Do you want to hurt her even more than you have?"

"She'll forget me, she'll be all right . . ."

"Listen," I said then and shifted, heard Hugh bumping
against the settee and angling off toward the other end of
the arbor, "Fiona is not perfect. She's made mistakes. She's

246

been accused before of husband-stealing. Wrongly, of course, but accused nonetheless."

"Don't say it, boy."

"And do you think Fiona approves of everything I do? Well, she doesn't. We've had our differences. If she knew how you really feel about Catherine and me, and if she thought you were right and I was to blame for the way you feel, Fiona would be the first to take your side. In that case there would be no argument. If Fiona told me to give Catherine up, I would give her up."

"You're to blame. By God, you're to blame . . ."

"Fiona's judicious. If you put it to Fiona, she would tell you immediately that without malice and without superiority I'm not to blame. She would say that since Catherine is not using me to revenge herself on you, and since I am not having sex with Catherine for malicious ends of my own, then your defeat, chagrin, antagonism—whatever you feel—is your responsibility, not mine."

"Anguish. Just anguish. The point of the pike in the scrotum . . ."

"You need a little reassurance, Hugh. That's all."

"Take my wife and give me reassurance . . . But it's no good, boy, no good."

"Hugh," I said and moved another few steps, "let me tick off the possibilities. OK?"

"There's nothing you can say. Nothing."

"First of all, if you insisted on having Fiona to yourself, at least for a while, she would agree. She wouldn't like it, but she would be willing to go against her better judgment, if you insisted. And Catherine would understand. And so

247

would I, despite the inconvenience and despite the fact that Catherine and I have already decided against that kind of indulgence for ourselves. That's how it would be. It could happen, but it won't. We both know it won't."

"Don't suggest it, boy. My God . . ."

"Or suppose you were sentimental enough to disappear, as you put it. In that case you'd be deserting Catherine, the children would suffer, Fiona would send me off to bring you back. This isn't going to happen either."

"So I don't count. Don't count at all."

"Or suppose we just continue on as we are, and Fiona's right about the two of you. If it turns out she's made a real mistake in you, she'll get along. No one is more self-reliant than Fiona."

"I know that, boy."

"But if I changed my mind, if I told Catherine you're hopelessly stubborn, vindictive and all the rest of it, and that from now on she and I wouldn't be having any more little sex-songs, not even once in a while—what then?"

"She'll thank you. So will I."

"Think what would happen," I said quietly. "Catherine would never trust either one of us again. She would never forgive you. She would never forgive me. I'd never hear the end of it from Fiona. You'd never know when Catherine and I might let go of ourselves and start the whole thing over again. Catherine would never forget what you did to her tonight. Your own sex life would be destroyed. Fiona wouldn't be able to bear the sight of you. Our wives would brood. You and I would always be embarrassed. We wouldn't be able to explain ourselves. We wouldn't be able to clear the air. You wouldn't sleep. I wouldn't sleep. The children wouldn't understand our silence. How long could it last? But why? All because of a few words from you? Just because you can't condone a little extra sweetness between Catherine and me?"

"You've got your manhood . . . Let me have mine . . ."

"It's one thing to deny Fiona. Fiona is strong. But it's something else again to try to tether your own wife the first time her natural instincts reach out to another man. Your rancid feelings are an affront to her harmless awakening. Do you think I'd ever treat Fiona the way you're treating Catherine? Don't you understand that Catherine won't be able to forgive what you did tonight unless I'm able to persuade her to? Can't you see that it will take the two of us, and Fiona as well? You need me. You need Fiona. But even if you had your own way, do you think it would help? Do you think you'd be able to forget the past? Catherine's body, my body, as you imagine them? What you think you hate, already exists—in two forms, yours and mine. If I swore off Catherine, your idea of what we've done together would go on snagging your inventiveness forever. So what good would it do? Your only hope is to understand at least something of my version of what's been happening. And if you can accept the past, and I think you can, then you won't have any reason to destroy the present."

"You don't know what you're asking, boy. You couldn't."

"Besides," I said slowly, "I'm not going to let you destroy it."

Within arm's length of each other? Trapped at last? Hugh listening to reason? Wiping wet beard and wet head of hair with the back of his hand? The empty bench, the empty settee, the darkness in which we faced each other, the sand like powdered bone, the clusters of invisible and uneaten grapes, the nearby sea, the silent villas, our two wives waiting for something or nothing out there in the night—standing quietly in front of Hugh I was aware of it all and of how little I was asking and how much it meant. Catherine accepting a few roses, Fiona smiling, Hugh rid of his unhappy load, I spared any further need to talk us out of our blue moods and free, disinterested, enjoying myself —why not? Why shouldn't it be? But Hugh was no longer dodging me and gulping air. Hugh was as close to me as I was to him. Perhaps there was already no further need to talk.

"If you think I don't know what you're feeling," I said, "you're wrong."

"Don't touch me. Keep your hands to yourself."

"Of course Fiona can be hurt like anyone else."

"What does Catherine see in you anyway?"

"What's Fiona see in you?"

"I'm not worth it, boy. Not worth it."

"Fiona feels otherwise, that's all."

"Maybe I'm too damn idealistic. What do you think?"

"Fiona's idealistic. She's just as idealistic as you are. That's why this impasse of yours is so unfortunate."

"I'm losing out all around, don't you see?"

"Fiona's idealism isn't prohibitive. It's receptive. It doesn't preclude sexual affection. It starts with it. That's the difference. Everything she feels for you is genuine. She has a lot more to regret than you do."

"I've deprived myself of the wife of a man who's already taken mine. That's plenty to regret. Plenty."

250

"Shout if you want to. But stop hissing at me, Hugh. You don't need to hiss."

"Your lust is fulfilled. My lust isn't. And between your lust and mine I'm going up in smoke, burning away."

"You don't feel any lust for Fiona. The idea's ridiculous."

"How do you know what I feel, boy? How?"

"I've seen the way you look at her. I've heard you laugh. I've seen her hand on your knee. I've seen your exhilaration. You've been pretty good to Fiona, as far as you've gone."

"She's on my mind. You and Catherine are on my mind."

"Anyway, I have never experienced simple lust. You haven't either. But of course there's nothing wrong with lust if there's nothing else. Fiona has known a few purely lustful men. But you're not one of them, Hugh. Believe me. As a matter of fact, if it turned out you were, she might be pleased. But you don't even feel any real lust for your peasant nudes."

"Listen, you're trying to force me into your bed so you can stay in mine."

"If you manage to benefit from this discussion," I said slowly, "the four of us will be better off. I won't deny it. On the other hand, if you don't learn anything from this talk of ours, if you can't free yourself from these crippling fantasies, naturally your dissatisfaction is going to rub off on the rest of us. I won't deny that either. Your clenched teeth would spoil anybody's idyls. Darkness can come to Illyria. It's possible. But even so, Catherine and I will continue to meet alone together just as frequently as we've been meeting until now. We will continue because of the clear emotional basis of our relationship. We will not stop because of the reasons I've already given you. Harmony is something all four of us can enjoy. I'd like to see Fiona happy. But that's your affair. Catherine's fondness for me is mine. It can't be changed."

"There's always the belt. There's always that damn chastity belt . . ."

"Yes," I said slowly, "the belt."

We swayed, we tottered. I released Hugh's shoulders, I heard Hugh sink to my vacated place on the stone bench. And was it finished? Were we done? But to what end? Was Hugh relieved or only more silently inflamed than ever? Was Hugh's poison draining or collecting? Who could tell?

With my usual care I fished for a cigarette, produced a flame, inhaled. And by the light of that little momentary point of flame I saw that Hugh's seated figure was bent and slack but that his thin and stony face was turned up to mine. In the next instant it had disappeared, but not before I noted the expression on Hugh's face, noted the upper teeth clamped over the lower lip and embedded in the blackness of the pointed beard. The flame died, the face disappeared.

"Listen," I said, "anything you want me to say to Catherine?"

I waited. The cigarette hung down and glowed. In the darkness I heard Hugh's breathing which had become no more than the timeless drift of air in and out of a small orifice cut in stone.

"It's easy," I murmured. "Give it a chance."

I turned, withdrew deliberately from my dark and silent arbor where Hugh now sat alone repeating my arguments, pondering my advice. There was a sweetness on the night air that engulfed my cologne, Hugh was behind me, I had done my best for the four of us. After all, if dawn did not find Hugh with his head in Fiona's lap or Fiona dozing with book and terry-cloth robe discarded and Hugh at her side, if dawn brought no harmony for the four of us to share, at least none of it would be my fault. I had done my best.

Dawn would tell. And already the seeds of dawn were planted in the night's thigh. For a moment I thought of diverting my single-minded intention from Catherine to Fiona, for a moment considered changing my direction and looking in on Fiona who even now was no doubt lying amidst the little illusionary halos of her thin candles and concentrating on the book in her hands. But no, I told myself, it would be better to return to Fiona after rather than before the whole thing was settled, better for me to let Fiona wait and leave Hugh on his own and trust to the dawn. My place was with Catherine—for her sake and mine. Clarity had never been more essential. My next step was clear.

"Well, I'm back."

"Where have you been?"

"With Hugh."

"He hates the whole thing."

"I talked with him. It's not so bad."

"We can't go on."

"Hugh's coming around. He's probably with Fiona right now."

"Whatever he does, it's over between you and me."

"Listen," I said slowly, "I told Hugh I'd never give you up. What you and I have together hasn't changed."

"We can't have any more . . . sex. But we don't need it, do we?"

"Of course we need it."

"I've hurt Hugh as much as he's hurt me. I can't face it any longer."

"You can forgive him for what he did tonight. So can I."

"It's over. That's all I can say."

"You know why I talked with Hugh. You know why I'm here."

"Don't touch me. Don't ask me to move."

"Catherine, I want you to stand up."

"Hugh made me put it on. He'll have to tell me to take it off."

"I'm speaking for Hugh. For his good and yours and mine. Now stand up, Catherine. You'll feel better."

Had I persuaded Hugh only to lose Catherine? Was what Hugh had said about losing out all around now going to apply not to him but to me? Because I realized that never had it occurred to me that Hugh's influence over Catherine might be as strong as mine, and now I could only admit my error since Catherine's tone was suddenly Fiona's tone and Catherine's argument was Hugh's. Apparently all the time I had been grappling with Hugh in the arbor Catherine had been aligning herself with her missing husband in this very room. Not from the start had Catherine ever pushed my hand away or allowed any thoughts of Hugh to come swimming into the picture of our nights together. Or not for long. Not seriously. And now? Was this the case?

Once again I removed my golden spectacles and deposited them in their usual place of safekeeping beneath the bed. Again I untied the silken sash and removed my decorous old dressing gown and shook it loose, draped it carefully across the front of the bed. Pajama top followed dressing gown, my chest was bare. I smelled the scent of the night dust and felt the warmth of the coming dawn already flowing in the walls around us and in the silent ranked overlapping tiles above our heads. Dry armpits, expansive chest, lingering acrid taste of the cigarette in my moistened mouth—here I stood, a mental and muscular presence prepared for love. Only this silent woman's aging but youthful lover composed and half undressed and ready once again for love.

"Catherine," I said in my clear low voice, "give me your hand."

I groped for Catherine's hand in the dark. And when at last I took hold of it, I understood all too well the limp fingers and unresponsive hand. I had expected no abrupt change of mind, no suddenly fierce grip. I understood her desire to be rid of the belt but also her reluctance to expose herself to the shame of it—even for me. No woman was less deserving of such abuse than Catherine, no woman less able to throw it off.

Yet I persisted and helped her up until she was on her feet and accepting if not returning my long embrace. I held her, again I smelled the faint smell of Catherine's hair turning gray at the roots, I understood only too well the power of that invisible garment which was as ephemeral as Fiona's panties but as forbidding as the cold fortress from which it had come. Bent as I was on removing that impediment to love, was I already the accomplice of he who had forced Catherine to put it on? Slowly and carefully I unbuttoned the phosphorescent top of Catherine's pajamas.

"Now stand still a minute."

Carefully and without urgency I pulled the tie-string of her pajamas and then sat down on the edge of the bed with my knees apart and Catherine rising tall and soft and passive between my spread knees. No emotionalism, I thought, no talking, no drama—only the open pajama jacket, the tie-string hanging loose, the pajama pants opened in front. The end of Hugh's violence was only this brief and matter-of-fact procedure smoldering, so to speak, with eroticism.

"Stand still," I whispered again. "Be patient. Trust me."

There in Catherine's room and seated on the edge of her bed in the heart of the night, aware of our breathing, our presence together, and smelling the bed linen which only yesterday or the day before I had helped Catherine hang on the line with Hugh's wet sailor pants and Meredith's sadly modest swimming suit, and conscious of myself as the quiet full-bodied lover who had made Catherine move a little more quickly through all this displaced banality, and conscious of the secreted dead remnant of Hugh's hostility and of the fact that I had not touched my mouth to Catherine's mouth all night—slowly I raised my hands, seized Catherine's hips, inserted thick but tender fingers between the skin of her hips and the waistband of her pajama pants and drew them down until somewhere below the knees they fell of their own accord and dropped in a soft and useless heap around Catherine's feet. But Hugh's accomplice? Yes, I was Hugh's accomplice. In all my strength and weight I was not so very different from Hugh after all. Because as soon as I pressed thumbs and fingers against the thin pitted surface of the iron band circling Catherine's waist, I realized that Hugh's despairing use of that iron belt must have occasioned a moment more genuinely erotic than any he had known with Catherine, with his nudes, or in his dreams of Fiona.

"But, Catherine, it's tight, so unbearably tight . . ."

Now with my two arms around Catherine's waist, and leaning forward so that my cheek was within inches of her bare stomach, slowly and deftly I gave that little brutal and rusted clasp the single expert twist that was all it took to pick the lock of Love and unfasten the belt. The belt came free, I peeled away the iron, I drew the short barbarous tongue from between Catherine's legs. And now what on Catherine's body had been Hugh's chastity belt alive with tension and cruelly snug, in my two hands was only a pathetic dangling contraption withered and faintly rattling.

"Well," I whispered, "do you still want me to go? It's up to you."

As if there had been no belt, no doubts, no problem, no anguished Hugh, no reason at all for hesitation, Catherine merely stirred herself within the limits of my embrace and took off her already unbuttoned pajama jacket and stepped out of the soft phosphorescent heap of her pajama pants and with one foot pushed them aside.

"Kiss me, Cyril . . . kiss me . . ."

Together we moved, together we sank down at last on that lumpy and earthen-smelling mattress until in time the fish began to flow, the birds to fly, the twin heavenly nudes of Love to approach through the night.

Would it stop? Would it ever stop? Catherine could not expel her breath forever, my emissions were limited in length and frequency. We could not go on. True radiance only end in the dark. Then why was the tempest still exploring the storm? Why was I still bulging from head to foot? Why was Catherine still holding her breath, why hugging my buttocks more tightly than ever, why biting her own lower lip? Would it never end?

But of course at this very moment I found myself becoming aware of change, heard Catherine sigh, felt her two hands sliding away, knew that on either side of me her two feet were again flat on the bed, felt my shoulders sagging and knew with deep pleasurable regret that suddenly the naked twins of our invented constellation were gone. The bed was still.

"Listen," I said at last, "remember that evening we saw the nightingale?"

"You're so good to me . . . You're so good to us all . . ."

"Or that time I spitted the lamb on the beach?"

"I love to hear your voice in the dark . . ."

"Tomorrow I guess we'll have to get Hugh into the water."

Later, much later, I awoke to the silence and bright light of the sun-filled room and sat up on the edge of the bed. I stood. I took my usual count of bottomless breaths of morning air. Smiling down at Catherine I decided to carry the pajamas but wear the old dressing gown. And then with chastity belt in hand and laces tied, eyeglasses adjusted, sash in place, pajamas carefully folded over my right arm, I left.

I paused in the open doorway of Hugh's villa. I paused on our side of the funeral cypresses. I paused in the arbor which was empty. I found a safe hiding place for the belt. I took a few more long breaths of the sun. All of Illyria was a chalky and yet verdant landscape drenched in champagne.

Within a half dozen paces of our narrow doorway framed in vines I found myself smiling into the gray-green steady eyes of my waiting wife. There stood Fiona in that doorway of white mortar and sprightly vines, Fiona wide-awake and up and around like me. I did not move, I drank her in, she watched me with familiar pleasure. Over her right arm she carried her folded terry-cloth robe, and except for the loosely folded robe was naked. How alike we were, I thought, knowing that for the moment at least neither one of us would speak and that Fiona was reading, as it were, the pajamas on my arm exactly as I was reading the robe on hers. Our two separate but similar nights were evident in our appearances, each of us was perfectly aware of the other's thoughts. I was exhausted but as fresh as ever, she was tired but tense. She knew that I had enjoyed my night hours, I knew that she could not possibly look the way she looked if she had spent those same hours alone. Her bright eyes, her obviously sore muscles, the somehow roughened texture of her hard and slender body—what else could they mean?

"Baby," she whispered, "come inside . . ."

I let fall the pajamas just as Fiona dropped her robe, quickly I seized Fiona's proffered hand and followed her through our vine-beribboned doorway and down the cool corridor to the room that was ours. Her slim bare feet were light on the stone, her trim buttocks were filled with purpose. Hand in hand and thigh to thigh we stood in the entrance to our sun-drenched connubial room.

"Baby," she whispered, "isn't he beautiful?"

I brushed thick lips against her tight cheek, I stared

down at Fiona's prize. What else could I do? Of course I had expected an empty bed, of course I wanted to hone the bones of our love. Even with her eyes on the naked man in our bed, Fiona was maneuvering our two hands so that the back of hers was caressing the shiny source of my song. But it was hopeless. It was out of the question. And yet wasn't this precisely what we wanted? This sight of Hugh coiled up like a naked spring and covered with the lip-marks of Fiona's kisses? Right now he was preventing Fiona and me from enjoying our version of what he and Fiona had so recently enjoyed. But at the same time he had proven my theories, completed Love's natural structure, justified Catherine's instincts, made Fiona happy when she had given up all her hopes for happiness. What more could I ask?

"Cyril . . . ?"

"Fiona . . . ?"

"I want you, baby. I want you now."

"We love each other. Agreed?"

"But he's going to wake up any minute and I have to be here. I love him very much. I really do."

"There's always tonight."

"We'll just have to see. OK?"

"Listen," I murmured, and kissed her cheek, "he can't catch up. But God knows we'll let him try . . ."

She gave me one quick glance, I smiled, she turned in girlish haste to the bed while I retreated down the corridor to the bright morning which in unaccountable silence was rushing faster than ever along the path of the sun.

Later, much later, though before the hour of noon, the four of us met again for a new first time at Fiona's small rickety breakfast table set up in the arbor, Hugh and Fiona emerging from the narrow doorway framed in vines at the very moment that Catherine and I made our entrance through the wall of cypresses. Hugh and Fiona came out shoulder to shoulder and with their hands full of Fiona's crockery, Catherine and I stepped forward with our arms about each other's waists. Yes, openly and freshly we came together in the arbor which was sweet and shaded and bursting with hymeneal grapes, a quiet and appropriate place for our reunion. Catherine was wearing her white pajamas, I had all the clothing I needed or wanted in my comfortable old blood-colored dressing gown, Hugh had borrowed my red-and-white striped cotton shirt which he wore extravagantly and unashamedly with his own long gray undershorts. Fiona topped us all in one of her nearly mid-hip pale green transparent nighties. Yes, frankly, happily we sat around the perfect square of that small rickety table piled high with Fiona's morning fare, sat smiling and eating and touching bare feet beneath the table. Catherine sighed and licked her fingers, Hugh coughed and put his hand on Fiona's arm, Fiona shivered and caught my eye and stared at my bland contented features with a limpid smiling intensity she rarely displayed. Never had she looked more the faun, more the woman. Never had I loved her more or valued quite so highly this special hovering shyness now felt by us all. But the food, wasn't there also something special about the food? Of course there was. How like Fiona on this morning of mornings to select from the garden of her imagination only those items which, according to superstition, were aphrodisiac. Just like Fiona to fuse in one stroke her feminine wisdom and my sensible view of sex.

"Well," I said, lifting high my glass of cold white wine, "let's drink to us."

"To us, baby. To us . . ."

"Hᴇ's ɴᴏᴛ ᴛʜᴇʀᴇ."

"What?"

"I mean it, baby. He's gone."

"Catherine too?"

"She's still asleep. But he's not with her. He's gone. He's just not there."

"Well, look around. He can't be far."

"I've looked for him already. Everywhere. Something's wrong."

"Why don't you come on back to bed awhile. OK?"

"All right, baby. I'll go alone."

So before I could pull on my frayed white ducks and reach for my old white woolen sweater (no time to search for underpants or shirt, no time for shoes), Fiona had already given me her quick hard sign of disapproval and summoned all her usual self-reliance and walked out of our room, disappeared into that loud dawn wind that almost never blew but was blowing now. Hard-faced, hair untended, barefooted, wearing her crumpled but sporty mid-thigh trench coat open over a short white modest sleeping gown, skin and eyes still bearing the marks of a recent dream—in all her fleeting vividness she too was gone, as if she had not roused me by my naked shoulder, had not stood over me and spoken, had not given me a glimpse of what I took to be undue agitation, had not brought me this latest and, I thought, trivial news of Hugh.

First from our darkened room. First to abandon without a qualm our bed. First to find Hugh missing and not merely absent from Catherine's side at the outset of the very day we planned to row the children to the chapel on our little nearby island. First to dart like a golden arrow into the clear and pointless energy of the high wind. That was Fiona, my all but clairvoyant wife, who now, I saw, was once more rushing out of sight through a rift in the wind-blown frieze of cypresses. But I was not far behind her, sleep-ridden and heavy and half dressed, and though I did not catch up with her until she stopped for a moment amidst the first chalky stones of that dead village.

"Don't worry," I shouted through cupped hands, "we'll find him, wherever he is . . ."

For an instant longer I stood there squinting, rubbing my sleep-filled belly, fighting the wind, staring at the invisible spot where the trees and my wind-tossed wife had merged. Why wind? Where was it coming from? How could it blow with so much power and yet no direction? I swayed, I listened, I shaded my eyes, knowing that Catherine was indeed asleep and that Fiona's haste was justified but futile and that the light itself had turned to wind or that the wind had somehow assumed the properties of the dawn light. We would make no joyous expedition to the island chapel, that much I knew. But if Catherine was still sleeping, at least her children were pathetically and ironically awake. Because with my first deliberate step in pursuit of Fiona, hands in pocket and breath hard won, I heard their piping cries high on the wind—or thought I did. And what were they trying to tell me, those senseless cries, if not the worst?

There was no reason to hurry, no time to lose. Behind me I left the twin villas now equally desolate, though one was occupied and one was not. Ahead of me lay the white sea and the narrow beach heaped up with the ominous splendor of all those uncountable spears of light and drowned in the silent velocity of the wind's voice. Instinctively I turned left toward the village, I who was never a partisan to disaster now preparing in full consciousness to share with Fiona all the simple practicalities of pure disaster. My feet did not bleed on those sharp rocks, I did not run. But I knew what was coming and moved forward quickly enough to be of what help I could to Fiona.

"Wait," I shouted, catching sight of her and waving, "you can't do him any good alone . . ."

Did she hear me? Did she read my lips or take into account the meaning of my upraised hand? Was she standing there restrained in flight against that white wall out of need for me, out of concern for me, or only to collect her amazing energies and indulge herself in one moment of distraction for the sake of her fear, her plan, her determination? I approached, she waited, I saw the skirts of the tan coat beaten flat to the wall and the white gown beaten between her thighs. There in the driving light and silent wind at the entrance to the village, she might have given me the briefest smile of welcome, recognition, affection. But she did not.

"Fiona," I said clearly and gently, "I'm not to blame . . ."

"I'm not blaming you, baby. How could I?"

And then she jerked away her perfect shoulder, jerkeu away the features of her face baked hard in seriousness, took back the fragment of attention she had given me, turned and ran off abruptly toward the center of the village. And now I ran. Yes, I kept pace with Fiona below roofs of fungus-green or rouge-red tiles and past rows of crooked and tightly shuttered windows. We smelled the fetid smell of the black canal. The wind glazed the chunky white façade of the squat church. At least there were no short and robust leather-suited figures to point to our bare feet and curious attire and to shout *croak peonie* or *crespi fagag* in the wake of our progress up that village street.

"Listen," I said, "why don't you wait down here? I think you should."

Had she forgotten her many visits to that room above? Had she forgotten my own brief visit or two? Had she for-fotten the rusty hinges, the knotholes, the formidable latch, the oddly polished surface of that rough wood? Was she oblivious to the significance of a closed door? But none of it meant anything to Fiona, who without listening or even hesitating merely used her shoulder against the sagging street-level wooden door and with one blow knocked it ajar.

I followed her into that brutal darkness. I was right behind her as she climbed. She stumbled, I heard her breath come back to me in short unhappy gasps. It was cold in the stair well, but we were safe at last from the wind.

"Hugh? I'm here, baby, I'm here . . ."

Yes, she was there. And I was there. And Hugh was hanging in the corner. Fiona, not I, yanked open that second and final low door of wide wooden planks. Fiona, not I, ran forward immediately into the filtered gray light of that

265

small sloping barren room and initiated Hugh's abortive rescue, with both arms embraced his naked waist and attempted to raise him up and relieve the tension of the rope on his neck. We arrived together, entered that little cold sloping room together, faced together the stark and unavoidable sight of Hugh's nude body hanging amidst all his photographs in the corner nearest the inevitably shuttered window on the canal side of the room. Yes, Fiona and I were competitors for Hugh's life from the first moment we intruded upon the scene both of his art, as he called it, and his death. And I too was active, except that I saw in a glance that the rope was much too thick and much too tight for Fiona's courageous efforts, no matter how sensible they were on the surface, and understood at once what Fiona in all her intensity and devotion could not perceive— that our only hope was to cut him down immediately. So rather than join her in the corner, where now she was making soft agonized sounds of comfort, I turned instead to Hugh's enormous homemade worktable and with a single heave cleared it of pans, traps, labyrinthine pieces of equipment, glass-stoppered bottles. Quickly I dragged it into position beneath the great rusted hook which, like a beckoning iron finger, held the end of the rope. And noting the open eyes, the smile on the open mouth, the sweat still fresh on his pitted brow, the glossy photograph clenched in his good hand, the white feet side by side and suspended only a few inches from the floor, quickly I stood on the table and freed the rope and helped Fiona lower him gently, swiftly, to the bare floor that was now Hugh's crude temporary bier. We needed light, so in passing I smashed my elbow through the frail slats of those rotted shutters which Hugh in his love of darkness always kept closed. And when I withdrew my elbow and turned, still heavily in motion and using up no time, no time at all, I saw that that sudden long splintered shaft of light was falling directly on Hugh's face and on Fiona's swift hands already reaching for the rope at his throat.

Together we knelt at either shoulder, Fiona and I, together and in silence did all we could. But Fiona's fingers, not mine, broke the spell of the noose, though I raised Hugh's head so that Fiona was able to remove forever the hairy loop of that rope which was thicker than my two thumbs. And Fiona, not me, attempted without respite to blow life into that strangled man. Her face was low, her left hand was pillowing the back of Hugh's head, her right hand was lightly braced against his chest, she was trying to breathe both for herself and Hugh. But here? Now? This confined space? These thick walls? This cell so bleak and at the same time so lurid? This broken light? This wreckage? This white body stretching as if from one end of the room to the other and welted with thin tendons that would never again relax? Was it possible? Was this the same Hugh who had danced one night for his children and taken his pictures and smiled at Fiona and carried Catherine into Illyria and thanked me solemnly for the song of the nightingale? Could even Hugh have made this miscalculation and closed all our doors? Fiona was not a woman to waste herself, or to expect senseless occurrences to make sense, or to blind herself to what she did not wish to know or punish herself for what she could not have. She was hardly a woman to display grief or to attempt to restore what had already been destroyed. But for once Fiona, still kneeling at what she knew full well was not even a final kiss, was behaving out of character, and I was glad. Until she spoke, which in the next instant she did, and even when she spoke, obviously Fiona was grieving, remembering, flying once more down the whole long road of eccentricity with Hugh. Before she pulled her mouth from his, before she sat back on her heels and looked at me, before she could notice what I was doing, quickly I plucked that cracked and shiny photograph from Hugh's rigid grasp and thrust it from sight.

"It's no good, baby. He's dead."

"At least it was an accident. At least he wasn't trying to kill himself . . ."

"For God's sake, I understand."

"It was bound to happen. If not now then later."

"Listen, baby, I'm going to Catherine. You can do the rest."

AND VIRGINITY? THE ADOLESCENCE OF THE VIRGIN? THE stiff pictographic story of downcast eyes, clear water, empty hands, light the color of cut wheat? Is all this mere chaff in the wind of the practical lover? Mere fading sickness of men like Hugh? Unreal? Perhaps. But sex-singing is hardly possible without the presence of the frail yet indestructible little two- or three-note theme of innocence, and though I am anything but insensitive to boring technicalities and dangerous by-products (religious inventions, martyrs ampu-

268

tating their own breasts with stolen swords, and so forth),
nonetheless I have always defended the idea if not the fact
of purity and have always felt warmly inclined toward the
sight of narrow beds and young girls carrying clay pots to
massive fountains. Fiona understood what I meant. Did
Catherine? Does she now? After all, there was a time when
all our days were only memories of hours that had not yet
passed and each one of us was in some way virginal. Lounging on all that remains of Fiona's old settee, I wonder if I
could put the adolescence of the Virgin into words for
Catherine. In the twilight should I lead her back again to
the chapel of the wooden arm and let her look for herself?
Tomorrow, I tell myself, smiling through my own thick
smoke, or the day after.

But virginal? Four large virginal human beings? The suggestion is not that I myself ever experienced the slightest
preference for virginal over nonvirginal girls or women. The
suggestion is not that my wife or Hugh's could ever suffer
significantly by comparison with the young and half-naked
shepherdess chasing across the sunburnt field after her
shaggy goats. No, one body does not diminish beneath another, there is no amorous oil to lose, the woman bathing in
her blue pool renews not her flesh but her readiness.

Yet even now I see once more the adolescence of the
Virgin herself, those few still scenes discovered only toward
the end of our idyl and in that very chapel where Catherine collapsed in grief on those cold stones.

Look up there, Fiona. Proof enough?

Sketches. Only a half dozen or so crude sketches of innocence joining the thick wall to the vaulted darkness, small
panels of hazy paint invisible except when, once a day and

thanks to some cosmic situation and the faulty construction of the squat church, the sun at last becomes a thin blade that slips beneath each of my brief glimpses of the Virgin and for a moment illuminates the three hooded attendants and their rigid and yet somehow submissive charge.

At first glance the wordless story is simply barren, undecipherable, says nothing. And yet to the patient viewer the colors begin to speak, the plaster glows. That yellow stroke? Her gown. And the purple pear? A vessel filled to the lip with water undoubtedly. As for the large dark object held with apparent effort by the attendant bound and hooded in the ocher-colored robe, it is a hairbrush, obviously, though the yellow figure of our young Virgin has no hair while the brush itself resembles nothing so much as a crude, gigantic iron key for a medieval lock. But the color is the important thing, the yellow that dominates each scene— now blond, now sandalwood, now gold, now the yellow that flows in cream, now the color carried in the furry sacs of unmoving bees. The skin of the tree is yellow, the stiff gown is yellow, the bare feet, one of which is missing in the third frame, are pale variants of the small female lemons that once hung from a white branch but now hang from nothing. Is it the color of truth and adolescence? The color of youth removed from the context of age? Simply the color of innocence? The Virgin hue? I suppose it is. And so one figure supports the shoulders and one holds the feet while the yellow but now horizontal girl remains as stiff as ever: she is rising. But the third attendant, ocher-colored, robed and hooded, is sitting on the end of the bed with his wide back to the day's first event. Or the Virgin stands upright and faceless in a large receptacle of ancient wood: she bathes. But nonetheless she is still clothed in the yellow gown, no water flows from what must have once been a bucket tilted above her head. Or among leafless trees she walks with hands held as if for some illuminated book: she prays. Yet trees, book, attendants are now invisible. And in this frame our yellow Virgin has suffered the same decay as the surrounding plaster and is all but gone.

Yellow was Fiona's favorite color. I have seen Hugh's narrow eyes downcast in the midst of his craving. Catherine's face did not betray her longing. Even at night the four of us walked in that light the color of cut wheat.

T HE SUN CASTS ORANGE DISCS ON THE SEA, OUR NIGHTS ARE cool. From three adjacent wooden pegs on my white wall hang a dried-out flower crown, a large and sagging pair of shorts, the iron belt—and is it any coincidence that all my relics are circular? Who can tell? Everything coheres, moves forward. I listen for footsteps.

In Illyria there are no seasons.

New Directions Paperbooks—A Partial Listing

For complete listing request complete catalog from
New Directions, 80 Eighth Avenue, New York 10011

† Bilingual